'Til Death Us Do Part

Thanks!

To everyone who supported me in this journey, thank you very much.
I couldn't have done it without you.

To everyone who did their best—knowingly or unknowingly—to not
support me in this journey, thank you very much. I really couldn't
have done it without you.

CHAPTER 1

The cold refreshing mountain air made Vicky Golden feel alive.

She pushed hard cresting the ridge close to the summit, near-freezing wind chilling her lungs with every inhale. Watching her footwork on the snow and ice, she used her peripheral vision to scan the landscape ahead.

She loved Mt. Shasta. Could spend days—and often did—hiking alone, basking in the serenity above fourteen-thousand feet.

Not today.

"Dean," Vicky said into the two-way radio clipped to her shoulder. "You and Schroeder head south. Come up around the east side of the crash site. Brian and I will continue in our current direction."

Static crackled over the radio. "You're the boss," her business partner and fellow rescue team member answered. "How many people are we looking for?"

"Three. Duff plus his two passengers." Shadows appeared on the terrain as yet another wind shift played with the clouds. Vicky tightened the drawstring on her hood. Strong blast. Could be what downed the helicopter.

"Let's get a move on, boys," she said. "This storm's

coming in faster than predicted."

"Roger that. Dean out."

Vicky's breath steamed in the air as she and Brian picked up the pace down the ridge, slipping a few times on the soft, mushy snow at the lower elevation.

To the east, about a hundred yards, a dark speck against a white background caught her eye. She confirmed her suspicions with high-powered binoculars. A small copter lay sideways in a crater, having tumbled about a thousand feet down the slope.

Not far from the wreckage, the pilot walked erratically. She recognized the Celtic cross on the back of her friend's jacket weaving left and right.

Toward a crevasse!

Vicky sprinted, Brian hot on her heels. She gasped as she covered the distance, digging the toe points of her crampons into the slick surface. The gear bag on her back slammed against her spine in rhythm with each stride.

Pieces of sheered rotor blades stuck up in the snow. She weaved around them while keeping an eye on her stumbling friend. Another few feet and the crazy old Irishman would drop into the chasm. Springing from her position, she grabbed him before he stepped off into air.

Her pulse pounded in a combination of exertion and apprehension as she pulled him to safety. Sluggishly he raised his head to look at her.

Piercing blue eyes. Long, straight nose. High cheekbones. Stubborn jaw. All revealed a European aristocratic lineage.

Not Duff. A face she hadn't seen in eight years.

The last face she expected to see.

Ever.

Christiaan.

Her blood ran cold.

After what he'd put her through… what he'd taken from her… what he'd *done* to her, she should push him into the crevasse herself.

And let him die.

Christiaan's body began to shake violently, gasping for air. He was going into shock.

Dean's voice crackled over the radio. "Steve and I are at the crash site. We've got Duff and one guy still strapped into the bird. No sign of a third."

"I've got him." Vicky forced herself back into rescue mode. "Radio Rescue Air One that it's too soft to land here. They'll need to drop a rescue harness."

"Got it."

Christiaan struggled for air.

"Slow, deep breaths," she instructed. "In through your nose, out through your mouth."

"You…" He reached up and touched her cheek. "You're…" The seductive Dutch accent stoked a gently growing fire within her. The memory of lying in his arms tore through her like a bolt of lightning.

Ice crystals kicked up by the arriving rescue helicopter cut at Vicky's face. She covered Christiaan with her body to shield him from the razor-sharp pieces.

In less than a minute, the crystals blew off, and Vicky focused on getting this man as far from her as possible.

She grabbed the rescue harness dangling above, pulled the device over the semiconscious Christiaan, then secured it around his waist and legs. She signaled "go ahead" to the winch operator. Only after jerking the harness tight did Vicky notice her husband staring at her.

The cable pulled taut. He rose into the air, screaming "Brianna."

No. She's dead.

Christiaan floated in and out of a conscious dream state, the boundary between reality and fantasy blurred.

Clad only in black lace, Brianna came to him. She topped him, pulling at his clothes like they were on fire. His hands explored her back, her waist, her hips. She sat up and removed her bra, her fingers skimming the sides of her breasts before throwing the garment aside.

Hard nipples teasing him, he reached to touch them. But she forced his hands to her hips and purred for him to remove her thong and follow her lead. He pushed her back, slipped the fabric down her long legs, then tossed it aside. Her long brown hair glowed like muted fire. Passion burned in her gray eyes.

He positioned himself above her. "Mijn minnares. My lover. Tell me what you want."

Her firm lips parted against his own. "Yo, bro," erupted from her throat.

His precious Bri faded.

"Yo, bro," a man's voice said. "Rise and shine."

Sunlight streamed through the bedroom window, robbing Christiaan of the first erotic dream he'd had of his wife in a long while. Forced to confront the intrusion, his eyes soon adjusted then scanned the room.

Although luxurious, the king-sized bed barely accommodated his six-foot, four-inch frame. The clothes he'd dropped on the floor last night after checking out of the emergency room were gone. His briefcase lay closed on top of the dresser. The alarm clock on the nightstand showed 1:00 PM.

Potverdomme! How long had he been out?

Reaching under the covers, he ripped the now-very-warm ice bag from his bruised and swollen knee and pitched it into the corner of the hotel penthouse.

Enough rest. He needed to get back to work. Had to save his company.

Yanking the covers off, he leaped out of bed. But freedom had its price. His head began to pound, his right knee buckled, and every muscle in his body throbbed.

Scratch the ten-mile run from today's to-do list.

"Whoa." His best friend Baz Yager caught him before he hit the floor. "Doc said you need to rest for the next several days. Several means more than one, bro."

"I'm fine." At least Christiaan thought so. He remembered everything up to being thrown free when the helicopter bringing him from the airport veered out of control. Nothing else until he awoke in the ER.

"Unfortunately, that's all the get-well time I can afford," he said. "I can't get this project back on track lounging around in bed."

"Serves you right. I told you you didn't need to fly all the way over here. Everything is under control." Baz helped Christiaan back onto the bed. "You listen to me about as much as you did Duff when he told you to buckle up."

"If I'd known falling out of the sky was on the itinerary, I would have." Christiaan snickered then winced as bruised ribs protested. "I'm taking a nice, safe taxi back to the airport. How is the Irishman, by the way?"

"Pissed about his broken wrist, kicking himself for loaning you his good-luck jacket." Baz dropped into a nearby chair. "Swears that's why we went down. So much for the luck of the Irish, huh?"

"What about you?" Christiaan asked.

"A little sore, but ready to work. However, *you* could use some serious recuperation time. Why don't you head back to Amsterdam? Let me do my job. I'll email you daily updates."

"I'm not going home until I'm satisfied the Mineral Springs project is on track. The future of VL Holdings depends on it." *I refuse to lose another precious thing because I failed to take action.* Christiaan pointed at the dresser. "Hand me my briefcase, please."

Baz shook his head. "Not 'til you promise that once you're satisfied everything is under control, you'll leave it all to your more-than-capable VP of development... *moi.*"

"Promise."

Baz dropped the briefcase onto the bed then disappeared into the living room.

Christiaan spun the combination on the lock and flipped the case open. He grabbed his phone and scrolled through his messages, stopping only to read and reply to ones marked "Urgent." Unfortunately, the majority were marked "Urgent."

"ShastaWatch isn't letting up," he said. "I've got messages from at least twenty U.S. government officials telling me the group is bombarding them with phone calls, emails, and letters. I guess if the environmentalists aren't happy, nobody's happy."

"Oh, they're definitely not happy." Baz reentered the room and tossed the local newspaper in front of Christiaan. "Check it out."

Christiaan glanced at the front-page headline. "Summit Energy to Rape Mountain for Profit."

He shook his head at the media's audacity. "What? No room to add 'and Pillage'?" He read aloud. "Environmental group ShastaWatch condemned the President's administration for approving the development of a controversial geothermal project at Mineral Springs near Mt. Shasta. The group denounced the Department of the Interior and the U.S. Forest Service for giving the go-ahead to a project that threatens the area's already-fragile environment and historical significance. Officials contend the approval was justified due to increased demand for renewable energy. An anonymous source within ShastaWatch vows to do anything to stop the injustice."

"Good thing we established Summit Energy here in the States to manage our expansion into North America. Imagine what the tree huggers would be screaming if they knew a foreign company was involved."

"Yeah, the headline would read 'Dutch Conglomerate to Turn Greenspace into Greenbacks'." Christiaan tossed the newspaper aside. "Let's keep it Summit Energy as long as possible."

"Hey, your call. You're the big man in charge."

"Of a nearly bankrupt company."

"Hey," Baz said. "Who knew the ethanol market would collapse?"

Obviously not me.

Christiaan breathed deep and rubbed his temples. He

still wasn't sure what happened. Normally, he saw business opportunities like a psychic. But somehow, he'd underestimated operating costs and was now bleeding millions a month.

The Mineral Springs project had to be fast-forwarded soon. He was running out of cash.

And time.

Thanks to shortsighted... uncooperative... uncompromising tree huggers.

"So tell me about this group, ShastaWatch."

"Not much to tell," Baz answered. "No names, no office, no website, no phone."

"And no clue who runs the show."

"Not a one." Baz shook his head. "Even Lou couldn't find a trace."

Christiaan arched an eyebrow. "Wow, that means something if a former CIA agent can't dig up any info. But, this is a small town, and small towns don't have secrets. Somebody, somewhere knows something. We just need to find that somebody." *And fast.*

"But first..." He carefully swung his legs over the side of the bed. "I need to get dressed."

"Here." Baz grabbed a faded running shirt and worn sweatpants from a nearby dresser.

"Thanks." Christiaan let out a short snort. "Remember growing up how you could sweet-talk the nanny into telling us where my Christmas presents were hidden?"

"Ah, the Yager charm," Baz said with a twinkling eye. "Never met a woman I couldn't win over."

Christiaan cocked his head to one side.

"Okay, there was one." Baz tossed the clothes at his friend. "But I never had a chance with Brianna because she only had eyes for you."

For one awful moment, the memory of Bri's death flickered. The weight of her small gold wedding band on the chain around Christiaan's neck hung heavy.

He cleared his throat and refocused on the present.

"How about using the Yager charm to get some information out of the front-desk clerk?" Christiaan slid the sweats on, grimacing as he pulled a pant leg over his still-swollen knee. "The one who waves her ample chest every time we walk by."

"Or the hotel maid who wanted to give 'his majesty' her *personal* turn-down service. Or the emergency room nurse that offered to make a special house call to the Baron van Laere?" Baz shrugged. "I'll give it a shot. They may throw themselves at the clean-cut, button-down aristocrat, but they're always willing to let the ponytailed, rough nobody catch them."

Christiaan studied his best friend. He wished he could enjoy the attention women forced on him. It had been a long time since he'd enjoyed female companionship. But that would require tapping into the well of emotions bottled inside.

And that well was closed, permanently. He owed Bri that much.

"By the way, who rescued us yesterday?" Christiaan pulled on a shirt. He winced as he bumped his sore ribs.

"A local crew." Baz smirked as he leaned against the doorway. "And get this, according to the paramedics, the leader is a real hottie named Vicky Golden."

"We should track them down and thank them."

"Dibs on the hottie," Baz said. "Hey, you hungry?"

"Starving, but I've got too much work to catch up on to go out. Let's do room service."

"Lobster? Veal? Filet mignon?"

Christiaan raised a brow.

"Cheeseburgers it is." Baz headed toward the living room. *Next on the agenda… bathroom.*

Christiaan struggled to stand and managed to knock his briefcase off the bed.

An old photo of a young woman sitting on a picnic blanket fell to the floor. The image of the summer sun highlighting her long brown hair made him start. In shorts and a t-shirt, she posed for the camera, toasting the photographer with a drink.

Christiaan caressed the picture with his eyes. He'd snapped it a week after meeting Bri. The next day, he'd asked her to marry him.

Thank God she said yes.

Pain flared in his heart. As fresh as the day he lost her. He fingered Bri's ring.

Hot tears stung his eyes. *I'm sorry, <u>mijn minnares</u>. It was my fault. All my fault.*

CHAPTER 2

Close, but no cigar.

"Arrgh!" Vicky's fingers slipped from the handhold. Only this time her tired legs couldn't support the sudden weight shift. The automatic safety system caught the rope and slowed her descent. She dropped to the floor with a thud, arm muscles burning like fire. Her pride hurt worse.

She scowled up the length of the climbing wall built into the backside of the two-story indoor chimney. Small puffs of breath rose in the great room of her rustic lodge.

You're pathetic. Her typically fierce concentration had crumbled. Usually, extreme physical exertion kept the demons at bay. Christiaan's sudden appearance had them refusing to be controlled.

Why was he here?

Vicky couldn't stop the images tossing about in her mind. They reminded her of all she'd lost.

She wiped sweat off her face with a forearm.

No. Not lost. Taken.

By him.

Another "Arrgh!" bounced off the open rafters. Vicky flung the rope, sending the thick black line swinging back and forth.

In her wildest dreams, she never pictured her husband showing up on Mt. Shasta. Her Shasta. Her mountain.

What was he doing here? Passing through? Sightseeing? Pleasure trip?

The bigger question… why hadn't he come looking for her? To finish what he started eight years ago. Clearly, he'd recognized her on the mountain.

But he'd gone into shock. He might not recall anything.

Besides, Christiaan would never believe his mousey, overweight, afraid-of-heights Bri could be a mountain guide. Not in America. Not on Shasta. He was probably winging his way back home on the company jet, none the wiser.

Good riddance.

Too bad her heart—and her body—didn't share her mind's sentiment.

Vicky shivered. She slipped off her climbing harness and boots, threw on a fleece pullover, then headed into the kitchen. Pouring a cup of coffee, she glanced at her old-fashioned answering machine sitting on the island. Small price to pay for living so far from reliable cell service.

A red 5 flashed on and off, indicating how many calls she'd ignored since yesterday.

Go for it. She could use the mental break. Sliding onto a bar stool, she pressed play.

Beep. "Yo, Vic. It's Dean. We're short on hot chocolate, toilet paper, and duct tape for tomorrow's climb. Could you pick some up in the morning on your way into the office?"

Yes, dear.

Beep. "Hey, sweetie. It's Rainbow. Dean says you guys have a trip leaving tomorrow. I'll drop by your shop around breakfast. I tried a new tofu recipe I know you're gonna love. Ciao! Oh, by the way, a really nice guy joined my Yoga for Stress class today. He's perfect for you. I'll tell you about him when I see you. *Ciao!*"

When are you going to learn I'm not interested in dating or Austrian Curd Cake?

Beep. "Victoria, love. Duff 'ere. I owe ye fer savin' me arse yesterday. Wadda say I buy dinner fer ye an' thet blokes fer helpin' us? Can't fly fer six weeks 'cause of dis damn broken wrist an' damn FAA, so anytime works. Let me know."

Free dinner? You're on.

Beep. "Vicky, it's Kaitlin. I did a little research at the university law library. Summit Energy can sue us by claiming ShastaWatch is violating their right to use the property in an economically viable way. Considering we don't have any money for a legal battle, maybe we should reconsider our no-compromise position. What do you say, boss?"

No. Hell no.

Beep. "Vicky? David here. I just wanted to let you know that I'm going up to the Mineral Springs site this afternoon and take some pictures with my new telephoto lens. Who knows? Maybe I can catch 'em doing something we can use against them."

Great. Maybe we'll find something we can use to stop these creeps.

Vicky hit the delete-all button, then headed back into the great room, feet padding softly on the slate floor. Heat radiated from the grand fieldstone fireplace but failed to warm her soul.

She retrieved a worn manila envelope hidden behind a row of books on the mantel. Sitting on the raised hearth, she dumped the contents into her lap. Photos. Clippings. Memories.

From once upon a time.

The top image, of a handsome couple dressed in white, brought tears to her eyes. Their wedding day had been the happiest time of her life. With Christiaan at her side, life would be perfect.

Next, she paged through clippings from her journalism days. A profile of the Sierra Club's efforts to curb air pollution. A report on fraud and incompetence within the EPA. An in-depth piece about the potential environmental consequences of the Exxon Valdez oil spill.

And the feature she'd written about the new thirty-something CEO of VL Holdings, a family-owned European conglomerate into everything from oil exploration to shipping to retail. A puff piece she'd only consented to pen in exchange for the magazine agreeing to publish a four-part expose on the government's plan to grant power companies permits to develop alternative energy sources on Federal lands.

Stapled to the article was a copy of their marriage license, issued only a month after she'd interviewed him. Behind that was a picture from their last Christmas together. Christiaan was handsome, healthy, and happy. She stood next to him, overweight, miserable, and drunk. The photo was a chilling reminder never to trust love—or a man—ever again.

A small picture fell to the floor. Fuzzy and fragile, the tiny black-and-white print with its blurred fingers and hazy body outline was the only evidence of the miracle they'd made together. Vicky caressed the image.

"What happened to us, Christiaan?" The pain made her throat constrict. "What happened?"

Memories of her previous life flowed over her like an avalanche. Tears fell as she negotiated the maze of emotions surrounding yesterday's rescue. The phone ringing forced her attention back into the now.

Vicky breathed slowly. The knot in her throat faded. The pressure in her chest weakened. Once again, she'd overcome the pain without crawling into a bottle of Scotch.

The answering machine beeped. "Hey, it's Nelson," played through the speaker. "I talked with Beckwith today. The Congressman has decided not to support us on the Mineral Springs issue. Seems he talked with the Summit Energy people this afternoon. He thinks the company's proposed measures to reduce the environmental impact of the geothermal project are fair and urges us to accept them and move on. Call me when you get this message, and I'll fill you in on the details."

Argh! Vicky grabbed a log from the stack by the hearth and heaved it into the fire.

Destroying a pristine area, used by recreational visitors and Native American tribes for thousands of years, simply to turn a buck was not fair.

It was irresponsible, bordering on immoral.

Mt. Shasta and the surrounding land was sacred, a place that deserved protection at any cost.

The mountain was the anchor in Vicky's life. Her new life. And nobody would take that away from her.

Not again.

Summit Energy had no idea who they were dealing with. Vicky shoved her memories back into the envelope.

Rest in peace, Brianna. Rest in peace.

Vicky parked her clunker truck next to Dean's motorcycle then slipped through the back door of their Climbing for Singles business. She stifled a yawn.

Sleep had been erratic at best last night. After a few fitful hours, she'd given up and returned to the climbing wall until the wee hours.

Nothing a strong cup of motor oil her business partner called coffee couldn't fix. Slip into the back room, down a cup of sludge, and head out to meet the Romeos and Juliets on this trip.

The private office door lay open. Dean sat at the desk, talking on the phone. His long legs and size-thirteen feet stretched across the floor in his patented no-worries mode.

"Yes, sir," he said. "We'll make sure she gets plenty of material for her article."

Article? Vicky tensed. What article? She tossed the nine-roll pack of toilet paper at her partner's head. He deflected it with one hand while hanging the phone up with the other.

The roll of duct tape would have been harder to miss.

And hurt more.

"What's got you on the warpath this morning?" He stood then headed for the grind and brew in the far corner.

"Who was that on the phone? What article?"

"Nothing, Vic. Hey, I made some fresh coffee. Wanna cup?"

"Dean…" She aimed an evil eye.

"Okay, okay." He threw his hands up in surrender. "That was the managing editor for *Inc.* magazine. He wanted to make sure his reporter had arrived. She's going to do a small feature on Climbing for Singles."

"When we talked last week, I believe I said 'We'll see'."

Dean chuckled. "Which means no. Come on, Vic." He inclined his shaggy blond head. "This is a *major magazine.* Think of the publicity. It'll be great for business."

But not for her. What if someone recognized her as Brianna? Her looks had changed a great deal, but why tempt fate?

Biting her lip, she ran a hand through her short locks.

"Not the hair thing." Dean rolled his eyes.

"The hair thing?"

He pointed at her head. "When you're upset, you bite your lip, then push a hand through that red mop of yours."

"Call the editor back and tell him we've changed our minds."

"Can't." Dean shrugged. "The reporter is already here and ready to tag along on this trip. Besides, if we make a big deal about this, it looks like we have something to hide. This way, we have some control."

Good point. Besides, Christiaan usually avoided the media, especially from the States.

"I still *don't* like it." Vicky let out a sigh.

"Of course you don't," Dean laughed. "But you'll get over it."

He came around the desk and hooked an arm around hers. "Come on. Let's get the party started."

They walked out to where a dozen people wandered

the large main room of Climbing for Singles. A handful
stood next to the bulletin board, reviewing the itinerary for
the two-day climb leaving in a few hours. Another group
waited by the equipment room to be fitted with rental gear.

"Call me crazy, but man I love my job." Dean winked
at Vicky before making a beeline to a statuesque blond
struggling with her backpack.

Vicky laughed. She'd called him crazy five years ago
when he'd suggested they start a guide service catering to
unmarrieds. From the first trip, Climbing for Singles had
been a success.

And so, too, was Vicky Golden.

She checked her watch. A few more minutes then
they'd herd everybody into the classroom so Dean could
start orientation. A yawn escaped. First, she needed coffee.

"Hey, sweetie!" A way, *way* too-perky voice stopped her.

She turned to see Rainbow Sun Rubin, ShastaWatch
co-founder, self-proclaimed steward of Vicky's love life,
and the closest thing she had to a best friend. The
spontaneous and free-spirited yoga instructor loved
everyone. But threaten someone or something she was
passionate about, and Rainbow was like a mother bear
protecting her cubs.

"Hey, girl."

Rainbow held up a small plastic container. "I brought
some Pine Nut Seed Bars for lunch."

Vicky cringed. A vegetarian for several years, she ate
healthier than most people. But her friend was a devoted
raw foodie who believed man shouldn't eat anything
cooked. Today's entrée looked like something only a
squirrel could find appetizing. Maybe.

"They're rich in vitamins and enzymes." Rainbow
popped the top and shoved the container toward Vicky.
"Try one."

Vicky raised her hands in protest. "Too full. Maybe
later?"

"Oh. My. God."

Great. Now you hurt her feelings.

"Look, I'm sorry," Vicky offered. "I know you made these just for me, but I'm not—"

Rainbow shook her head and pointed behind Vicky. She turned around. Her breath caught short in her throat.

Oh. My. God.

The most unforgettable rugged face met hers, muscles clenched along the chiseled jaw line. Thick brown hair turned at the collar framed a pair of Windex-blue eyes. Every step toward her highlighted a powerful, well-muscled body in a worn leather jacket, unbuttoned white shirt, and tight faded jeans.

That regal bearing and self-assurance exuded wealth and power. Two basic requirements on any woman's turn-on list.

Vicky knew without looking that every female in the room wanted to be his.

Including herself.

Raw heat that had been lying dormant for years surfaced. Her breath hitched.

Covering the distance between them in three long strides, her husband stopped so close she could smell his distinctive male scent.

Their eyes locked. The same white-hot fire that had burned her when they first met fifteen years ago flamed again.

Heart hammering against her chest, she extended her hand.

"Hello, I'm Vicky Golden."

CHAPTER 3

Christiaan froze. He wouldn't have been more surprised if the statuesque redhead in front of him had introduced herself as Queen of The Netherlands.

"Hello?" The shapely beauty's hand remained extended. Her eyes narrowed.

He mouthed a reply, but nothing came out. All he could manage was to stand there and stare.

And stare. And stare.

Next to him, Baz voiced an appreciative "Whoa."

With a capital W.

The passing likeness to Bri when they'd first met was startling. Vicky's eyes were gray like his wife's, but the hue was different. Bri's had been sparkling platinum. These verged on stormy silver.

The differences were just as astonishing.

And stunning.

Vicky's features were much thinner, more defined than Bri's. The nose, pert, almost sculpted. Lips, soft and full. Her hair was short and a deep auburn color, not long and brown like Bri's.

His gaze dropped to the bright blue top clinging to muscled shoulders and toned arms.

Breasts, definitely smaller.

But still quite nice. His cock stirred.

"Hello?" she repeated. This time he detected a touch of annoyance. The voice was deep and devoid of Bri's native Texas twang.

Because this woman isn't your wife.

That simple truth failed to explain the immediate connection he felt with this incredibly beautiful woman. Or the sexual shockwave that shot through him.

Staring at her like a complete idiot wouldn't solve either mystery.

"Hello, my name is... is... ah... ah—"

"Christiaan," Baz finished for him. "And I'm Baz." He brought Vicky's hand to his lips and kissed her knuckles. "Forgive us for staring, Miss Golden. You remind us both of someone we used to know."

And loved.

Christiaan's rational mind finally kicked into gear. He held out his hand. "Miss Golden, this is a pleasure."

Her handshake was cold. Her facial expression even chillier.

"And you are?" Baz turned, repeating the chivalrous gesture with the woman standing next to Vicky. Definitely his friend's type. Long blond hair, pretty face, and dressed like the bohemians that frequented Baz's favorite Amsterdam coffee shop.

"Rainbow," she said between giggles. "Nice to meet you."

Baz winked. "The pleasure is—and I hope it also will be tonight—all mine."

Christiaan hoped his friend was making plans to probe the girl for information on ShastaWatch. From the look on Baz's face, that wouldn't be the only probing done tonight.

Christiaan turned his attention back to Vicky.

"Miss Golden, we're here to thank you for helping us yesterday."

She stood there, biting her lower lip and combing her right hand through that gorgeous auburn hair.

Something about the gesture intrigued him. He shook off the feeling.

"On the mountain?"

"Yes," Christiaan said. "From what everyone has told me, it could have been worse had you not reached me in time."

"You'd be dead." Vicky cleared her throat then gave the room a cursory glance before training her exquisite eyes on him again. "But you're not."

"Thanks to *you*." He smiled, but her expression remained as cold as the mountain she'd rescued him on.

"Excuse me, but I have work to do," she said, then nodded to Baz. "Mr. Yager. Rainbow, later." Vicky turned and strode off toward the back of the room.

What? That's it?

Being summarily dismissed was not something Christiaan Gerhard Cornelus Jan Stokman, Baron van Laere, was used to. Not even if the speaker was amazingly good looking, utterly fascinating, and temptingly kissable.

Women generally tripped over themselves—and each other—vying for his attention. They generally fell into two categories. Those who wanted to be filthy rich and those harboring a serious Cinderella fantasy.

Now, a third category... capable of single-handedly reversing the effects of global warming.

Christiaan studied Vicky's retreating back for a moment. Two questions popped into his mind.

Who the hell was she?

And why did he care?

"Wow, didn't the Titanic bang into her?" Baz said. "That's one cold hottie. She may look a bit like Brianna, but that's where the similarities end."

"You'll have to forgive my friend," Rainbow said. "She's normally not this—"

Frigid?

"—distracted."

"I understand. We did come unannounced." Christiaan stared at the doorway where Vicky had escaped. Should he wait here? Follow her?

The second option would be quite a challenge considering the hard-on fighting for space in his pants.

Another option? Forget her. If the Ice Princess couldn't thaw enough to acknowledge appreciation when it was given, screw her. He had bigger issues to deal with.

Like a cold shower.

"It's this awful situation with the mountain," Rainbow said. "It's got all of us tied up in knots, especially Vicky."

Not his problem.

"Those people at Summit Energy are such bastards."

His problem.

"Summit Energy?" Christiaan jerked his head toward Baz. From his face, he thought the same thing.

"Yes, those pigs want to build a geothermal industrial park that will degrade air quality, increase water pollution, damage living organisms, and threaten public health. But we are going to stop them."

"We are...?" Baz asked.

"ShastaWatch."

The proverbial thorn in Christiaan's side.

"And Miss Golden is a member?" he asked.

Rainbow nodded. "A founder. We started the group together, but she's really the driving force. Nobody's as passionate about protecting the mountain as Vicky."

A loud clap interrupted the conversation. "Okay, everybody." A scruffy young man started herding people. "Orientation time. Make your way to the classroom, please."

"Who's that?" Christiaan asked Rainbow.

"Oh, that's Dean. The other half of Climbing for Singles."

"Excuse me." Christiaan caught the man as he walked past them. "I didn't get a chance to finish my conversation with your partner. Is she in the back?" He nodded to where the Ice Princess had disappeared.

Dean shrugged one shoulder. "I doubt it. She probably

already left to take gear and provisions to the trailhead."

"How soon until she returns?"

"In a couple days. After this trip." Dean pointed toward the classroom. "Excuse me. Gotta get in there to get this show on the road."

"Of course." Christiaan nodded his head. "Thanks for your help."

The man returned the gesture and left.

"Am I getting this right?" Baz whispered in Christiaan's ear. "The hottie with the cold shoulder is the pain in our project?"

"So it appears," Christiaan said, his mind racing at lightning speed. ShastaWatch was the key to Mineral Springs. He either had to appease them or find a way to force their cooperation.

Success was now one step closer.

He knew who pulled ShastaWatch's strings.

Now he needed to find out how to yank Vicky's.

"Come on." Christiaan smiled at Rainbow then waved for Baz to follow him. "Let's take another chance on this mountain."

Was he nuts?

No, just desperate... unless desperately nuts was a socially acceptable condition.

Christiaan stood outside the Climbing for Singles building and zipped up his newly acquired down jacket to ward off the brisk wind. He smiled. Duff would probably have appreciated Christiaan making the purchase sooner and not tainting the Irishman's luck.

While they stuffed gear into their new backpacks, Baz peppered him with questions.

"Tell me again why we're doing this, bro?" his friend asked.

"Vicky is the key. She *is* ShastaWatch. A few days on the mountain will give me time to get to know her a bit and maybe devise a strategy to either make her happy so we can build our plant or get around her so we can build it."

"You think it'll be that easy?" Baz handed him a sleeping bag. "She didn't exactly thaw out for you."

"No, but on the mountain, with clients depending on her, the Ice Princess can't disappear like she did in there." Christiaan bent over to push the bag into his pack.

"Hey, Dutch Boys. I need your stuff in the bus… now," Dean said, carrying gear past them.

"Almost ready," Christiaan called after him.

Baz shook his head back and forth. "I don't know, bro. I don't see Ice Princess making nice with Prince Rape and Pillage." Holding up a set of metal spikes, Baz raised an eyebrow. "What exactly are these?"

"Crampons. You attach them to your boots for traction on snow and ice." Christiaan reached for the equipment and carefully wrapped them in a towel before putting them in his backpack. "But remember, Ice Princess doesn't know I'm Prince Rape and Pillage."

"Are you sure? Because from the look on her face, bro, if she could have frozen you stiff, she would have."

She did, metaphorically speaking.

"If Her Highness even suspected who we were—who I was—she'd have done more than sling a few verbal arrows. We'd have been tarred and feathered by now."

Baz laughed. "So her surprising immunity to the Baron catnip is simply a stroke of luck?"

"Real funny."

"Why do I have to go?" Baz squatted down to zip a roll of toilet paper into a side pocket on his pack. "Are we talking some Cyrano de Bergerac action, bro?"

"I may not be as smooth as you, but I certainly don't need lines whispered from the shadows." Christiaan folded a fleece pullover and handed it to his friend.

"No, but you *are* rusty. When's the last time you had to woo a woman, especially one not impressed by your money and title? Not since—"

"Bri, I know." Christiaan stopped packing to look up at

his friend. "But it's like riding a bike, right?"

"Yeah, well you haven't—" Baz made air quotes. "'Ridden a bike' since then either."

"I'm *not* trying to bed Vicky."

I'm not… right?

Baz's eyes narrowed. "If you're so confident you can sweet-talk her, why do I have to tag along?"

"Because if I do strike out, then the Yager charm gets to bat." Christiaan hoped it didn't come to that. The thought of Vicky and Baz together shot a stab of jealousy through him.

"I don't know, bro." Baz stood up and massaged his lower back. "We're not exactly over our last mountain adventure."

"Considering our timeframe and ShastaWatch's momentum, there's no other choice." Christiaan squatted to tighten the top drawstring on the backpack top. Pain knifed through his knee. He grimaced. "Nothing a handful of ibuprofen can't fix."

"Now's really not a good time for me." Baz gnawed his lip a moment. "I'm ass-deep in geological reports, environment impact studies, and spreadsheets galore."

Christiaan glanced up. "Which reminds me. Where is the operating costs-to-date report I asked for? I expected to see it earlier this week."

Baz tilted his head. "Accounting didn't send you the figures?"

"Not yet, but I'll need to see them as soon as we get back. Also, I'm still looking for a complete project status rundown, details on where we've been, where we are, and where we're going. I'm especially interested in estimates from the seismologists on when we'll move from final exploration to initial production."

"Yeah… yeah… I'll take care of that as soon as we get back, okay?" Baz bent over and focused on cinching his pack closed. "Are you sure you want me to go? I mean, I don't know how to use these crampon things."

"They'll teach you."

"Well," he snickered. "I planned to look for a pot of gold at the end of the Rainbow tonight."

"Her treasure will keep 'til you get back."

Baz sighed. "No matter what I say, I'm going, huh?"

"Yes."

"And this is strictly to save the project?"

"Yes."

"And nothing to do with Vicky?"

"Yes... I mean... no!" Christiaan stammered. Honestly, he wasn't sure. The connection he'd felt when she'd introduced herself was undeniable. He also couldn't reject the spark of excitement at the prospect of seeing her again.

Only because she stands between you and your company's future, right?

Vicky was strictly a means to an end. That was it.

Christiaan fumbled with the backpack's main zipper. He wished he could explain to Baz how desperate he was to ensure the project moved forward. He didn't like keeping secrets from his friend, but he didn't feel like burdening Baz with how dire the situation was.

"Well, let me make a few calls, move a few things around before my phone is as useful as a stone, bro," Baz said before wandering off.

Not a bad idea. Christiaan couldn't imagine decent—if at all—cell service on the mountain.

He pulled out his phone and dialed Lou Mancini, VL Holdings' security specialist.

One ring. "Talk to me."

"Lou, it's Christiaan. I need some background on a mountain guide out of Mt. Shasta City, California. The name is Vicky Golden. Late thirties, early forties, owns an outfit called Climbing for Singles."

"Business or pleasure?"

"What?"

"Is this for business or pleasure?" Lou asked.

"Does it make a difference?"

"Yeah, the difference between looking at financial information and criminal records or marriage records and civil restraining orders."

Christiaan hesitated. "Business. Strictly business."

"Okay, I can get you some basics by tomorrow. Give me forty-eight, and I'll tell you who her third-grade teacher was, what's her favorite Popsicle flavor, and whether she prefers boxers or briefs."

Fingers crossed for tightie-whities.

"Let's go, boys," Dean yelled from the back of a rusting yellow school bus.

Christiaan nodded in acknowledgment.

"I'll be out of touch for a day or two, Lou, so email me anything you find."

"Will do."

Christiaan slipped the phone into a pants pocket then hoisted his backpack onto his shoulder and grabbed Baz's.

"*Potverdomme!*" His bruised ribs protested. Christiaan bit his lip. He'd be fine.

As long as he didn't breathe.

"Come on." Dean motioned with his arm. "Let's get this party started."

Christiaan followed the guide to the rear of the bus. He tossed both packs into the back then followed Dean onto the bus.

Christiaan sank, literally, into an empty bench seat. On a comfort scale of one to ten, the duct-tape-covered beauty rated a zero.

Dean slid behind the steering wheel and pulled the lever to close the door. Baz jumped in right before it slammed shut.

"Sorry." Baz settled into the seat behind Christiaan.

Dean threw the bus in gear. "The adventure begins."

What an understatement. Christiaan stared out the window.

Intuition warned him that his world was about to turn upside down.

And he couldn't do anything about it.

CHAPTER 4

She'd done it again. Got away from Christiaan.

Through sunglasses, Vicky surveyed the cold, shallow snowfield she'd picked for base camp this trip. Good thing she'd decided on the early equipment run. No one had yet snagged the spot near a stone cairn large enough to protect them from the sporadic brisk wind.

Of course, she'd have had an easier time battling a hundred-mile-per-hour snowstorm than feigning indifference to the man she'd promised once to love for better or worse.

Who would have guessed what *worse* entailed?

The instant Christiaan's gaze had caught hers back in town, she forgot to breathe. Neither time nor age had softened his sculpted physique. Neither had it cooled the heat that ran through her body and pooled between her thighs every time she was near the man she loved.

Once loved.

Inches from him, the control she'd mastered over her emotions unraveled, almost. Then the sheer irony of the situation penetrated her psyche.

Christiaan saw her as a stranger. Even Baz failed to recognize her. Neither caught her "Mr. Yager" slip up.

Thank God.

Kudos to a drunk plastic surgeon and a old car without air bags. Dr. Zweit's skills had not only rebuilt her shattered nose but altered her face somewhat. The doctor tossed in a free breast reduction to avoid a lawsuit. Focused practice had eliminated the Texas twang.

"You about ready to head back?" Claude, a local college student who worked for her part-time, interrupted her thoughts. His breath turned into small white puffs as he pounded stakes into the ground for the last tent.

"Yes," she answered. Anything to get her mind off her husband. "Dean and the crew should be hitting the trailhead soon."

And by now—if there was a God—Christiaan was on his way back to The Netherlands, to Astrid's loving arms. His father must have been overjoyed when Christiaan had finally married the debutante chosen for him then sired the heir Vicky had failed to produce.

The heir she'd lost.

She kneeled to hold the last tent peg steady for Claude. Two mallet thwacks, done.

"Whoa!" he said, checking his watch. "This took longer than I thought. I'm gonna be late for class!"

She gestured to the trail with a nod. "Then let's go."

A swirl of snow whipped around Vicky as she offered a silent prayer to Mother Shasta. Forgetting Christiaan this time would be easier than the last. Eight years ago, her heart had shattered the moment she realized he'd given up on her.

He was dead to me then… still is.

Vicky worked her way down a few thousand feet of elevation, refocusing her thoughts on ShastaWatch and their efforts to protect the mountain.

Chief Running Bear would roll over in his grave if he knew the white man planned to tap his tribe's hallowed Mineral Springs area to provide energy. The property northeast of Shasta was sacred to his people. They believed the area's dozen or so hot springs heated by the earth's interior had the power to heal and renew.

Now, the world wanted to harness that gift to produce electricity.

The chief had fueled Vicky's love and respect for the mountain with stories about the mountain's legends, mythology, and folklore. His beliefs about the beauty of Shasta's mix of strength and vulnerabilities helped Vicky find herself.

She tipped her face into the sun. Unfortunately, the rest of the world didn't share the Native American's appreciation for nature. Jane and Joe Q. Public couldn't get past their never-ending energy needs. The government couldn't see past their own shortsighted political agenda. Summit Energy saw only hefty profits.

But they all underestimated ShastaWatch. The group was successful at stopping similar projects and would prevail again this time.

Vicky still had a few tricks up her sleeve. She'd learned a thing or two as the wife of a hard-nosed businessman. She wasn't about to let anyone take away the most precious thing in her life without a fight.

Not again.

A shortcut through the trees put her at the trailhead parking lot and an extremely out-of-breath Claude.

"You okay?" Vicky asked.

"Peachy."

A manic flutter of warblers and chickadees overhead announced a vehicle's approach. Loud backfire heralded the arrival of the Climbing for Singles bus.

Claude hopped into the bed of Vicky's old truck and tossed the last gear bags onto the ground. "You sure you don't want me to tag along to camp with these two?"

"Nah, I got 'em." She tossed him the truck keys. "Get your butt to class."

"Yes, ma'am. I'll be back late tomorrow afternoon to help break camp." Claude jumped behind the wheel, started the engine, then sped out of the lot.

Vicky crouched next to the pile of gear. Bungees that had secured the bags into the truck bed lay strewn about.

Behind her, one final exhaust bang told her Dean had parked the bus. She yanked a small red pouch from her jacket and spent the next several minutes rounding up stray cords.

Faint footsteps caught her attention.

"Miss Golden?"

She looked up to find a camera inches from her face. Gently, she pushed it away.

"Hi." The young woman offered a hand. "Paige Williams. *Inc.* magazine."

"How nice to meet you." Vicky shook the writer's hand then gestured toward the mountain range behind them. "Welcome to Mt. Shasta. Breathtaking, isn't it?"

"Yes, very."

"First time here?"

"Yes." The reporter snapped a few images. "I've read about McKinley and seen pictures of Rainier, but nothing really about Shasta."

"McKinley's higher and Rainier's famous, but Shasta… she's special." Vicky returned to gathering bungees.

"Why?"

"Because so many myths and legends surround her," Vicky said. "One story deals with the Lemurians, a super race who built a golden city called Telos in the center of Shasta."

"Come on. That's crazy," the reporter said over digital camera clicks.

"Not according to the locals." Vicky shoved the last of the cords into the red pouch, pulled the drawstring tight, then tossed it next to the gear bags. "Shasta Indians won't ascend above the timberline of *Waki-nunee-Tuki-Wuki*. Not out of fear, but—" She smothered the camera, once again pointed at her. "*No* pictures."

"Why?"

Because tempting fate is not for people supposedly dead. Vicky shook her head.

"Camera shy, huh?" the reporter said.

"Yeah, that's it."

"Okay." The reporter sighed. "So, are you from around here?"

"No." Vicky's brain snapped to full alert anytime someone asked about her past.

"Have you been a climber all your life?"

Vicky smiled, remembering tenacity was a reporter's best trait. Of course, it worked both ways.

"Hey, aren't you here to write about Climbing for Singles?" she asked. "Let's talk about that."

"A forty-year-old woman who summits mountains around the world *and* runs a successful climbing business would make a great feature story."

"No."

"You'll be famous."

"Don't want to be."

"Come on," the reporter laughed. "What are you afraid of?"

Spiders, cellulite, and someone from my past recognizing me.

Vicky forced a smile. "I just like my privacy. Write about anything else but me."

"And there's nothing I can say or do that will change your mind?"

"No."

"Okay, okay." The reporter raised both hands in surrender. "*No* pictures. *No* talking about you. *No* nothing."

"No is such a discouraging word." A deep accented voice caressed Vicky's ear.

Crap. She slowly turned and collided with a powerful, rock-hard, unforgettable body. She inhaled slowly, exhaled softly, and almost melted from his spicy masculine scent.

Double crap. She peered up. A wicked smile filled her husband's devastatingly handsome face. She swallowed.

Hard.

Triple crap.

Lucky for him those damn mirrored sunglasses had flown off her face when she'd bumped into him. Christiaan could drown in those eyes.

Beautiful.

Haunting.

Familiar.

"What are *you* doing here?" Vicky jerked back. The cool beauty of her tanned face contrasted with the hot anger chasing up her cheeks.

"Baron van Laere." A young woman holding a camera appeared at his elbow. "Paige Williams. *Inc.* magazine. Could I have a moment of—"

"What are *you* doing here?" The Ice Princess repeated, eyes blazing.

Christiaan flashed a coy smile. "Giving the mountain a second chance. I'm hoping she'll return the favor."

That curious American adage, "if looks could kill," seemed appropriate. Dead would be his current state if the daggers shooting from Vicky's eyes were real.

She plunged delicate fingers through gorgeous chestnut hair then nibbled a luscious lower lip.

Again. That movement.

"You... you're not supposed to be... be here," Vicky stammered. "Who said you could be on my mountain?"

"Your partner seemed to think it was a great idea, especially when we paid for everything in cash."

"We?"

"Myself and Baz."

"Dean!" Vicky whirled away, tripping over a small red bag in the process. A tangle of bungees fell at her feet. "He's gone *too* far this time."

Christiaan lowered his head to hide the laugh fighting to break free. A stray cord lay on his right boot. He handed it to the fiery redhead. When his fingers brushed her arm, she jumped like a wanted woman.

Wanted, all right. By him.

"Th-thanks," murmured Vicky, snatching the bungee from him and shoving it into the red pouch now in her hand. She flung the bundle into a nearby open backpack then pointed a finger at Christiaan. "*You* wait here while I straighten this out." A tremor touched her smooth lips. She snared the fallen sunglasses then stomped to the other side of the parking lot.

Christiaan chuckled. Round one of the mental wrestling match had ended in favor of the Dutch contender. He couldn't wait until the bell rang again. Until then, he'd survey scenery.

Framed by a forest of red firs and mountain hemlocks, Mt. Shasta soared in the background, surrounded by clouds. A symphony of bird songs and nature melodies proved a fitting soundtrack to the picture.

The midday sun burned bright, but the temperature remained low. Cold air tickled the hairs inside his nose. A small breeze picked up, sending a handful of loose snow into his face.

"Baron van Laere?"

Much to his disappointment, the reporter hadn't moved from his elbow.

"Paige Williams. *Inc.* magazine. I'd love to interview you."

"Please, call me Christiaan."

"Okay... Christiaan..." She stepped closer. "What is the head of one of Europe's largest conglomerates doing on Mt. Shasta?"

Wishing all reporters wore bells around their necks for easy identification.

"Sorry, no interviews."

"Are you here looking to expand into the U.S.?"

"No," he answered, hoping his laugh diffused the truth of her speculations. "I'm simply here to enjoy some long-overdue time off."

"You said something about giving the mountain another chance. Are you referring to the accident you were involved in a few days ago?"

Potverdomme! He'd paid a lot of money to a lot of people to ensure the crash never made the news.

"How did you—"

The reporter leaned back, eyes unblinking. "Are rumors about your company true?"

"Rumors? What rumors?"

"That you're in serious financial trouble. That since your wife's accidental death, you've lost your golden touch. That your family's century-old enterprise is nearly bankrupt."

Christiaan struggled to maintain his composure.

"Sweetheart..." Baz walked into view, two packs slung over his right shoulder. "You don't build a billion-dollar holding company without—as you Americans love to put it—pushing the envelope a bit. Besides, what better assets to be born with than blue blood in your veins and a silver spoon in your mouth?"

"And you are?" the reporter asked, the corner of her mouth twisted in obvious exasperation.

"Bastiaan Yager, right-hand man extraordinaire and designated sherpa to His Grace." He brought the reporter's hand to his lips and kissed her knuckles. "But you may call me Baz. All my friends do."

"Okay... Baz." She pasted on a happy face, but her body language told a different story. "Are you willing to talk to me about the troubles at VL Holdings?"

"No, but I'd love to show you what—"

The reporter jerked her hand away, muttered something about him being a pain in her butt, and walked off.

"—going Dutch really means." Baz nodded toward the departing woman. "Hmmm... two angry women in one day. I guess the Baron thing just doesn't play well with some American chicks."

Especially not one that knew way more about

Christiaan's current situation than she should. Where was the reporter getting her information? And why was she focused on him?

"I gather the Ice Princess isn't happy we're on her mountain," Baz said. "She looked at me like she wanted to remove my testicles with her bare hands. The reporter looked like she wanted to do the same thing to you, bro. Let's bag this, head back into town, and keep our boys safe and sound."

"I'm *not* leaving," Christiaan snapped. He wasn't going anywhere until he had a clear-cut strategy to either appease or circumvent Vicky Golden and her merry band of misguided environmentalists.

The reporter he could handle. Vicky? He wasn't so sure.

Fear and anxiety knotted inside him. He needed to push this thing along and hard. Assets were running out. Another six to nine months, and he'd be bankrupt.

The Mineral Springs project had to get started. The company was all he had left in this world.

Christiaan watched the object of his frustration and fascination storm back across the parking lot.

She was the key to everything.

Igniting his hormones was a side benefit.

Or a curse.

He hadn't held such an inexplicable fascination with a woman since...

Bri.

But Baz was right. They may look somewhat alike, but the two women were as different as night and day.

Vicky stopped within striking distance.

Ding. Ding. Round Two.

Christiaan took a step back, half expecting an eye-dagger thrown at his throat.

"Everything seems to be in order," she said, her tone chillier than the air around them. "Welcome to Climbing for Singles, gentlemen."

The Dutchman takes Round Two.

"Let's go." Vicky grabbed the gear bags she'd tripped over earlier and tossed them onto her back. "We need to get everybody moving so we can be settled into camp before dark."

"Would you like me to help you with those?" Christiaan asked.

She leaned into him and jabbed her index finger into his chest, missing his sore ribs by an inch. "I don't need or want anything from you, Baron… van… Laere."

Ding. Ding. Round Three.

CHAPTER 5

Rock. Vicky. Hard place.

Yep, I'm between 'em.

Vicky sat on the fringes of the group, sipping hot Chamomile and toying with the zipper on her jacket. Soft moonlight mixed with the warm glow from the campfire, illuminating everything in muted amber tones. The evening meal finished, Dean served his version of an after-dinner liqueur… warm cider.

"Guaranteed to warm your insides and land you in a tent not your own." Dean grinned like a Cheshire cat. "It's not the cider that does it. It's the whiskey I use to 'cool it… off.'"

Vicky laughed. He needed a new line. That one was at least four years old.

Dean started a word game for the romantic hopefuls gathered around the campfire.

"My name is Dean. I come from Detroit. I drive a Dodge, and I like to eat deviled eggs." He turned to his right. "Your turn."

"My name is Baz Yager. I come from Breda. I drive a BMW, and I like to eat *broodjes*."

"*Broodjes?*" Dean asked.

"Rolls," Baz answered.

Voices and laughter faded in and out as Vicky peered at her husband, seated near the fire. Between him and Baz sat a voluptuous, surgically enhanced blond with a tush you could bounce quarters off.

Of course, the incessant playboy Baz vied for the bimbo's attention. However, she seemed intent on gaining Christiaan's.

Who didn't seem to notice. He sat focused on the flames, fingers steepled against firm lips, sculpted face set in determination.

Why are you here?

"You're up, Paige," said Dean.

"Okay. My name is Paige. I come from Pasadena. I drive a Porsche, and I like to eat pizza."

For a man in his early forties, Christiaan had the physique of someone half that age. Broad shoulders flexed as he removed a snug jacket, revealing an even tighter long-sleeve sweatshirt and a gold chain that disappeared inside the collar.

Firelight accented a firm chest that tapered to a lean, muscled abdomen. Snug-fitting pants emphasized his long, powerful legs.

Vicky's heart skipped a beat. His chiseled cheekbones mesmerized her. His dark expression, provocative.

Her body responded. It was impossible to look at him and not want to run her hands— No, tongue all over that body.

She hadn't done that to any man before Christiaan.

Or any man since.

As if reading her mind, Christiaan stared in her direction. His square jaw tensed visibly.

Why are you here? Why am I still here?

Because Claude took her truck and she couldn't drive the bus. Plus, canceling the trip at this point would have caused more questions, especially from that pushy reporter.

"Dutch," asked Dean. "You game?"

"Why not?" Christiaan answered. His gaze remained focused on Vicky. "My name is Christiaan. I come from Catrip. I drive a Charon, and I like to eat *chocolade*... chocolate."

Vicky wrapped her hands around her tea mug in a futile attempt to steady herself and her emotions.

Man, I need a drink.

If only she could run her fingers through his thick brown hair. If only she could taste the warmth of his mouth. If only she could feel the sensation of his hands on her bare skin.

If only she could be his Brianna again.

If only he hadn't stopped loving her.

"Okay, who hasn't gone yet?" Dean said.

"I don't think Vicky has taken a turn." Christiaan's eyes burned deep into hers.

She retreated further into the darkness.

"My turn! I haven't gone either!" The blond and her breasts bounced. "My name is Heather. I come from Hollywood. I drive a Hummer, and I eat jalapeños."

Everyone laughed. The blank look on her face confirmed Vicky's earlier assessment. Heather's IQ was about the same as her bust line... forty-two.

Christiaan leaned over to explain. "Jalapeños start with a J."

"Really? Are you sure?" The blond patted his knee.

Then let her hand rest there.

A shot of jealousy stabbed Vicky. Serves her right. Her fingers drummed against the mug.

She should have taken off the moment Christiaan bumped into her at the trailhead. No, she should have disappeared when he showed up at the Climbing for Singles office.

Vicky shook her head. Why defy all logic and place herself in danger?

She didn't have an answer... at least not one that made sense.

A cold shiver spread over Vicky as she remembered the events that ended her marriage and her "life". Even now, the horrific truth that murder seemed easier than divorce pierced her heart like a dagger.

He's the reason you're "dead".

She sipped at her Chamomile tea, now lukewarm, but still soothing.

The reporter had called him Baron van Laere. Obviously, he'd finally inherited his father's title. Astrid must love her new spot in Dutch society. Had she produced the heir and spare yet?

Over the rim of her mug, Vicky caught Christiaan staring at her again, his expression vague.

Why are you here?

He clearly didn't recognize her. So, if he didn't know who she actually was, why was he following her?

Unconscious attraction?

Perverse fascination?

Romantic motivation?

Too many questions. Not enough answers.

From the other side of the fire, Baz followed Christiaan's gaze. He stared at her intently before refocusing his attention on the blond.

Obviously tired of being ignored, the bimbo turned aggressive. She tried wrapping an arm around Christiaan, who winced when she brushed against his rib cage.

Vicky's breath caught in concern. His injuries were worse than he let on. She should have insisted he return to town. Or at the very least, had someone carry his backpack.

Stop caring about him. He stopped caring about you a long time ago.

This wasn't going to work. Vicky had to stop thinking like Brianna the victim and start seeing things as Vicky the survivor.

She needed a plan.

Hiding in the shadows, watching the over-siliconed, over-botoxed, over-bleached blond paw at Christiaan,

Vicky weighed her options.

Stay here and risk discovery.

Or hightail it off the mountain and out of town before anyone was the wiser.

Vicky twisted the mug in her hands. She methodically analyzed each alternative.

Neither promised much hope of success.

A curse escaped her lips, the breath clouding in the cool air. Taking off now and disappearing would only arouse suspicion, especially Christiaan's. Not to mention placing her clients' safety in jeopardy.

But staying and tempting fate wasn't feasible either.

Or was it?

Christiaan saw her as a female mountain climber with a major-bitch attitude, a complete one-eighty from her former self.

She grinned mischievously. Why not hide in plain sight, right underneath his nose? He'd never suspect a thing.

His precious Bri was dead, *right?*

She'd only need to keep her distance for one more day. Once they hit town again, he'd head home, climbing trip over.

Vicky smiled and relaxed the grip on her mug.

After all, why else would he stay?

Can you get close to a snarling tiger without her handing you your balls on a silver platter?

Christiaan studied Vicky, alone on a large boulder. The soft glow of the campfire played over her face, accentuating the strength of her perfect features.

And her intense but secretive expression. She sported a smile, but not for one minute did he believe the Ice Princess was melting.

Since their heated exchange at the trailhead, she'd avoided him. On the rare occasions their eyes had locked, she'd stare at him, almost into him, then turn away. An odd sensation—intimacy mixed with pain—stabbed at him. It was hard to ignore.

And incredible arousing. Christiaan groaned in the back of his throat.

The dancing flames entranced him, like the woman in question. Brilliant... spellbinding... intense... Get too close and get burned.

He was already sizzling and ready to go up in smoke.

The last time he felt this strong for a woman, he'd faked an injury to gain her sympathy.

Christiaan smiled. The cheap ploy during his rugby match had worked. Bri interviewed him for some silly article while he iced the invented trauma. They ended up spending the entire weekend in each other's arms at a secluded beachside house in the Caribbean. They married a week later.

Now he really was injured and highly doubted Vicky would offer any sympathy. She was likely to harm him more.

Christiaan peered at the redhead sipping tea. Her body language conveyed "don't screw with me", but something in her face revealed vulnerability. Somewhere, someone had wounded her soul.

Who could be so cruel?

"Knock knock," Dean said, laughing.

"Who's there?" The reporter asked from her spot on the other side of the campfire.

"Ben," Dean urged.

"Ben who?"

"Ben Dover."

Christiaan snickered. The crowd's laughter encouraged the amateur comedian.

"Knock, knock," Dean said.

"Who's there?" someone asked.

"Broccoli."

"Broccoli who?"

"Silly girl. Broccoli doesn't have a last name."

This time the crowd split between chuckles and jeers.

"I've got one," the reporter said. "Knock, knock."

"Who's there?" Dean said.

"Police."

"Police who?"

"Police stop telling me these stupid knock-knock jokes!"

More laughter.

"Knock, knock." Baz joined in the fun.

"Who's there?" asked Christiaan.

"Amsterdam."

"Amsterdam who?"

"Answer the damn door. It's freezing out here!"

Corny, but Christiaan couldn't help laughing.

Even the Ice Princess chuckled.

His gaze riveted on hers. The pleasure lighting her face caused a familiar clutch in his groin. She couldn't possibly know the affect she had on him, but he nodded in appreciation anyway.

Vicky shivered, but Christiaan sensed the intensity wasn't from the cold mountain air. Then her expression did an emotional one-eighty.

Iceberg dead ahead, Captain.

"I've got a joke," the reporter offered. "A drunk calls 911 on his cell phone to report his car's been broken into. Outraged, he explains to the dispatcher, 'They've stolen the stereo, the steering wheel, the brake pedal, even the accelerator!' He's instructed to remain calm and wait for an officer to arrive. Minutes later, the officer radios in. 'Disregard the call,' he says. 'The drunk crawled into the backseat'."

Everyone fell apart at the punch line. Everyone except Christiaan. Drunk jokes weren't funny. Then again, he'd been married to a drunk. And nothing Bri ever did as one was funny.

Sad. Hurtful. Never funny.

Vicky wasn't laughing either.

Obviously, the reporter found alcoholism hilarious. "A

car sped off the highway, went through the guard rail, bounced off a tree, and finally shuddered to a stop. A witness to the accident helped the miraculously unharmed driver out of the wreck. 'Goodness, ma'am,' he gasped. 'Are you drunk?' 'Of course,' said the woman, brushing the dirt from her shirt. 'What the hell do you think I am… a stunt driver?'"

The whole group howled.

"I got one," Dean said. "A drunk walks into a bar…"

Vicky jerked to her feet, one hand on her mug, the other jammed into her pants pocket. Christiaan read her mind as easily as he could his own.

Unbelievable.

She turned and headed into the darkness.

"Vicky, wait," he said, jumping up to follow her. A whirl of snow hissed past him as he caught up and placed a hand on her shoulder.

She answered without turning around. "I'm tired. I have no energy left to trade clever barbs with you." Slipping from beneath his grasp, she headed toward her tent.

"How long have you been sober?"

Vicky stopped dead, her warm breath swirling in the cold air. "I don't know what you're talking about."

"Yes, you do."

She whirled around. "How?" The pain of discovery etched on her face could move a mountain.

"Your refusal to partake of the spiked cider. Your response to the drunk jokes." He stopped to take a deep breath. "Look, it's nothing to be ashamed of."

"Recovering alcoholic…" she said, running a hand through her hair and nibbling the corner of her bottom lip. "Not exactly a title to be proud of."

"Beating the bottle is an impressive accomplishment," Christiaan said. "Don't let anyone convince you otherwise."

An eight-year burden lessened as he suddenly offered words and understanding he wished he'd shared with his wife. Before he'd lost Bri, her drinking had escalated. After her death, he finally understood how she'd crawled into the bottle. He'd married an American who failed to produce an heir. An inadequacy the van Laere family constantly mentioned no matter who was within earshot.

If only he'd recognized her descent into depression.

If only he'd stood up to his father.

If only he'd shown her love instead of contempt on their last night together.

"It takes courage to fight the demons of alcohol," he told Vicky. "My wife died before I could tell her that, and I've regretted it ever since."

A tender moment passed between them. Vicky's hand eased from her pocket. Something peeking out from her fist caught the moonlight. Whatever the item, her white-knuckled grip suggested it meant more than anything to her.

Palm outstretched, Christiaan stepped closer. "May I?"

Like a frightened rabbit, she stood as if trying to decide whether the source of the danger she sensed was directly in front of her or buried deep inside.

He was prepared to say goodnight and leave when she reached out and placed her fist in his hand.

The touch fired a shot of raw desire through him. Vicky must have felt the heat, too, because she immediately dropped the item into his hand and stepped back.

A small gold coin with raised lettering lay in his palm. Portions of a triangle with Roman numerals VII etched in the middle appeared worn as if rubbed many times. The words "One Day at a Time" appeared on the reverse.

"What is it?" he asked.

"My AA anniversary chip. My sobriety sponsor gives me a new one each year I manage not to take a drink."

"A silent reminder of your commitment?"

Vicky nodded.

Christiaan fingered the chip. "VII. Seven years of sobriety?"

"Seven very hard, torturous, but worth-it years."

"From the worn surface, I'd guess your eight-year prize is due soon."

Piercing platinum eyes looked up at him. A flood of emotions ambushed Christiaan. Some about Bri. Some about Vicky. Many conflicting.

Before he realized what he was doing, Christiaan grazed her cheek with his free hand. "Eight years is a long time. Congratulations on making a new life for yourself."

Vicky drew back, her expression now as cold as the light snow swirling around them. She snatched the coin from his hand.

"Like I had a choice." She glared at him like the highlight of her day would be to scratch his eyes out.

"Wait," Christiaan said. "I didn't—"

She strode past him, her jaw set, eyes straight ahead. What had upset her? He was as clueless as the blond who'd hung all over him earlier.

Baz appeared from the shadows as Christiaan debated whether to follow her or not.

"Imagine that," his friend said. "An alcoholic."

"You overheard?"

"Yes, and may I say you're brilliant, bro?" Baz placed a hand on Christiaan's shoulder. "The way you keyed into her weakness. Got her to reveal her secret, then tested her embarrassment level. Now we have what we need to make her toe the line."

"What are you talking about?" The small hairs on the back of Christiaan's neck bristled. He wasn't exactly sure where this was headed, but the sinister undertone of the remarks was clear.

"It's not a sobriety chip. It's a bargaining chip."

Christiaan stared at Baz. "You're suggesting blackmail?"

"Yes, I am. Think about it, Chris. She's obviously ashamed of her alcoholism and probably would do anything to keep it hidden. Threaten to take her secret public, and she'll call off the ShastaWatch dogs."

The idea's tentacles wrapped themselves around Christiaan's mind. Extortion wasn't his style. He preferred using intelligence and reason to achieve his goals.

A stab of conscience pierced his gut. Stooping to smear tactics was the act of a desperate man.

Which is exactly what he was. Without Mineral Springs, he'd lose everything.

VL Holdings was all he had left.

And if pulling something underhanded would save it, so be it.

The last time he failed to fight for what mattered to him, he lost her to fate and a deadly explosion.

Christiaan glimpsed Vicky saying goodnight to everyone then entering her tent.

Bri's face flashed across his mind. If anyone had dared use her alcoholism against her, he'd have killed the person.

Yet, that's exactly what Baz proposed.

Shame twisted at Christiaan's gut. If Bri was alive, she'd be so disappointed in him. He reached for the gold band hanging from his neck.

For the first time in eight years, he thanked God she wasn't.

CHAPTER 6

From his perch on the mountain, Christiaan stared at the breathtaking beauty before him.

And the scenery on Shasta wasn't bad, either.

Thirty feet away, Vicky sunned herself on a flat gray boulder. Like a Greek priestess paying homage to the gods, she raised her face to the heavens, sun-kissed hair teasing a slender, kissable neck.

The tight, sweat-drenched top and form-fitting pants revealed a body honed by hard work, perseverance, and passion. A visual of him using his tongue to prove that theory kicked his dust-covered libido into overdrive and begged for attention.

Potverdomme! Eight years is too long to be celibate.

Christiaan dismissed the vision and shifted enough to give his erection room to breathe. Enough thinking with the little head. Right now, he needed to use the one sitting on his shoulders to focus on more pressing, rational thoughts.

Sorry, boy.

Since the deep freeze last night, the closest Christiaan got to the Ice Princess was one "Good morning" and two "Watch your footing" on their way up the mountain. Only a few hours until they returned to the real world and Christiaan wasn't any closer to her or an acceptable strategy than when he started.

He eyeballed the group. Everyone lounged on various outcroppings, eating peanut butter sandwiches. Baz sat perched on a smaller boulder next to the reporter. Dean entertained them with tales of his climbing exploits.

"Okay, so, I'm just about to lose my footing. I literally push away from the mountain, jam my axe into the ice, thus saving myself and my team." Dean blew on his fingernails then buffed them on the front of his shirt.

"Tell us another one," the reporter asked, holding a digital recorder closer to him.

"Okay." He jumped into some story about Joshua Tree National Park, a rockslide, and a former Miss Oregon "with a body like a walking fantasy".

Christiaan yawned. He'd been up half the night pondering his situation and his conscience. His sore ribcage a fading memory thanks to an overdose of ibuprofen, he leaned back in time to see a hawk glide in circles across the blue sky. Many an afternoon as a child had been spent like this, gazing at white billows drifting overhead. A young Christiaan would whine about the burdens of wealth and privilege while a young Baz grumbled about the burdens of poverty.

Christiaan snorted. The roles would be reversed if the Mineral Springs project failed. Baz would relish the juxtaposition.

Christiaan bolted upright. Mineral Springs would not fail. He hadn't leveraged everything he owned to lose it to a cold, vindictive woman and her eco-misfits.

Vicky stretched forward in a yoga-like pose, gently touching her forehead to her knees. He glimpsed a red thong peeking out from her climbing pants and barely stifled a thick groan from the back of his throat.

A sinfully erotic cold, vindictive woman and her eco-misfits.

"So when I said Joshua spanked me hard, she called me a pervert," Dean explained. "She didn't understand I was saying how the climb had completely worn me out."

Everyone laughed.

"Any other interesting stories?" the reporter asked.

"Well..." Dean checked his watch. "Maybe one more. My best climbing story includes Vic. We were part of an expedition support team in Alaska. Vic adding McKinley to her Seven Summits string, and me along for the ride."

"Seven Summits?" Christiaan asked.

"The highest peaks on the earth's seven continents. Kilimanjaro in Africa, Elbrus in Europe, Aconcagua in South America, Kosciusko in Australia, Vinson in Antarctica, McKinley in North America, and, of course, Everest in Asia. Something like only four hundred climbers have completed them all."

A collective "wow" rose from the crowd. Christiaan agreed.

"Vic's only missing one... Everest," Dean answered. "Anyway, we're on day three, ferrying oxygen tanks, when one of the locals who's ahead of us loses his footing." Dean paused for effect. "The metal tanks he's carrying on his back shift and knock him unconscious."

"Wow!" The reporter leaned in closer.

"Wait, it gets worse. I was directly behind him, so his body hit me first and got entangled in my pack. The tanks I'm carrying jar loose and fall away as both of us go sailing straight down the mountain." Dean gestured with his hands.

"You must have been moving at a pretty good clip," Baz said.

"Flying. I couldn't stop myself 'cause I'd lost my ice axe when the dude hit me."

"So what'd you do?"

"Actually, *I* didn't do anything." Dean nodded his head toward his partner. "Vic did. She was about fifty yards behind us. Saw us falling, dropped her pack, and—to this day I still can't believe it—anchored herself to the mountain with her crampons then drove her ice axe straight through my pant leg into the surface."

"While you were falling?" someone asked.

"Yes. With a free hand, she grabbed me—now remember I still had the out-cold guy strapped to me—and we came to a bone-jarring stop. Once I caught my breath and my bearings, I got myself semi-anchored, as best you can with a hundred-fifty-pound dead weight hanging on you. Vic radioed our position, and we were airlifted out within the hour."

Silence covered the group. Everyone's mouth, including Christiaan's, opened wide enough to walk an elephant into. They all turned to stare at Vicky.

Who was still in seated-forward-bend-with-winking-thong pose.

"Yo, Vicky." One of the guys in the group yelled, giving her thumbs up. "Balls of steel, babe. Balls of steel." The entire group exploded into laughter.

Vicky sat up, the corners of her lips curved. Her high, sculpted cheekbones rose as she laughed, the animation enchanting. "Never leave home without it." She patted the thin axe hanging from her hip.

No denying the woman possessed a hefty set. Climbing mountains, performing superhuman feats, and serving as Mother Nature's pit bull took balls.

But last night she'd revealed a weakness. One prime for exploitation.

Baz walked over and sat down next to Christiaan. "'Local Climbing Hero Former Drunk' would make a great headline, bro," he whispered. "ShastaWatch supporters would read that over their morning coffee and drop like flies by afternoon tea."

Christiaan nodded. "It's a half-truth and a cheap shot."

"No worse than her claim that Summit Energy plans to rape the mountain."

"I understand what you're saying, but I'm still not comfortable with this," Christiaan answered, touching the wedding ring hanging under his shirt. "Bri would be so disappointed in me."

Baz crossed his arms and stared into Christiaan's eyes. "She's dead, Chris. Dead. Move on."

Even now, the words stung like salt in an open wound.

"Look at it this way," Baz said. "We're not *actually* going public with the info, merely threatening to. Vicky will call the dogs off to keep her secret, I get to do what I came here to do, and Bri rests in peace."

Christiaan sighed and looked away. His life had always been based on honesty, integrity, and fairness.

But now he had no choice. Too much was at stake. Using Vicky's alcoholism to his advantage may be deceptive, exploitative, and unethical.

But not illegal.

Christiaan glanced at Vicky. She turned and held his gaze, those luminous gray eyes boring into him.

Those eyes.

Vicky would never forgive him.

Neither would Bri.

Vicky cursed life in general as the late morning sun warmed her body. Already twenty degrees higher than when they'd started this morning, the temperature continued to climb.

Along with her anxiety.

She tried to refocus her thoughts and breathe in the wondrous landscape. Unfortunately, Mother Shasta could do nothing to soothe the emotional turmoil provoked by her husband's presence.

Last night had rattled her. What had possessed her to talk to him let alone pull out her AA token?

Christiaan's manner had reminded Vicky of the day they met. He'd charmed her with good looks, a disarming personality, and that elegant Dutch accent. They'd fallen in love that day and had been inseparable.

Until...

The dull ache in her heart and the unsettling between her thighs underscored the situation.

She chuckled to herself. Situation. Sounded so innocent. Forgetting to pack soap, that was a situation. Misplacing a canteen of water, that was a situation.

Pretending you're somebody else to the one person who knows—correction, knew—you better than anyone? That was a nightmare.

A red-tailed hawk screeching overhead penetrated the mental fog surrounding her. Checking her watch, Vicky refocused her mind and rose from the rock.

"So Dean," the reporter asked. "How long have you and Vicky known each other?"

"A couple of years. Vic just showed up one day. A real gumby. Had never done anything athletic in her life. I taught her how to climb." He laughed. "Of course, first I had to get her over her fear of hei—"

"Hey, guys." Vicky jerked to her feet and clapped her hands together. Hopefully, the sound had masked Dean's last remark. "We really need to get moving."

He checked his watch. "Vic's right. Time to head down."

"Don't forget to put everything back into your packs," Vicky reminded everyone. "That includes garbage. Pack it in, pack it out."

She shoved the empty wrapper from her nutrition bar into a side pouch and shrugged on her jacket then gear. To her left, she caught a delightful view of Christiaan's backside as he reached for a banana peel on the ground. Her heart pounded.

Wooden shoes make for great buns of steel.

"Vicky, I need your help." The reporter walked up and dropped her backpack on the ground between them. "I think I broke this."

"Let's see." Vicky hoisted the pack onto a nearby boulder and identified the problem. A shoulder strap had somehow gotten loose from its cinch strap buckle. "Not broken, just unraveled."

"Gee." Paige shrugged her shoulders. "I don't know how that happened."

I hope she's a better reporter than a liar.

Vicky smiled then began the tedious job of rethreading the strap through the multitude of slots on the buckle.

"Dean tells me you're pretty active in a local environmental group. ShastaWatch, is it?"

"I thought we agreed you weren't going to write about me," Vicky answered without looking up. She didn't want to make a mistake. Loose equipment could be a climbing hazard.

"Can't we at least talk about your group? I'm sure you guys could use a friend in the media."

Good point. ShastaWatch could use all the help they could get in their fight against Summit Energy.

"What would you like to know?" Vicky asked, threading the strap through the last two slots.

"In your opinion, what's the greatest threat to Mt. Shasta?"

"Not what, who," Vicky said as she double-checked her work. "Real-estate developers. Power companies. Politicians wheeling and dealing for campaign contributions. They're all environmental rapists."

"You don't pull any punches, do you?"

"Not when it comes to saving my mountain." Vicky pulled to ensure the strap would hold then looked at Paige. "Right now, I'm trying to stop the building of a geothermal industrial park at Mineral Springs, a pristine and sacred Native-American Indian site. The federal government and the power company holding the drilling leases say 'don't worry, it's okay... it's renewable energy... it's green energy... it's safe'."

Vicky stood. "But it's not okay. Geothermal is not green... geothermal power plants emit low levels of carbon dioxide, nitric oxide, and sulfur. It's not renewable... locations may eventually cool down as there's only so much energy that can be stored and replenished in a given volume of earth. And it's not safe... earthquakes in Europe, China, and Australia are known to have been triggered by nearby geothermal facilities."

"Wow, you're pretty fired up about this."

"Yes I am. For over twenty years, power companies have tried to tap Mother Shasta's volcanic highlands. She deserves to remain pristine and untouched for generations."

"How do you plan on ensuring that?"

"By declaring war on Summit Energy." Vicky handed the backpack to the reporter.

"You sound pretty sure of yourself," a Dutch accent said behind her.

Vicky turned to find Christiaan and Baz standing there. She was not going to get into a debate with those two. Neither had ever been interested in social causes. They always sided with business.

"Okay, everyone." She checked her watch. "We need to get moving." *Now.* Vicky needed to get some physical space between herself and her husband.

Mental space wasn't so easy.

She couldn't stop herself from gazing at his tall length. The straps hugging his chest made heat pool low in her stomach. In six years of mountain climbing, she'd seen hundreds of male chests framed by gear. But not one had prompted an overpowering urge to slip her hands under clothing to touch bare flesh.

None. Until today.

Vicky swallowed a deep breath and tried to erase a vision of her lips playing with the muscular ridges of his abdomen. Only a few more hours until the torture was over. Goodbyes would be said, and she could escape to her lodge to forget everything about the last two days. Forget the pain. Forget the pleasure.

Forget Christiaan.

"When your bag is packed and on your back," Vicky

said to the entire group. "Double check your crampons are secure and free of any ice buildup then file into line behind me. Remember, pay attention and watch your footing."

Just her bad luck, Christiaan and Baz were ready before anyone else... including Dean.

"Gotta siphon the python." A slow grin spread across Dean's face before disappearing behind a rock.

"*Hij is gek*," Christiaan said directly behind her.

"Yeah, he's crazy," she replied.

Christiaan smiled.

A devastatingly dark, sinful smile. The expression still took her breath away, just like the day fifteen years ago when she arrived in Amsterdam to interview him. An afternoon of watching him play rugby turned into a long weekend in the Caribbean. Four incredible days—and nights—of love, romance, and passion still today left her breathless at the memory.

Oh, their passion. Smoldering. Tantalizing. Intoxicating. Vicky clung to the images like a climber dangling from the edge of a crevasse.

She turned to head the crew down the mountain, and a spray of snow blew off a nearby rock to kiss her face.

She'd fallen in love with Christiaan the moment they met. He was Prince Charming to her Cinderella, introducing her to a world unlike her own humble existence in Texas.

He'd defied his father to marry her.

He'd insisted she accompany him on his travels to discover investment opportunities all over the world.

He'd refused to blame her for their failure to conceive a child.

Then everything changed. She choked back a tear. He betrayed their love for Astrid.

Vicky's foot caught on something, pitching her body forward.

What the he—?

Off balance, she stumbled and immediately grabbed for

her axe. Chunks of falling ice and rock stung exposed flesh as she slid down the steep slope. On her back, she was fighting gravity.

And losing.

Gaining speed, she flipped onto her stomach, bent her knees, and jammed the axe point into the thick snow.

She skidded to a stop less than forty feet from a sheer drop-off.

"Vicky!" Dean's baritone cut through the other voices calling her name.

She struggled to get as much of her weight over the head of her axe, but Mother Shasta refused to cooperate. Rocks dislodged by the fall rained down. An extremely sharp one bit into her hand and she lost her grip.

No!

Her only hold on the mountain was gone.

Vicky slid closer to the drop-off.

Dig! Dig! Dig!

She clasped her hands together against the slope to accumulate snow in them and distributed her weight evenly. The combined movement created friction and slowed her descent. She hammered her elbows and knees into the surface. Slow. Slower.

Stop.

She jammed the steel toe points of her crampons into the mountain and took a deep breath. Heart beating like a jackhammer, she sized up the situation.

Not good.

A loose, palm-sized rock perched inches from her hand. She reached out, twice, to grasp the support. Just out of range.

Shifting slightly, she stretched again. Fingertips scraped the rough edge. Still too far.

Risking shoulder dislocation, she shot the hand out again. Little more... little more... finally, she closed her fingers around the stone.

Got it!

Vicky stabbed the crude axe into the surface, using the stone to work her way back up the slope. Anchor right toe hook into snow. Push. Dig in. Slide right foot up. Repeat.

"Hold on! I got ya."

Heavy breathing covered hers. Powerful hands grabbed hers.

Christiaan.

He caught her arm and dragged her back onto the trail. Once safe, Vicky threw her arms around him, her heart thumping against both their chests. Their breaths were ragged. For a few seconds, only the howling wind broke the silence.

Danger over, adrenaline withdraw set in. Vicky began to shake.

"Shhh," he whispered, tightening the embrace. "I got you now."

The warmth of his body enveloped hers. This is where she belonged. Here, in the arms of her Prince Charming.

"Vic!" A gruff voice called out. "Vic!"

She pulled away as Dean rushed toward them. He glared at Christiaan then motioned for her to sit on a nearby boulder. "What happened?"

"I'm not sure. Did anybody else fall?"

"No," Dean answered, squatting beside her to check for injuries. "You okay?"

"I'm fine, really." She nodded. "Just a bit shaken up."

"Man, you disappeared like a puff of smoke in a windstorm. What happened?"

"I lost my balance... somehow." The answer made no more sense aloud than in her head.

"The Dutch Boys were right behind you." Dean looked at Christiaan. "You guys see anything?"

"No. What's that line you Americans like to use...?" Christiaan smiled. "Accidents happen?"

A cold shiver ran through Vicky.

"Accidents happen," she repeated, but wasn't sure if she believed it.

CHAPTER 7

Christiaan was supposed to be having fun.

He wasn't.

"Here's to life, love, and the pursuit of fun," Dean said, raising a beer mug into the air. "From this day forward, may your arms never be empty and your bed never cold."

A dozen glasses clinking in toast cut through the din of the crowded roadhouse on a busy weekend night. Their Climbing for Singles trip successfully completed, everybody agreed to clean up and meet here for a few rounds of drinks, compliments of Baz.

Christiaan sat at the far end of the long group booth, nursing a Scotch, hoping to derive by sheer divine intervention a way to save his company.

Unfortunately, God wasn't divulging any secrets.

He traced the rim of his highball glass with a fingertip. His situation had gone from bad to worse.

Scratch that. Bad to dire. At least, that's how he felt after talking to his corporate attorneys.

Baz slid into the booth next to Christiaan, third Scotch in his hand.

"Was that Duff I saw you talking to at the bar?" Christiaan asked.

"Yep." Baz drew a long, slow swig from his glass. At this rate, he'd be on his fourth in less than a minute. Christiaan still nursed his first.

"How's he doing?"

"Fine," Baz answered then took more Scotch. "Duff's always *fine*."

"Did you invite him over for a drink?"

"No, but knowing Irishmen like I do, it's only a matter of time until he comes over and asks."

Baz was probably right. Christiaan knew a few Irishmen, too.

"Tell me again why the attorneys want to put Mineral Springs on hold," Baz said.

"They suggest we cease all work at the site until we can appease ShastaWatch. A show of good faith that might prompt the group to work with us."

Baz eyed Christiaan. "Work with us? They refuse to even talk to us. What makes you think they'll suddenly agree to some type of arbitration?"

Christiaan didn't. But he was running out of options, time, and money.

As well as patience. He hated to admit it, but blackmail seemed the only possible solution.

"Stopping isn't an option!" Baz slammed a hand on the tabletop, anger flashing across his face. Mugs, glasses, and plates rattled. Talking ceased. He smiled, waved "sorry" at the startled table, then lowered his voice.

"A delay now could cost us a bundle," Baz growled. "That meddling bitch is ruining everything. She has to be stopped, soon. Very soon."

Christiaan peered over at said bitch.

Vicky had surprised him, showing up to celebrate with the group, especially in this setting. A few spots down in the booth, she nursed a Shirley Temple.

"I need a refill, *mijn schatje*." Baz flagged their waitress with his empty glass. "Another round for the table... compliments of this good-looking Dutchman."

Almost wearing cutoff jeans and a tight t-shirt, the young woman rattled off their order.

"Let's see, that's two pitchers of beer, an Appletini, a strawberry Margarita, two scotch-on-the-rocks, and a kiddie cocktail, right?" She pointed to Vicky's drink.

"Yes." Vicky nodded.

"I'll be right back," the server said then scurried off.

Christiaan pulled a long taste of Scotch. The whiskey burned his throat.

Pale amber.

Single-malt.

Bri's drink of choice. And since her death, his.

He glanced over at Vicky, in deep conversation with the reporter. Vicky was as much a mystery tonight as she had been yesterday. Lou's first-round background check hadn't uncovered much. Nothing scandalous. Nothing noteworthy. Nothing even remotely interesting.

Nothing on the boxers or briefs question either.

None of this made sense. How could such a vibrant, adventurous, willful woman live such a plain-Jane life?

"Christiaan." Paige now turned her attention to him. "You're a businessman. Vicky says that people who see this planet as a commodity are in direct opposition to those who see it as a community. Therefore, compromise is impossible. What do you think?"

Christiaan considered possible answers. He needed something vague and elusive. Nothing to suggest a connection to Summit Energy. Now was not the time to tip his hand.

Not yet.

"Compromise is possible," he answered. "Provided everyone is willing to make concessions."

"Like realigning a thirteen-mile power line to lessen the impact on a thriving osprey habitat? Or setting aside a few hundred acres as designated green space?" Vicky leaned forward and tapped her finger on the table. "That's not a compromise. That's a travesty."

Obviously, Congressman Beckwith had forwarded Christiaan's latest offer to ShastaWatch. Obviously, they weren't interested.

"Is that the project you told me about earlier, Vicky?" The reporter peered over at Christiaan. "Mineral Springs?"

"Yes." Vicky nodded. "ShastaWatch will fight until the power company gives up."

"Then you're in for a hell of a war, princess," Baz slur-blurted out. "You have no idea who you're dealing with."

Christiaan shot his friend a quick look of warning.

"Tell me." Paige's eyes moved from Baz to Christiaan. "Exactly *who* is she dealing with?"

A heavy guitar cord cut the air, followed by a drum roll. Christiaan prayed the sound had drowned out the question.

"All right!" Dean shook his fist in the air. "Sounds like the band's ready to play again."

The lights dimmed, and a seductive rhythm purred through the speakers.

"Exactly *who* is she dealing with?" the reporter repeated.

Christiaan jerked Paige onto the dance floor before she could say anything else. He slid his arms around her waist. She popped her hands on his butt.

Uh-oh.

They swayed silently for a few minutes as other couples filled the floor.

"Nice move," she said. "Drag me away before I reveal your little secret."

"Secret? What secret? I just wanted to dance." Christiaan peered into her face, praying he looked as sincere as he hoped he sounded. "Just love this song."

"You're a brilliant businessman, decent dancer, and lousy liar. You're also Summit Energy."

Someone had done her homework.

"Look, I don't like wasting time," she said.

No confusion there considering the firm grip she had

on his butt.

"I'm tired of chasing petty-ass feature story sidebars, writing routine corporate profiles, and going to banal business conferences." She squeezed Christiaan's left butt cheek. "I need a real story about real issues. One that will make my editors take me seriously."

"Good luck with that."

"Don't patronize me." She squeezed the right butt cheek. "I know who you are, why you're here—"

"I told you on the mountain, I'm simply here to—"

Paige stretched up on her toes to whisper in his ear. "And that you need this project to save your company."

Where was this girl getting her information? Maybe Lou should consider hiring her.

"You know what else I know?" She flicked his ear with her tongue.

Christiaan pulled out of mouth reach. "That the human tongue is a veritable breeding ground for an infinite number of germs?"

"Cute." The reporter laughed. "You're funny. I like that."

Good. For a minute there, I thought you weren't interested.

Christiaan gazed over at the woman he wished was groping him. Vicky accepted a fresh Shirley Temple from the waitress. Paige followed his line of sight.

"So that's it. You don't want her to know why you're really here."

Not yet.

"What's it worth to you?"

"Excuse me?" Christiaan asked.

"Give me exclusive access to your story and..." She wiggled her eyebrows. "...you, and your secret is safe with me."

"I'm not sure I understand." This was more his friend's territory than Christiaan's.

WWBD... What would Baz do?

"Okay, let me spell it out for you. You give me everything I want... *and I mean everything*... and in return, I don't tell Vicky that you're the environmental rapist she's trying to send packing."

Blackmail was getting rather popular around here.

"Come on, what's it worth to you, Baron van Laere?" the reporter pushed. "How far are you willing to go to protect your secret?"

Good question.

Baz winked at Christiaan as he slid a fresh Scotch in front of Vicky.

"Obviously, whatever it takes."

Vicky's eyes connected with Christiaan's. A hot ache grew in her throat. That angular handsome face. Those extraordinary cobalt eyes. The sexy grin that could charm the pants off any woman in the room.

Including her. She crossed, then uncrossed her legs. Then she shifted in her seat. Nothing she did could satisfy the itch that needed scratched.

Her vulnerability to him disturbed her. On the mountain, after he'd pulled her to safety, she'd melted into him. Like a rock tumbling down a steep mountainside, she was powerless to resist. Even now, the fire spreading through her body could barely be contained.

Vicky swallowed hard, but the lump forming in her throat as she watched her husband slip an arm around another woman refused to go away.

The thought of him with any female burned deep. Especially that whore Astrid. The memory of discovering them in a passionate embrace haunted her still.

Across from Vicky, Baz swirled his drink glass, ice cubes tinkling against the side. When he took a sip, she could almost feel the whiskey burning down her throat, matching her mood.

Pale amber. Single-malt.

Her favorite.

Vicky stared at the tumbler.

"Care to dance?" The sweet aroma of Scotch on Baz's breath overpowered her, singing to her like a siren.

"No." She didn't want to dance. She wanted to leave. No, she *needed* to leave. Vicky shoved her chair back. *Now.*

"Victoria, love." A thick Irish brogue coming from a devilishly handsome, somewhat arrogant, but ultimately friendly body carrying a half-empty beer pint pecked her cheek then slipped into the seat next to her. "Fancy meetin' ye 'ere at thet pub."

"Hey, Duff. How's the wrist? Downing a few pints to dull the pain?"

"Well, certainly can't 'urt." The Irishman grinned. "No worries. I'll be back flyin' before ye know it."

Vicky tapped the cast. "Can I sign it?"

"Of course, love." Duff handed her a black marker.

Shamrocks, pots of gold, and the Irish flag engulfed most of the cast. "I told you Mother Shasta would make you pay for those low summit flybys." Vicky drew a heart next to a sunburst with two upside-down Fs inside it and two Irish words underneath it. "A little revenge on her part?"

He laughed. "Well, it wouldn't be thet first time a lady wanted revenge on oul' Duff. Dutchie 'ere tells me ye had some trouble with thet lady yourself earlier today."

"Baz told you?"

"Aye. Lucky fer ye thet Baron Boy was thar to save ye. Who knows what might have happened, eh?"

"Yeah," Baz said, raising his glass in a mock toast. "Prince Charming to the rescue."

Vicky stole a look at Prince Charming. He guided the reporter around the dance floor perimeter, smiling as she whispered into his ear.

Vicky clutched the sobriety token in her pocket so hard the ridged edge dug into her palm. What made her think this was a good idea? To come to a bar? With the man responsible for her death and quite possibly involved in today's "accident"?

"My goodness, love. Tha' looks brutal." Duff touched

her wrist with his tattooed ring finger.

She hadn't noticed it before. A golf-ball-sized bruise where Christiaan had caught her.

"It's nothing," she said.

"You really need to be more careful," Baz cautioned. "Prince Charming won't always be there to protect you."

The man had no idea.

Vicky's breathing shallowed as she fought for control of her mind. Her body. Her sobriety.

She traced a finger down the outside of Baz's drink. The whiskey looked so inviting. One sip would erase this pain.

Vicky's hand closed around the glass.

"Come on, you need to dance." Christiaan snatched her from the booth. He stepped behind her, placed his hands on her shoulders, and pointed her toward the dance floor.

"You're not trading almost eight years of sobriety for one minute of empty comfort," he whispered in her ear. "The price is too high."

Vicky couldn't argue with that. Not in the state she was in. She offered no resistance as he pushed her forward.

They stopped at the edge of the dance floor. Christiaan stepped around to face her. His gaze wandered over her slowly, like a caress. She lost herself in those gorgeous blue eyes, and her hunger for him doubled.

For the first time in a long time, she felt alive.

Vicky sank into his arms like she'd never left. Like the last eight years had disappeared.

Her husband wrapped a strong, powerful arm around her waist and drew her closer. The familiar smell of the man she'd fallen in love with intoxicated her.

They swayed to the music, the action around them ceasing to exist. Only them.

"Isn't this better than Scotch?" he whispered, warm breath on her ear sending shivers down her spine.

Much better.

His heat seared her emotions. Her body burned with an astounding intensity as she ran her hands over his broad chest. Memories of being as physically close as a husband and wife can be rushed over her. She collapsed against him.

Christiaan explored the hollows of her back. His breath caressed her shoulders like a warm summer breeze. A shiver of passion awakened.

Their dancing slowed as Vicky pressed her hips against his arousal. Christiaan growled and pulled their bodies even closer.

He buried his hand in her hair and brushed his lips across her forehead. Cupping the back of her head, he ran his thumb down her jaw line to her chin before bringing it up to gently stroke her bottom lip.

His breath fanned her face, teasing her, taunting her.

She looked up into her husband's eyes and saw something that stunned her. Recognition? Regret?

Desire.

Christiaan dipped his head and brushed his lips across hers. She moaned as his tongue traced her mouth. Her lips parted, and he accepted the invitation.

Hmm. Better than she remembered.

Their tongues swirled against one another, each exploring the other. Heat washed over Vicky, and she intensified the kiss. She was Brianna again. In the arms of the man she loved. Nothing, no one could separate them again.

Something caught her arm and jerked it, hard.

"I need to talk to you," Rainbow said.

"Can't it wait?" *Please.*

"No." Her friend struggled to push herself between Vicky and Christiaan. Vicky clung to him, not wanting the dream to end. Her hair caught on his watch. The spike of pain brought her back to reality.

Christiaan pulled away, an odd look on his face.

The music had stopped, everyone's eyes fixed on the commotion.

Vicky smiled then dragged Rainbow outside. She waited until the door swung shut before letting loose.

"What's wrong with you!" Vicky yelled.

"Look!" Rainbow shoved a stack of photos at her. "Here are the shots David took out at Mineral Springs. He emailed them to me, and I printed them out so I could study them. You, *obviously*, didn't look at them at all."

"I haven't had time yet," Vicky said. "I'll look at them tomorrow, okay?"

"No! Now!"

Vicky took them, squinting to see in the poor light. The first couple of shots were taken from a ridge overlooking the site. They showed people milling around one of the mineral springs the property was named for.

"What are you so worked up about?" Vicky asked.

"Keep going," Rainbow said.

The next two showed a half dozen men in hardhats next to a large drilling rig and tall stacks of pipe. "What? They're test drilling already?"

"That's not the big surprise. Look here." Rainbow grabbed at the stack of pictures, knocking them to the floor. Both women kneeled in the sea of images. Rainbow studied each one, looking for what Vicky couldn't comprehend. She hadn't seen her friend so worked up since Rainbow discovered the traveling circus abusing the elephants.

Rainbow snapped up the photos, slipping them one by one into her hand like a poker player. In one quick minute, she had her run and shoved the winning hand at Vicky.

She scrutinized the top picture. A forklift was off-loading shrink-wrapped pallets of large sacks. The next image showed numerous pallets stacked between a storage building and an office trailer. Yet another showed equipment she couldn't identify parked near the main access road.

David had obviously used his new telephoto lens for the next one. In the photo, two men stood near the front gate, holding what looked to be a large blueprint. A tree branch obscured the pair a bit, but one face was clear enough to identify.

Baz.

Vicky could barely breathe.

"That's one of the cuties I met in your office yesterday." Rainbow tapped the photo with a finger.

Vicky flipped to the last picture, already sure what she was about to find.

In this one, the other man's face was turned toward the camera.

Blood roared in her ears.

"And that's the other one. If I'd have known who the bastards were, I never would have told them about you, me, and ShastaWatch."

Christiaan.

"Vicky, I can explain," a Dutch accent behind her said. He'd followed them outside.

She held up her hand to cut him off. "No explanation necessary."

He was the enemy.

He was Summit Energy.

And he was ruining her life... again.

CHAPTER 8

Vicky had escaped death, conquered alcoholism, and fooled everyone into believing she was dead.

Yet, she couldn't manage to make a stinking pot of coffee.

Was that five scoops or six?

The sound of ShastaWatch members squabbling between themselves drifted into the kitchen. After last night's grand revelation at the roadhouse, Vicky had called an early-morning emergency meeting. The handful of people that could make it now sat in her living room, brainstorming ideas on how to stop Summit Energy.

How to stop Christiaan.

She yanked the paper filter from the basket, showering coffee onto the counter.

Crap.

Vicky brushed the scattered grounds into the garbage then grabbed the scoop and started counting over again.

Too bad she couldn't start last night over again.

What a sucker she'd been.

Everything Christiaan had said and done over the last two days was an act. Pure and simple. He'd needed to gain her trust to find a weakness. So he could take everything away from her again. Their son's sonogram flashed through her mind.

Another scoop of coffee hurled into the basket.

"Crap! Was that five or six?"

"Five." Rainbow appeared in the doorway, Starbucks cup in one hand, serving platter filled with heaven knows what in the other.

"I see you're indulging this morning." Vicky nodded toward the venti.

"Yeah." Rainbow crossed the room and pulled up a stool beside Vicky. "After last night's great adventure, I figured I'd earned a double chocolate iced soy chai latte with extra cinnamon."

Last night. Vicky had refused to listen to anything Christiaan said. Stunned by the revelation he was the rat bastard ShastaWatch was fighting, she'd escaped to her lodge while Rainbow tore him a new one. Another minute in his presence and Vicky would have killed a fifth of Scotch, easily.

Or Christiaan, easily.

"Anything exciting happen after I left?" Vicky slung another scoop of coffee into the filter. "Like spontaneous penile dismemberment or self-inflicted castration?"

Rainbow laughed. "No, he pretty much clammed up. Just stood there, waited until I'd said my piece then wished me a good night and walked off."

Ahh, the legendary van Laere self-control and politeness. Valuable assets for business. Significant liabilities for marriage.

"Now, his cute, ponytailed friend…" Rainbow continued. "*He's* another story."

"What?" Vicky asked.

"Well, after Baron von Rat Face sauntered off, Rat Face-In-Waiting was all over me, saying we'd 'made a connection' at Climbing for Singles the other day and how badly he wanted to buy me a drink." Rainbow shrugged her shoulders. "Figured I might learn something valuable we could use for the cause, so I chilled out and let him spend his money."

"Way to go, Mata Hari." Vicky snapped the coffee basket into place and punched the on button. "How'd it go?"

"I learned a few things that might help. Between his Dutch accent and Scotch-soaked speech, he tried to impress me with his job title—executive vice president of development for VL Holdings—who, by the way, is really behind the Mineral Springs project. They just used the name Summit Energy to avoid attention."

That explained why Vicky hadn't made the connection.

The sweet aroma of brewing coffee filled the kitchen. Vicky watched the liquid drip slowly. What other secrets could Christiaan be hiding?

"I found out some stuff about Baron von Rat Face, like he owns the company and he and Baz have been best friends since childhood," Rainbow said, taking a sip of her latte. "By the way, care to explain how you and his highness ended up in each other's arms last night?"

Venti order. Vicky stifled a yawn. She'd lain awake all night looking for an explanation herself.

Nothing yet.

"No, I don't." Vicky busied herself by grabbing non-dairy creamer and the sugar bowl from a cabinet. She placed both next to a dozen coffee mugs on a serving tray on the counter.

Rainbow peered at her sideways. "Okay, I'll let it slide for now, but eventually I want details."

Another sip of latte then she continued. "We have another round of drinks, flirt a bit... yadda, yadda, yadda... Then he asks me if I'd like to go back to his suite for a Dutch treat."

Vicky rolled her eyes.

"Yeah, corny line, but I think, what the hell? He's attractive, he's hooked in with Summit, so with a little pillow talk I might learn something we could use to run these guys out of town. Plus, Mars is in my eighth house—Scorpio—so the sex would be mind-blowing." Rainbow shrugged her shoulders. "Hey, wouldn't be the first time I've used sex to protect the mountain."

"No," Vicky said. "There was the time you kept the real estate developer occupied so he missed his meeting with the Forest Service. Bye, bye proposed townhouses."

"Yeah, Gordon. He was fun." Rainbow smiled. "So, while Baz and I are walking to my car, I ask him about Mineral Springs, and he starts bitching about how Christiaan has so much riding on this project that he's personally handling stuff Baz usually does. How did he put it?" Rainbow tapped her bottom lip with her finger. "Umm, 'Christiaan is so far up my sphincter I'm gagging on his shoelaces'."

"Nice visual," Vicky said. "Did you talk about our objections to geothermal energy?"

"Yeah, while we drove back to his hotel. He gave me the usual stuff. How the project would revitalize the economy, provide jobs, supply much-needed renewable energy... yadda, yadda, yadda."

"And cover the landscape with toxic sump ponds and transmission lines," Vicky added. "Fill the air with steam plumes, chemical odors, and noise from well-drilling and construction. Destroy the spiritual and cultural significance to Native Americans."

"I mentioned all that. Of course, he gave his 'personal guarantee that we'll do everything possible to protect the environment and the cultural history of the area'."

"That and four dollars will buy me a frappuccino at Starbucks." Vicky crossed her arms and leaned against the kitchen counter. "They have as much interest in protecting the environment as I do climbing Everest naked."

"He was emphatic about their devotion, saying they were already on site conducting tests to comply with EPA requirements. When we got back to his suite, I showed him David's pictures and asked him to explain exactly what they were doing. He showed me where engineers were mapping old-growth trees, taking ground water and soil samples, even conducting an endangered species assessment."

"Really?" Vicky asked. "Looked like a lot of people and equipment for just simple testing. I'm guessing they're already drilling."

"I thought so, too, so I asked him to explain exactly what was in the rest of the pictures. But Romeo didn't want to talk anymore, so..." Rainbow smiled. "We didn't."

"You got your Dutch Treat?"

"Yeah, three times," Rainbow giggled. "Then this morning, as he walked me to my car, I asked if he and Baron von Rat Face would consider taking us on a tour of the site, show us exactly what they're doing."

"And?"

"He said no. Then he leaned in, kissed me, and said 'Tell your fearless leader we'll do whatever it takes to build the Mineral Springs plant. *Whatever.*' Then he turned on his heel and left."

A chill raced through Vicky. She didn't want to contemplate the possible permutations of "whatever".

Kaitlen, a law student and ShastaWatch's defacto legal counsel, popped into the kitchen. "The natives are getting restless. Coffee soon?"

"Almost." Vicky handed the serving tray to her. "Take that, and I'll follow with the pot in a minute."

"Sure." Kaitlen headed back into the living room.

"Wait, my eggplant and hummus pita chips will go great with that!" Rainbow raced after her, platter in hand.

Vicky turned to stare out the large picture window onto the pristine landscape surrounding her lodge. A wave of déjà vu swept over her.

Christiaan backing her into a corner. "Or-else" threats thrown at her like baseballs. Nowhere to turn. No one to turn to.

Brianna had no choice then.

Vicky had them all now.

She grabbed the java and marched into the living room.

A "Yeah, caffeine!" chorus greeted her. Vicky sat the pot down on the stone sofa table and found an empty spot on the warm hearth. Everybody stopped talking long enough to fix coffee. When they settled back down, Vicky started the meeting.

"Okay, everybody. We now have a name and face to our enemy, how do we stop him?"

"According to Sun Tzu in *The Art of War*," Nelson, a local college professor, spoke up. "'Know thyself. Know thy enemy.' So, I googled him this morning." He poked at his iPad. "I stored it offline since *somebody* doesn't believe in having wifi in her far-off mountain hideaway. Okay, listen to this… Christiaan Stokman, Baron van Laere, is—"

"Oooh!" Phoebe, a waitress from the local diner, squealed. "A baron? Do we have to curtsy when His Grace enters the room?"

Vicky shook her head. Too many romance novels. "Go on, Nelson."

"Van Laere is CEO of VL Holdings, a multibillion-dollar holding company with annual revenues of \$2.3 billion, the company ranks forty-seven on Forbes magazine's list of the top 600 international private companies."

"VL Holdings? I thought we were dealing with Summit Energy," Phoebe asked.

"Subsidiary." Kaitlen chimed in. "Probably to avoid any kind of foreign-ownership prejudice when applying for government grants and funds."

"And it's legal?" Lance, an herbalist, asked.

"Yes. Questionable, but very much legal."

"So, we have a wooden-shoe blue blood, a multibillion-dollar company with an identity problem, several government agencies with renewable energy tunnel vision, and—," Nelson stopped to let Vicky read an email from their inside source at the California Energy Commission.

"As of late yesterday, a pledge of \$50 million over sixty months to Summit Energy if the Mineral Springs plant is operational in four years." Nelson shook his head. "We haven't a prayer."

"All hope is not lost." Vicky rose to her feet and began pacing. "We need a bargaining chip. Something to force Christiaan to rethink his position."

"I could hand out flyers at the diner like Rainbow did at the yoga center last week." Elbows on thighs, Phoebe cradled her chin in her hands.

"Been there. Done that. Nada difference," Rainbow answered.

"What if we hold a big rally in the city park? Something festival-like, with music, games for the kids, an information booth where we could educate everybody on the problem—" Lance began waving his hand. "Oh! We could blow up a big picture of van Laere and have people throw darts, and give away pri—"

"Whoa, there, P.T. Barnum," Kaitlen interrupted. "We don't have enough time or budget to put something together like that."

Nelson cleared his throat. "What about a news conference at the site? Present our concerns and let public opinion take it from there?"

Kaitlen whistled. "Hello? Didn't we try that already? All the major media outlets in the state told us not to bother them with typical treehugger stuff. Only in California could something like this not make the news."

"Too bad we don't have a video of van Laere driving a big honking SUV while drinking inorganic coffee from a styrofoam cup and tossing disposable diapers from the window into a landfill... *that* would get their attention," Phoebe said.

Kaitlen wagged a finger. "But I think you might be onto something."

"What do you mean?" Vicky stopped pacing.

"Van Laere might think twice about building here if he thought bad publicity could cripple his position," Kaitlen explained.

"Like what?"

Kaitlen's brows furrowed. "Something so-o-o big, so-o-o negative that public opinion would turn against him. Something that would make the government reconsider their position and stop Summit Energy dead in their tracks."

"I don't know." Lance sounded unsure. "That's not really playing fair."

Van Laeres aren't bred to play fair.

"He's not. Why should we?" Kaitlen grabbed Nelson's iPad. "What else do we know about this guy?" She silently read, stopping periodically to offer a line or two aloud. "Forty-two years of age... only child... law degree from Leiden University... MBA from Erasmus University Rotterdam... took over family business at age 30... lost American wife, the Lady van Laere, in an accidental explosion... no children..."

No *children.* Memories of losing their son slashed through Vicky's chest as easily as a razor. Doctors had attributed the miscarriage to chromosomal abnormalities, but she knew the real answer was stress. From her husband's family. From her husband.

"You okay?" Rainbow's hand on Vicky's shoulder drew her attention. "You look like somebody died."

Somebody had.

Her baby. An innocent life lost to the selfishness and greed of a man convinced he was above the law. To an assassin bought and paid for by a coward. To a woman blind to the reality of her marriage.

"Christiaan murdered his wife," Rainbow said matter-of-factly.

"What?" Vicky stared at her friend in astonishment. She'd never told anyone she suspected Christiaan had had her murdered instead of simply divorcing her.

Or at least had tried to have her murdered.

"No, it says here in the article that it was an accidental explosion," Nelson corrected.

"No, it was *m-u-r-d-e-r*," Rainbow countered in a deep,

suspenseful voice then broke into laughter. "Come on. Accusing Baron von Rat Face of killing his wife would definitely put the wolves on his scent."

Bewilderment clogged Vicky's thought processes. Hearing her "death" discussed was strangely refreshing. And unnerving.

"I... um..." Kaitlen cleared her throat. "I was actually thinking more along the lines of closet communist, corporate fraud, sexual harassment. You know, stuff that's hard to prove or disprove. Something just to get people talking."

"But it doesn't matter if it's true or not," Rainbow said. "We just have to create the perception it is."

Brianna *was* dead. Her hopes and dreams buried by Vicky eight years ago.

"Are you sure it'll work?" Nelson held up Christiaan's picture. "He doesn't look like a killer."

No, he didn't. The man who had asked her to marry him a week after they met wasn't a killer. The man who had unknowingly apologized to his wife for not supporting her sobriety wasn't a killer. The man who had swept her into his arms last night and made her feel love again wasn't a killer.

"Who does look like a killer nowadays?" Rainbow shrugged her shoulders. "Besides, we'll have won the hearing by the time the truth surfaces."

Vicky traced the bruise on her wrist. The man who betrayed their wedding vows was a killer. The man who had arranged for her car to explode while she was in it was a killer. The man who had pushed her down the mountain yesterday was a killer.

"I don't know," Lance said. "Accusing a man of murdering his wife just doesn't seem right."

"Ruining Mt. Shasta for financial gain isn't right either," Rainbow answered.

"We'll need to be ready for a frontal assault from his PR people," Kaitlen interjected. "I doubt he'll turn tail and run that easily."

No, not Christiaan. Not a van Laere.

"But we'll be out front first," Nelson offered. "We'll grab the headlines before he's had a chance to formulate a strategy. He'll be playing catch-up for a couple of days."

"By then, hopefully, enough damage will have been done to his reputation that no one will want to work with him." Kaitlen grinned mischievously. "He'll have no choice but to give up on Mineral Springs."

"Exactly." Rainbow clapped her hands. "Let's vote. Everyone in favor of accusing Baron von Rat Face of murdering his wife say 'Aye'."

A round of "ayes" blanketed the room.

Vicky hesitated, torn by conflicting emotions. Part of her wanted the truth to come out, for the entire world to know that she had survived her husband's assassination attempt. But another part wanted Brianna to stay dead because Vicky had become the strong woman Brianna had only dreamed of.

"Opposed?"

Silence. *Should I say something? Stop this?*

"Operation Wife Murderer carries."

Too late.

"Now what?" Nelson asked.

"I'll take it from here." Rainbow stood and headed into the kitchen, cell phone in hand.

Vicky caught her arm. "I'm… I'm… I'm not so sure about this."

"All war is based on deception," Rainbow said. "Nelson isn't the only one that can quote *The Art of War.*"

Christiaan stood at the picture window in his suite, working on his third cup of coffee. Outside, Mt. Shasta still hid part of sunrise behind her majestic peak. Pastels washed across the mountain range, promising a peaceful day.

Peace. That was something he could use right now.

In the window frost, he traced a circle around the

towering mountain. His future lay there. He could feel it. Exactly what was in store for him wasn't as easy a draw.

Christiaan washed a hand over his face. The nine-hour time difference worked against him. Afternoon in The Netherlands had produced an inbox filled with messages. Bankers reminding him about upcoming balloon payments. Attorneys with ridiculously low buy-out offers from competitors. Accountants concerned with balance sheets. That damn reporter insisting he call her back.

The wolves were nipping at his heels. If he didn't get this project closer to happening, he'd lose everything. Out in the cold, like standing on Mt. Shasta in nothing but his underwear.

He wrote in the frost on the window. H-E-L-P-L-E-S-S. *Haven't felt like this since Bri—*

"Yo, bro. You're up. All ready to go for a run?"

Christiaan erased his musing before turning around. Baz strolled into the room, long hair hanging wet from the shower, pulling a t-shirt on, that stupid tattoo staring at Christiaan. One summer with relatives living in Ireland and Baz thought he was a soldier for the cause.

"Nee. Too much on my mind." Christiaan gestured toward the room service cart. "Brunch?"

"Just caffeine. You'd have slept like a baby last night if you'd have followed my lead at the bar." Baz grabbed a cup of coffee before settling into a leather high back. "Summit Energy would be a secret, and Vicky Golden's drinking problem wouldn't."

Christiaan winced at the honest assessment. His friend was right. One chivalrous gesture had cost them much-needed leverage, leaving the Mineral Springs project vulnerable.

"A few sips of Scotch and we'd have had what we needed to force her cooperation. What exactly were you thinking, pulling her away like that?"

"I don't know." Christiaan shook his head. She'd looked so vulnerable. So lost.

He'd had to stop her.

Christiaan refilled his cup then sat down across from Baz, touching Bri's wedding ring in the process.

"I know what you're thinking," Baz said. "But Vicky isn't Bri. She doesn't need saving. She just needs to get out of the way."

"I know." The picture Vicky had thrown at him last night lay on the coffee table. He cringed, remembering the look of betrayal on her face when she realized exactly who she was kissing.

Christiaan slid the photo in front of him and studied it. The shot was taken the day after the helicopter crash. Despite his injuries, he'd insisted on a complete site tour by the project manager Baz had hired. The number of workers and equipment already on site had astounded him.

In the background of the photo, two men were unloading boxes marked "Blasting Caps" and stacking them into the storage building.

"I thought we were using vibration trucks instead of explosives for seismic testing."

"We were, but..." Baz leaned forward to see what Christiaan was pointing to. "But we couldn't get any decent readings, so now we're leaning toward the old-fashioned way." He grabbed his iPad from the table and sat back into the chair.

"And the drilling rig?"

"Ready for when we begin," Baz answered without looking up.

Christiaan stared at the photo. No doubt, Vicky and her ShastaWatch cronies would use this to strengthen their position. How exactly they'd do that remained to be seen.

"Take a look at this." Baz snorted then turned his iPad around so Christiaan could read the screen. He pointed to a headline on an online newspaper.

"Trump Triumphs: Treehuggers in Boulder Drop Lawsuit. Controversial Development Back on Schedule."

Maybe Christiaan needed to call The Donald and ask

what his secret was.

"See if you can find one that says 'van Laere van Luck: Crazy Woman Learns the Word Compromise. Much-Needed Geothermal Project Back on Course.'"

Baz laughed. "If there is, I'll find it. I have alerts for anything with van Laere in it."

The image of Vicky at the bar, defending her position, popped into Christiaan's head. Such fire. Such passion.

He'd tasted that and wanted more. Much more.

However, last night's grand revelation ended any hopes of that. What a shame. No chance to bury himself in her hair. No chance to bury himself in her arms. No chance to bury himself in her—

Strains of Blackberry Smoke's "Good One Comin' On" began to play from Christiaan's phone. He pulled it from his pocket, checked who was calling, then hit "answer".

"Lou, tell me you have something good."

"I wish I could," the PI answered. "Don't really know anything more than what I emailed yesterday. Can't find a trace of information about your Vicky Golden anywhere."

"She's not *my* Vicky Golden. Are you telling me she just appeared on this earth one day?"

"It's a theory," Lou said.

Christiaan leaned forward. "Like she's hiding from something?"

"Or someone," Lou answered. "A good set of fingerprints would help me identify your mystery lady."

"She's not my— Never mind. Any suggestions on how to do that with a less-than-cooperative subject?" Christiaan couldn't imagine Vicky offering to give him anything with her prints on it.

Except maybe a one-way ticket out of town.

"Find something she's touched, a drinking glass, a piece of paper, anything then get it to me. If her prints are in the system, I'll have an answer in twenty-four hours."

Christiaan's eyes locked onto the photo.

"I have something already. It'll be in your hands within

hours."

Lou whistled. "Must be nice to have a private jet at your disposal."

"Call me with an answer as soon as possible, and I'll buy you your very own," Christiaan said before cutting the connection. Next, he texted his pilot instructions then got the photo ready for pickup.

"Um, bro," Baz said, tapping the screen of his iPad, tilted toward Christiaan. "You might want to check this out."

He glanced at the tabloid website on screen. His friend's obsession with American trash mags was almost pathological.

"Pics of nude celebrities are your thing, not mine." Christiaan grabbed the plastic liner from an empty trashcan and an overnight envelope from the desk. He covered the photo with the bag then slipped it into the thin container.

"Chris." Baz shoved his iPad in front of Christiaan's face. "*Now.*"

Christiaan read aloud the headline blaring across the screen. "Like Father? Like Son? Did Billionaire Playboy Choose Murder Over Divorce to Save Millions?"

Anger shot through Christiaan like wildfire. Everything about Bri's death washed over him like the horror happened yesterday. He continued reading.

"Questions recently surfaced regarding the death eight years ago of real-estate mogul Baron van Laere's wife, before he assumed the title. She died instantly when the car she was driving exploded mysteriously. A subsequent police investigation determined a gas tank leak caused the freak accident. Accident or history repeating itself? It seems the previous Baron lost his first wife to a strange horseback riding accident. At the time, speculation he had her murdered to avoid a massive divorce settlement arose, but were never proven.

Could the current Baron have decided life with an alcoholic who'd failed to produce an heir was unbearable and borrowed a page from his daddy's cure-to-marital-ills playbook? A divorce could have cost him millions. Perhaps murder was cheaper?"

The byline read "Paige Williams".

The reporter. She'd found her story.

"Wow." Baz leaned back in his chair. "Suggesting you had Bri killed to protect your fortune is cold. I mean I know you can be cheap, but—" Christiaan shot him a glare that would have melted polar ice.

"Nothing the police found in their investigation suggested I lost her to anything but an accident." Christiaan turned away and began pacing, slowly, restlessly. "A horrible... freakish... devastating... accident."

"You know that and I know that, but I can't vouch for the rest of the world. It's only a matter of time before this hits the major news outlets."

Nobody wants to do business with a murderer. There goes my reputation, my project, my company.

"Why now? After so long?" Baz asked.

Christiaan washed a hand over this face. "Last night, that reporter threatened to expose Summit's identity if I didn't give her an exclusive to my story.... and my body."

"Pfff. Figures. Women love the Baron thing." Baz grabbed his coffee cup and headed toward the room service cart. "Hell hath no fury like a woman scorned."

"Yeah, but why this?" Christiaan said. "She already sniffed out stuff about the company's finances. Why not go with that?"

He walked to the picture window. The sun was now above the mountain, its rays making the snow crystals hanging from the window shine like diamonds.

"Why dredge all this up? Who needs me to look like a reprehensible monster?"

"Man, we so don't need this right now," Baz said. "Not when we're still butting heads with ShastaWatch."

Christiaan watched in the distance as a line of climbers headed out to the mountain.

"*Potverdomme*! I know who's behind this!"

CHAPTER 9

The late morning sun warmed Vicky atop her favorite meditation spot, Serenity Rock. Already ten degrees warmer than her arrival an hour ago, the temperature continued to climb.

Along with her anxiety.

Publicly accusing Christiaan of murder was an incredible risk, as irrevocable as suicide. Technically, she wasn't the one to accuse him. Rainbow had greased the wheels with the reporter. After a good bit of cajoling, Vicky added a few details. Enough for Paige to add one plus one and come up with three.

Vicky hated to admit it, but satisfaction had swept over her earlier when she'd clicked on the link the reporter had forwarded. References to Christian's father's marital woes were a nice touch. The "perhaps murder was cheaper" line... priceless.

Now her head swirled with confusion.

"Oh Mother Shasta—" Vicky whispered. Her emotional control close to shattering under the immense strain. "Did I do the right thing?"

She took a long drink from her canteen. Regret? A smidgen. What was the Dutch saying Christiaan used when business negotiations were running rough? *Zonder strijd geen overwinning.*

No victory without a battle.

Vicky could only imagine the look on his face when he read the article. That granite scowl, tight lips, hardened tendons along his jaw standing out like cables.

Exactly how he looked the last time she saw him before she "died".

Their worst fight ever. The Baroness, Christiaan's stepmother, had thrown a lavish birthday party for him at the estate. She'd made all the arrangements, including the seating charts. Christiaan sat next to Lady Astrid Kroon, the Dutch blue blood his father would have preferred as a daughter-in-law. Brianna was stuck on the other side of the banquet hall next to Sir Boring as Hell.

Throughout dinner, Christiaan's attention never strayed from Astrid. Every smile, every look, every "innocent" touch on his arm whittled away at Brianna's hard-sought sobriety.

However, the first Scotch in six months did little to soften the blow of overhearing the Baroness tell a friend that her stepson's silly infatuation with that barren American trash was finally over. Once the divorce was through, Christiaan would marry Astrid. The Baron would then reward his son with keys to the van Laere empire.

The Baroness had laughed. And if Brianna refused to cooperate, well, "there were other ways to end a marriage".

So, the rumors she'd heard over the last year were true. Christiaan and Astrid *were* having an affair. Brianna's suspicions were confirmed later when she stumbled across the pair embraced in the shadows of the ballroom balcony. No amount of Scotch could ever make Brianna believe her husband was only "consoling a friend" about her father's recent death.

She'd lost it, accusing Christiaan of betraying their love, planning to get rid of her. He berated her for falling off the wagon. She screamed he was replacing her because she couldn't get pregnant. He yelled that her drinking had made her paranoid, so unlike the woman he'd fallen in love with.

In a fit of rage, Brianna shouted, "Your life would be so much better if I was dead, wouldn't it?" Christiaan, already halfway out the door, paused to glance over his shoulder. His face a mix of fury, desperation, and control.

"Yes."

With that one-word answer, he was gone. She never saw him again.

Until now.

Vicky lay back on the giant rock to watch the blue sky and passing clouds. Her daybreak ritual of renewal failed to lift her spirits. Mother Shasta could do nothing to still the turmoil inside.

Christiaan's face flashed into her thoughts. His blue eyes crinkled in laughter. His sensual mouth curved in pleasure.

A sigh escaped Vicky's lips. Desire still coursed through her veins like liquid fire. Her mind relived the velvet warmth of his kiss on the dance floor and all it had promised. She'd fallen for him again. Despite all rational thought.

"Mother Shasta, if I could turn back time, I would. We were in love once, promising to be together 'til death us do part."

A vow her husband had taken literally.

Now the matter of her death was back in play. What would happen next? What would be Christiaan's next move?

His initial reaction would probably be to strike out and disable the enemy. Then his boardroom training and royal upbringing would kick in. "Never complain. Never explain." His stepmother had repeated that mantra so many times to Brianna that she was surprised it hadn't been tattooed on her forehead.

She hoped he followed the same path he'd taken eight years ago. After the press beat him and his family senseless, he'd issue a statement then quietly retreat.

And her mountain would be saved.

As well as her heart.

Something blocked the sun from Vicky's eyes. So close a warm breath caressed her cheek.

"I... know... who... you... are."

The words struck her like a bolt of lightning.

Christiaan. Lost in her wallowing, she hadn't heard him approach. How long had he been there?

"You do?" was all she could squeak out.

"Yes. I. Do." He stared her down with eyes dark with rage. "Did you really think it would be that easy to hide from me?"

Vicky rolled to her left, found her footing, and jumped to her feet, keeping the boulder between herself and Christiaan. Unfortunately, the tactic also meant the only escape route was behind him.

Or through him. A well-placed headbutt could smash his nose or at least stun him, buying her at least five, ten seconds. Twenty, tops.

She bit her lip then brushed a hand through her hair. "How'd you find me?" Vicky met his gaze, her chin set, ready to make her move. She hoped fierce showed on her face because adrenaline had her voice wavering.

"I didn't. But your partner did. Something about a morning ritual that sets your day on the right path?"

Today obviously being the exception. Damn Dean and his big mouth.

"Look... I—"

"Shh... relax," he purred, touching her face.

She remained still as he traced the outline of her cheek. His warm touch made her tremble. From fear? Desire? Anticipation?

"Do you really think me capable of murder?"

Vicky tried to look away, but couldn't. All she could do was study his face. A picture of anger and pain. Desperation and determination. Passion and desire. But not murder.

A primitive instinct of self-preservation welled up in her.

Get real, girl. You didn't think he was capable eight years ago and look what happened. She needed to get out of here.

Vicky pulled away from his touch and rocked her head back. This was gonna hurt.

"I'm surprised at you. A smart, capable, determined woman such as yourself stooping to cheap theatrics."

Vicky froze. "What?"

"You heard what I said."

"Wait a minute." Her hand brushed through her hair. "What did you mean when you said you knew who I was?"

Christiaan straightened and crossed his arms. "You're one of those people who stoops to desperate tactics to divert attention away from a baseless position."

She laughed.

"You find manufacturing a ridiculous story about my marriage funny?" he said with a scathing stare. "Dragging my late wife into this was reprehensible."

Her secret was safe.

"I'm sorry." Vicky struggled for seriousness. "I don't know what you're talking about."

"Spare me the mock stupidity. The reporter couldn't have made the leap from alcoholism to murder without your help. You're the only person outside my family who knew details like that."

Vicky could see him mentally kicking himself for opening up to a stranger the other night. But thank God, he saw her as a stranger.

"Let's say you're right," she admitted. "Why are you here? What do you want?"

"Back off the smear campaign. Back off Mineral Springs. I need this project to move forward... NOW."

Desperation played on his face. His control seemed to falter.

Vicky straightened to her full height, crossed her arms, and drew back her shoulders. She hoped the fierce stance made up for the nine-inch height difference. "No," she answered.

"I'm running out of time and patience." He stiffened for a moment then spoke with an arctic calm. "Tell me what I can do to make you back off."

"Pack up your circus of destruction and move on."

"I'm not leaving," he said. "I've spent too much time, money, and effort to abandon this project."

"Then you're stuck between the proverbial rock and a hard place. You can't build without ShastaWatch's approval, and you can't get that without my help. And *that* will never happen."

A sense of triumph flooded through her. For the first time since marrying Christiaan, she had the upper hand. His life may be better because Brianna was dead, but Vicky would do everything in her power to make it worse.

He leaned forward and stared directly into her eyes. The cold determination burning there sent shivers down her spine.

"One way or another..." Christiaan whispered, lips curved in a dangerous smile. He slipped a finger beneath her chin. "I *will* build Mineral Springs, and there isn't anything you can do about it."

Vicky drew a shaky breath, her earlier bravado fading. *Zonder strijd geen overwinning.*

She could claim victory for the first battle, but the war was far from over.

"*Potverdomme.* You remind me so much of my late wife it's scary." Christiaan turned on his heel and headed down the trail.

Scary? Try deadly.

The sweet smell of blackberry bushes tickled Vicky's nose as she carefully slipped through a tangled stand bordering the Mineral Springs property. Grabbing a handful of the dark fruit in passing, she tossed the berries into her mouth and savored the rich, sweet black nectar.

Another of nature's beauties lost to bulldozers if Christiaan won.

The confrontation at Serenity Rock still had her a bit unnerved. Christiaan had always been passionate about business, but his emotions for this particular project bordered obsessive.

Vicky shivered though the air was humid. How far would he go to make sure his project happened? How far would she go to make sure it didn't?

Right now, at least trespassing plus breaking and entering.

A red-tailed hawk screamed overhead. The majestic bird met Vicky's stare and circled, riding the wind on slow, measured wing beats. It disappeared over the ridge toward Summit's temporary base of operations.

Was Mother Shasta sending a message? What you're looking for is over here?

Vicky picked her way along the west ridge, overlooking the meandering river below. Christiaan's plans were to divert the flow underground to extract heat from the buried hot volcanic rock. What's the loss of a major source of water for California to ensure all the Starbucks in LA have enough juice to blend frappuccinos?

Through gnarled Ponderosa Pine and Incense Cedar trees she caught sight of the breathtaking Little Glass Mountain in the distance. Here, an unbroken field of jumbled and jagged rock that once flowed as lava from the mountain ten miles away lay. For centuries, local tribes gathered snowflake and rainbow obsidian here to make sharp-edged tools. Now, rock hounds risked broken bones, lacerations, and rangers hiking the flow to add the extremely sharp natural volcanic glass to their collections.

The beauty of Mineral Lake's crystal clear water burst through the trees further down the ridge. Once the center of a volcano, the lake had challenged many an Indian brave over the last several thousand years to earn his warrior status by diving three hundred feet to the bottom and retrieving a stone. Medicine men still used the lake to practice their arts, believing the creator descended from nearby Mt. Shasta to bathe in the lake, thereby giving it healing powers to cleanse the body and soul. Unfortunately, they had to wait until nightfall to conduct ceremonies to avoid motor homes and boaters.

Further down the ridge, Vicky started down a well-worn path that snaked around boulders and old-growth trees to Mineral Springs Highlands. Here, Christiaan planned to build his geothermal project, covering up to eleven square miles with power plants, well fields, steam pipes, roads, and transmission lines.

Halfway down the path, a natural bridge served as the starting point to a series of caves and tubes formed when molten lava began to cool at the surface while the interior continued to flow. Multilayered and extending for miles, the highway of caves once served as an Indian stronghold against enemies, especially U.S. Army soldiers. The rough terrain, irregular pathways, and sharp rocks used as weapons enabled the Indians to defeat any force, even if outnumbered. Unfortunately, battles to protect their homeland now often took place in courtrooms, where they usually lost.

From the bridge, Vicky spied the large drill rig and pipe stack from last night's photos. The area sat quiet, no one in sight, the drill still. Lunch time. Great timing. Fingers crossed everybody had hit town for a bite to eat.

Beyond there, sat the temporary trailer serving as Summit's site office. That was her best bet to find something that could help her fight Christiaan. No idea what exactly, but it was worth a shot.

Vicky headed down a narrow path lined thick with blackberry bushes that followed the contours of the rock face to the bottom. She'd been here many times with Chief Running Bear to partake in one of the numerous steaming mineral springs dotting the area. On two occasions, they stumbled upon bears lunching on the blackberries.

The Chief said the tribes believed that the energy that heated the springs had a spiritual origin and should not be tampered with.

Too bad she didn't have time to relax. A long soak in the thermal waters would feel fabulous right now.

Vicky reached the bottom and stepped into the clearing when a rustling in the bushes caught her attention. A bird? A squirrel? A bear?

"Victoria, love, fancy meetin' ye 'ere."

Duff. Her breathing eased.

The Irishman stepped out from the greenery and wiped a bead of sweat dripping from his graying brow. Soaked clothes clung to an older, but still well-muscled body.

"You look like you've been running a marathon," Vicky said. "But we both know better." The only thing she'd ever seen him dash for was another drink.

Duff laughed, pulling his t-shirt from his sweaty chest. "Took a dip in wan of those springs everybody raves 'bout. Tot it might make me oul' wrist feel better." He knocked on his cast.

"Isn't that what a few pints are for?" She smiled.

"Aye, couldn't 'urt," the Irishman answered. "What do ye say we go get a few, love? Ye look like ye could use a bit o'feelin' better."

"I can't. I... I..." *Come on. Think. Think.* "I'm going to take a dip myself." Hopefully into something that would make her worst nightmare disappear.

"I'll join ye." Duff grinned and winked. "Can't think a better way to spend a grand afternoon such as dis tha' gettin' hot with a lovely young lass."

Biting her lip, Vicky pushed a hand through her hair.

"Um... well... I... I prefer to take mine naked," she spit out.

"Me, too." He winked again.

Vicky let out a short snort at the possibility of seeing Duff in the buff, colorful tattoos and all. The majority of the female population of Mt. Shasta would give their eyeteeth to be in her shoes right now.

Vicky would gladly hand over all thirty-two pearly whites not to be. Even with a smile on his face and a casual stance, the fifty-something was tough, basic, and vaguely primitive. But he was a friend, that's all.

"Look, Duff, you know I like you, but I..."

"No harm, love," he offered. "But be careful. Ye never know what you might run into 'round 'ere."

She exhaled in relief. Yeah, he got the message.

"I'll be careful," Vicky said.

The Irishman flashed that infectious grin, then his face grew tight.

"An' I suggest you stay away from thet caves, especially thet wans 'ere at ground level."

She looked at him funny. "Why?"

"Crazy things can happen thar. Remember a couple of months ago, when those two wee'ins wandered in, lookin' fer a bit of excitement an' adventure?"

And they'd found it. Poor boys. The young teens had remembered a flashlight, but not fresh batteries. Her rescue team had been alerted after the boys hadn't returned home by nightfall, and one of their mothers found an email outlining their plans to find Indian treasures in the centuries-old caverns. Vicky hadn't been the one to find them but had ridden in the helicopter to the hospital and listened to their stories of banging, lights, and voices.

"I already warned a couple of Indiana Jones wannabes I saw lookin' 'round. Crazy newlyweds. Totally clueless to how dangerous those caves can be."

She nodded her head. "Don't worry. The only hot water I want to get into is right over there," she answered, pointing toward her favorite mineral springs a few feet away.

"Okay then, love. Enjoy." He smiled, waved goodbye, and walked off.

"No peeking," she called out.

His boisterous laugh echoed off the rocks.

Vicky waited five minutes, then headed toward the trailer. Passing by a silent drill rig— which looked a bit dirty for not "being in use"—she weaved around the pallets of sacks she saw in the photos last night until finally reaching her intended destination.

Sneaking alongside the trailer, she peered through a window. No lights. No signs of life. She tried the door. Locked.

No problem.

Vicky slipped off her backpack, unzipped a side pocket filled with odds and ends, and retrieved two paper clips. Thanks to an overnight jail stint for disorderly conduct at an anti-mining protest in San Francisco, a granola bar, and a hungry, but friendly cellmate in for burglary, Vicky learned how to pick a lock. In seconds, she was inside.

Thank you, Slick Fingers Selma.

A flick of a switch and light flooded the trailer. Based on the crap stacked, packed, and strewn about, storage was the main function of this building. Vicky weaved her way around, scanning everything in hopes something might prove useful.

A door at the back opened into a small office. An old table with a desktop computer at one end, two old filing cabinets, and three worn chairs covered the majority of floor space. Maps, charts, and photographs papered the walls.

Your typical job site. Nothing notable. Nothing telling so far.

Vicky jerked at the drawers of each filing cabinet. Locked.

Again, no problem.

She bent down, tilted one cabinet backwards, and pressed up on the metal locking bar. Click. Unlocked. The move worked on the second one, too.

Thank you, Magnum P.I. reruns.

Vicky rifled through each drawer. One held a stack of what appeared to be thermal images of the Mineral Springs area. Another contained long, folded strips of paper that looked like EKG readings. Other drawers were filled with file folders marked everything from Federal Filings to Time Cards.

In the bottom drawer of one cabinet lay two unmarked cardboard tubes. Twisting off the end of one, Vicky slid the contents out and laid everything flat on the table. Atlas-sized maps segmented into grids were covered with different colored dots connected by odd-shaped ovals. Another sheet had similar markings as well as either red or green plus signs.

The other tube contained various multi-colored maps of North America, some marked in meters, some in degrees Celsius, and one marked with numbers followed by a formula of some kind.

Vicky shook her head, more confused now than when she'd broke in.

And you were expecting…. what? A file marked "Damning Evidence. Take Me?"

Sure would have made life easier. She was no expert, but nothing here seemed unusual.

Stuffing everything back in, Vicky pushed the locks in then headed for the 21st-century's version of the filing cabinet.

One press of the power button and the computer hummed to life. Within minutes, the VL Holdings logo appeared on screen. She accessed the file management area and scanned file names, some in English, others in Dutch. Unfortunately, not one was named "Damning Evidence."

However, one called "*An todhchaí*" stood out.

Hmm... What language is that? She clicked on the file.

A Password Required box popped up. Christiaan was CEO, so he'd probably have complete access to everything. The only secret code she could remember was their joint ATM PIN. Vicky typed in "Brianna."

The computer answered with "Incorrect Password."

Duh. Wrong wife.

She tried "Astrid."

"Incorrect Password."

Hmm, what would Christiaan use? She tried his mother's name, Ingrid. His father's, Gerhard. The name they'd picked out for their son, Pieter.

Password Required. Password Required. Password Required.

So much for my future.

Okay, so maybe he didn't have complete access or his passwords have gotten more sophisticated.

She tried a file named *"Diord Fionn"*. *Hmm... don't recognize that one.* Password Required. "Costs to Date." Password Required. "Marketing Strategy." "Another File Name." "Another File Name."

Password Required. Password Required. Password Required.

Biting her lip, she went to Programs, clicked on the Internet browser, and accessed the History file. Unfortunately, all she found was the basic stuff anyone would expect to find on a corporate computer, including a few porn sites, trash mag sites, and You Tube videos. She read over the complete list, but nothing stood out.

On a lark, she clicked one of the You Tube links. Up popped an animation titled "How Fracking Causes Earthquakes." Vicky watched as little trucks on screen pumped wastewater from the fracking process into drilled injection wells. Next, the liquid pushed through a deep layer of rock. Soon, the fluid leaked into nearby fault zones, causing them to slip and unleashing an earthquake.

"Damn. That would suck." She made a mental note to ask Rainbow if she knew anything about the Die Frackers Die group behind the video. Vicky wouldn't mind asking them if they knew of any fracking activity in the Shasta area. Considering the numerous surrounding fault zones, it would be worth looking into.

Flipping the computer off, she headed over to take a closer look at the maps and whatnot hanging from the office walls. Satellite images and geochemical surveys of the Mineral Springs site covered one side. Everything looked written in code. USGS... geopressure... MEQ... MW... Vicky wrote the alphabet soup down on the notepad from her backpack. She'd Google them at the office later.

On another wall, a large standard Forest Service map of the area was marked off in grids. Vicky counted at least five strangely shaped green crosses pinned to the surface. To the right hung a clipboard with a sheet titled "Drill Sites." Each line corresponded to one of the green crosses and listed today's estimated depths. Most figures were in the five- to six-mile range.

"I knew it! I knew they weren't just exploratory drilling." Through her research, she'd learned geothermal test wells rarely exceed three miles. Vicky fought the urge to rip the incriminating sheet off the clipboard for evidence. No need to hand Christiaan direct proof she'd been here. She'd simply mentally file the information for future reference.

A quick check of her watch told her she needed to get out of there. Christiaan's men would be back from lunch soon. She glanced quickly at the remaining maps before retracing her steps. Relocking the door, Vicky slung her backpack over a shoulder and headed toward the drill rig. Maybe a little sabotage to a few hydraulic lines could delay the project until ShastaWatch could find a way to end this nightmare.

Within minutes, the mission was complete. She weaved her way around half-full pallets and headed back up the ridge. At the natural bridge, Vicky stopped at one of the caves to grab a handful of blackberries from bushes framing the dark opening. Lots of boot prints and wheel marks in the dirt at the entrance mixed with bear tracks. The bears were obviously looking for berries. The people, adventure and treasure.

Hmm... Indiana Jones wannabe couple? More like Dancing with the Stars wannabes.

A huge whiff of air brushed over her as a hawk dove inches from her head.

"What the—" Vicky ducked as the bird swooped again, enormous talons grasping perilously close to her cheek. Her right foot slipped on loose stone. She caught herself, or so she thought, before pitching forward. Scrambling to remain upright, she found herself tumbling down the mountainside.

Debris rained down from all sides. Vicky came to rest precariously on a thin, flat ledge. Heart pounding, she clung there. Blood trickled into one eye, making it burn. A sharp, jabbing pain exploded from her arm.

The cause? A large boulder had her right arm pinned against the rock face.

Vicky struggled to get free. A sharp pain ripped through her arm with each yank.

Taking a deep breath, she shoved against the boulder. Nothing. Another deep breath. She tried lifting with her knees pressed under the rock. Nothing.

Vicky reached her left fingers down to touch her right hand. The contact barely registered. She tried wiggling the thumb. Nothing.

The lack of bone-splitting noises when the boulder hit probably meant no broken bones. No blood dripping from behind the stone was a good sign, too.

She was simply stuck.

Visions of the mountaineer forced to cut his forearm free with a dull knife a few years ago ran through her head. She had a knife, too.

In her backpack.

Which was no longer hanging from her shoulder.

Along with her radio.

Vicky ran the free hand through her hair and looked around. Her ice axe still hung from her hip! *Never leave home without it.*

A rustling in the bushes above caught her attention.

"Hello?" Vicky struggled to see what caused the noise, but her trapped arm gave her a limited field of vision. "Is anybody there?"

The noise stopped.

"Please, I need help."

More rustling, then silence.

"Help?"

Nothing. Probably an animal foraging for food.

A sharp twinge of disappointment hit her then she began to laugh. First, playing James Bond, searching for the missing piece to a puzzle that could stop Dr. No from taking over the world. Then, asking an animal for help. The stress of dealing with Christiaan was driving her crazy.

She slid down and sat on the ledge as best she could. "Okay, Vicky," she said aloud. "Pull it together. Let's calmly and rationally assess the situation."

Average survival time on Shasta without water is five days.

Subtract two days due to lack of shelter.

Three days.

Never mind being a sitting duck for a hungry bear or craving-a-midnight-snack mountain lion. Of course, her tone-deaf rendition of Mamma Mia could be her saving grace.

Who needs Bear bells?

Vicky let out a half-hearted chuckle. She assumed she'd stay alive until someone found her. The odds?

Not good.

That help from heaven above would take pity on her poor soul and send rock-eating Goran to feast? Considering the creatures were characters in a video game... a hundred to one.

That she could telepathically contact Dean and let him know she was in trouble? Considering her partner could barely manage the voices already inside his head... seventy-five to one.

That somebody would happen along this way and rescue her? Considering most people obeyed the "No Trespassing" signs, and she was one of a few who knew the only trail here... fifty to one.

That at some point she'd be missed and a search party sent out? Considering she didn't have another Climbing for Singles trip scheduled until the end of the week and Rainbow was already two hours into her yogathon fundraiser... ten to one.

That she would die here? Even money.

Grabbing her ice axe, she started pecking away at the boulder. At this rate, she have it pounded down to rubble in a month or two.

"Mamma Mia, here I go again. My my, how can I resist you..."

CHAPTER 10

Christiaan stared out the diner window, neither interested in the ham sandwich sitting in front of him or the phone on silent lying next to it. He wasn't hungry, and he wasn't in the mood to deal with any more calls or emails about Bri.

His PR department could handle that. He had enough on his plate today. Vicky Golden had declared war, and he still scrambled for a battle strategy.

He'd spent most of the day since their confrontation putting out fires. Her little stunt had cost him hard-won confidence with his lenders, requiring some fast-talking to prevent them from calling in his loans.

She'd also damaged the delicate truce he'd negotiated with various government officials. Assuring them he wasn't a murderer and could be trusted had taken all the diplomatic skills he'd learned from his father.

Christiaan stared into his cup. This Dutch Boy was going to need more than his finger to save the leaking dyke that was his company.

Potverdomme, Vicky. Potverdomme!

"Sorry, I'm late, bro."

He looked up in time to catch Baz sliding into the

other side of the booth.

"Where have you been?" Christiaan asked. "When I got back to the penthouse, you were nowhere to be found."

Baz grabbed a menu. "Just doing what needs to be done."

"Like dealing with problems caused a la Vicky Golden?"

"Yeah," he answered, not glancing up.

"Like subcontractors not wanting to be associated with a murderer?"

"Yeah..." Baz shook his head. "Exactly." He caught the arm of the waitress walking by. "Hello there..." He smiled, stroking her arm while he glanced at her nametag. "...Phoebe. How about some of that great coffee I smell?"

"Of course." She smiled. "Want something sweet to go with that?"

"Like you perhaps?" Baz winked. The waitress flushed all the way to her ears. "I'll settle for a cheeseburger... for now."

"Yes, sir." She wrote the order down. "Are you a baron, too?"

"No." Baz rolled his eyes. "I'm not."

"Oh." She frowned then left.

"You should have lied. She'd have been all over you," Christiaan said. "I only got her to stop calling me 'Your Grace' about five minutes ago."

"I don't need your advice or your title to get women." Baz leaned back and extended his arms across the top of the booth seat.

"No, no you don't." Christiaan's lineage had always been a sore point with Baz, especially when it came to most people's reactions over the years.

Christiaan changed the subject. "So, who's looking to pull out of the project?"

Baz straightened. "Nobody yet. Everybody just wants to hang tight 'til this thing plays out... one way or another."

"Like I have time to 'play'."

"Whoa, man. Why so worked up? This isn't the first time we've been ambushed with headlines."

Christiaan stiffened, his face tight. "Attacking the project is one thing," he said then turned to stare out the window. "Vilifying Bri's memory is another."

"So it got a little too personal this time. You'll live."

Christiaan eyed his friend for a long moment then shook his head. "You have no idea what it's like to be prime fodder for the media."

"Of course I don't, *Baron* van Laere." Baz's eyes narrowed. "No one cares what the lowly gardener's son does."

"They should." Christiaan smirked. "Your antics would keep them splashed in ink for years."

"But my blood doesn't run blue." Baz bowed his head then rolled his hand in front to pay homage to Christiaan.

"I'd trade you any day."

"Right. If it were only that easy," Baz answered sarcastically.

"Here ya go." The waitress placed a cup of coffee in front of him. She turned to Christiaan. "Do you need anything, Your Gra— Christiaan?"

"No," he answered. "Thank you."

Baz followed the swing of her hips as she walked away. "That, my friend, could take your mind off your troubles."

"For about ten minutes."

"Ten *seconds* maybe, considering how long it's been since you had sex." Baz laughed then began tapping on his phone, humming some old pop tune Christiaan couldn't quite place.

He had no interest in his friend's latest sex candidate. Vicky was all he could think about. He needed to do something about her. The problem was he also wanted to do something *with* her, *to* her.

His big head wanted one thing. His little one, another. How could a woman he'd only met a few days ago affect him at an emotional depth he'd let die with Bri?

"Great... this keeps getting worse." Baz turned his phone around so Christiaan could see the screen. Google News results on his name had hundreds of articles in just the last several hours. The first few entries filled the screen.

American Press Hints Freak Death No Accident
Baron Silent On Wife's Untimely Demise
Could van Laere Death Be Ruled A Homicide?
No Body, No Evidence, No Murder Say Dutch Authorities
Eight Years Ago: van Laere Reaction to Wife's Death said Fake
Baron Admits Better Life with Dead Wife

Christiaan sighed. He wasn't surprised. Once the first story hit, it was just a matter of time until his family's name was dragged, covered, and buried in the mud.

Anymore of this and no one would want to work with VL Holdings.

And he'd be bankrupt.

He threw his napkin onto the table and leaned back in his chair. "This thing is getting out of hand. Maybe I need to face the truth that this project isn't going to happen."

"No, we can't stop now." Baz's eyes shot up like a deer caught in the headlights.

"I know you've been working hard on Mineral Springs for many years," Christiaan said. "But if we pull out now, before this gets any nastier, maybe I can salvage what's left of my company. Sell the property. Auction the leasing rights." Neither option tasted palatable.

"No, not when we're so close." Baz dropped his phone to the table then began rubbing the back of his neck with one hand. "We need this, Chris. I really need this."

Oh no. Not the "don't-make-me-beg" face. Obviously, his friend had once again spent his bonus before he earned it. What was it this time? A car? A house? A woman?

The previous three times this happened, Christiaan had advanced Baz the money to cover his debts. This time, Christiaan didn't have anything to advance. Everything he owned and borrowed was leveraged against Mineral Springs's success.

"So...?" His friend stared at him expectantly.

Christiaan needed time to think. To figure out his next move. Everything was falling apart faster than a Kleenex in a rainstorm. He needed to regroup, to figure out his next move.

And, what exactly, to do about the infuriating, exasperating, intoxicating Vicky.

"Look, you said it yourself," Christiaan explained. "Everybody just wants to hang tight until this thing plays out. Let's put everything on hold and take a few days to see if we can talk Vicky into—"

"Into what?" Baz slammed his coffee cup onto the table. "The bitch isn't interested in talking. Hell, the only thing she's interested in is screwing up my life."

"It's just a few days—"

"Damn! Your women ruin everything." Baz slammed his fist on the table. Coffee flew everywhere.

With one hand, Christiaan snatched his phone from the table. With the other, he grabbed a handful of napkins to keep the liquid from running onto him.

"Sorry." Baz dabbed at the coffee seeping into his shirt. "Better clean this up before it stains," he said, heading for the men's room at the back of the diner.

Baz's phone sat in a puddle of coffee. Christiaan picked it up and wiped the device with a napkin before dropping it into his shirt pocket.

The waitress appeared with a rag and began clearing the table.

He scanned his phone screen. Lou had called, so he dialed the PI.

He picked up in one ring. "Talk to me."

"Lou, it's Christiaan. You called?"

"Yeah, just letting you know the package arrived. I had one of my guys meet the plane and deliver the photo to the lab."

"Great," Christiaan said. "How soon until we know something?"

"Can't say. Let me give my guy a call. I'm gonna put you on hold for a minute."

Christiaan heard a click followed by silence. The waitress smiled as she finished cleaning up the mess. With his free hand, he pulled Baz's phone out of his pocket. Hopefully, the coffee bath hadn't damaged the device. Finding a replacement in this small town would be next to impossible.

Good sign. The screen burned bright.

The phone suddenly blared Blackberry Smoke's "Sleeping Dogs". Caller ID showed the caller was from the environmental engineering firm hired for field-testing. Probably calling to give Baz grief about the media reports.

Might as well handle this himself. Christiaan hit answer and held the device to his free ear.

"Mr. Yager? Chuck Lape," a male voice said. "I'm calling to reiterate my concerns."

"Chuck, it's Christiaan. I understand your concerns, but let me assure you—"

"Mr… um… Baron van Laere? Oh, man, I must have dialed the wrong number."

"No, no you didn't," Christiaan said. "Mr. Yager… Baz had to step away for a few minutes."

"Mr. Yager…" The seismologist cleared his throat. "Mr. Yager was quite clear I was only to talk to him."

Christiaan shook his head. *Baz and his ego trips.*

"Well, Mr. Yager works for me, and since your concerns are with me and my past, don't you think I'm the one you should be talking to?"

"Sir… Mr… Baron…" Chuck stammered.

"*Alstublieft*… please, call me Christiaan."

"Christiaan… my concerns aren't with you. They're with the unmapped fault zones. As I—"

"Christiaan?" Lou's voice echoed in the other ear. "You there?"

"—mentioned to Mr. Yager in my report, transpressional rupture of a main strike-slip fault could infer—"

"Hello? Christiaan! You there?"

"—to accommodate relative motion between several tectonic plates, rupturing an unmapped north-dipping fault—"

"Hold on," Christiaan said.

"Christiaan," Lou growled. "My guy says—"

"—and causing a significant seismic threat for the surrounding continent. That's why I cautioned—"

Potverdomme! He couldn't focus on either man's information with both talking at the same time.

"Hold on!" Christiaan repeated.

"—Mr. Yager against the use of explosives—" Obviously, the seismologist was on a roll. Christiaan let the man ramble on in the background while he focused on the priority at hand.

Vicky Golden.

"—the lab's pretty backed up," Lou continued. "They're promising something in twenty-four to thirty-six hours tops."

Christiaan let out a frustrated sigh. So much for a quick offense. Back to playing defense. The waitress set two fresh cups of coffee and Baz's cheeseburger on the table then disappeared.

"In the meantime," Lou said. "I'll get up to speed on your wife's case."

"That's right. You weren't working for me then."

"No, I was fishing for Blue Marlin off the coast of Costa Rica."

Christiaan laughed. Lou hated fishing, but that was his cover story anytime anyone delved into his background. The security chief had shared few details about his past, so Christiaan was fairly certain that eight years ago Lou had been either been chasing al-Qaeda terrorists in Afghanistan or IRA extremists in Europe.

"Now you're just fishing for an unknown woman's identity," Christiaan said.

"A much easier and safer job, my friend. I'll let you know something about the photo as soon as I do." Lou cut the connection.

Agitation mixed with anxiety. Christiaan fought the urge to scream.

"The situation, if handled incorrectly, could end badly.

If you'll—"

Oh, yeah. He'd forgot. The seismologist.

"Chuck, I have to go," Christiaan said into Baz's phone. "I'll have Mr. Yager call you to discuss it further."

"Of... of course. Thank you." The seismologist hung up, and Christiaan set both phones down on the table.

Lost in a mental fog, he traced a finger over his coffee cup.

Baz slipped into the booth, wet spots on his shirt.

"Sorry I lost it."

"No problem," Christiaan offered. "Believe me, I understand your frustration."

"Yeah." Baz focused on putting sugar into his coffee. "So, who was that on the phone?"

"Lou. He still doesn't have a fix on this Vicky Golden."

"International terrorist? Professional assassin?" Baz laughed. "More like corporate whistle blower or alcoholic looking for a new start."

"Or eco-terrorist in hiding from sabotaging an oil rig to protect the whales or blowing up a housing project to save the owls." Christiaan tapped the side of his cup. "Anything like that would explain her keeping such a low profile."

Baz smiled as the waitress returned with a bottle of ketchup. "Sorry about the mess," he offered.

"Don't worry." She waved a hand. "Accidents happen. Can I get you anything else?"

"The check and your number—" Baz winked. "Phoebe." She giggled and walked away.

Christiaan let out a slow, impatient breath. False accusations and innuendo were tarnishing his name, damaging his reputation, and insulting his wife's memory. Yet here he sat, waiting for something, anything concrete enough to fire back with dignity. He felt as effective as a eunuch at an orgy.

"You know what you need?" Baz asked between bites of cheeseburger.

Christiaan raised an eyebrow. "If you say thirty seconds

with Phoebe, you're fired."

Baz laughed. "No, you need to go for a run."

Not a bad idea. His knee and his ribs were feeling better. Obviously, nothing significant was going to happen this afternoon. An hour or two of sweat and uninterrupted thought could be just what he needed to clear his mind and focus on the problem.

His problem. And possibly his obsession.

Vicky.

"Sounds good." Christiaan stood, tossing his napkin on the table. "I could use a break from the phone calls and emails."

Baz put his hand out. "Then leave your phone with me."

"Okay." Christiaan gave him the device. Baz slipped it into his pocket.

"By the way, here's yours." Christiaan slid Baz's phone across the table. "I saved it from the coffee bath."

"Thanks."

The waitress walked by with a huge tray of food and dropped off their lunch ticket.

"You'll get that, won't you?" asked Christiaan.

"And then some." Baz grinned and held the check out to show Christiaan the scribbled signature—complete with a heart instead of the "o" in her name. Her phone number and "I get off at 5" were written underneath.

Baz growled a low, sexy sound. "Then I'll get her off about 5:15, 5:30, 5:45, 6—"

"I get it, I get it." Christiaan held up a hand. "Have fun. I'll see you back at the penthouse."

He headed out the door humming that stupid pop tune and cursing Baz for putting it in his head.

Ten kilometers ago, the last place Christiaan planned on ending up was Mineral Springs. Yet, here he was, running down the rough-hewed access road they'd cut into the property. Maybe while he was here he'd stop by the site office and see if that report the seismologist had mentioned was lying around.

The seismologist! Christiaan had forgotten to tell Baz the guy had called. No problem. He'd call Baz from the trailer. A quick sprint had him there in two minutes.

Problem. The site office was locked. Wow, talk about efficient. Baz must have called everybody as soon as Christiaan had left the diner.

In the stillness, the distinctive sights and sounds of nature echoed around him. Crickets chirping in the tall grass. Cicadas humming from the pines. Deer rustling in the bushes, feasting on honeysuckle blooms. The deep rhythmic tenor of Christiaan's breathing blended in.

The more time he spent around Mt. Shasta, the more he appreciated Vicky's passion for it. Development of this property would allow others to appreciate the mountain, too. All it would take was compromise.

Not Vicky's strong suit.

A piercing scream stole Christiaan's attention. Overhead, a red-tailed hawk soared. Wings extended, the bird rode the wind, swooping down to within a few feet of him. The creature circled twice then disappeared over the trees.

Christiaan envied the bird. Go where it wanted, when it wanted. A freedom he never enjoyed. Being born into nobility and privilege meant being born into a world of archaic rules of behavior, dynastic family obligations, and scandal-loving media. A world Baz had always yearned to belong to. A world Brianna had trouble fitting into. A world Christiaan could never escape from.

His thoughts jumped to Vicky. A woman who fought passionately for her beliefs. Christiaan laughed. She'd set his world on fire. Evidenced by how she'd lit his kindling last night while they danced.

He'd taken her into his arms, and it felt incredible. Like she belonged there.

He'd instantly hardened. Vicky either didn't notice, didn't care, or didn't mind. No denying that when he'd kissed her, she'd kissed him back with equal ferocity.

The memory aroused him, forcing him to slow his pace. A guy could get injured running in this condition.

Christiaan checked his watch. He'd sweated for close to two hours. Time to head back. He turned around and set out toward the highway.

The hawk he'd seen earlier swooped down, inches from his head. A mother protecting her nest? He ducked and waved the bird off.

It wasn't fazed. The hawk charged again, squawking loudly. Scenes from Hitchcock's *The Birds* flashed through Christiaan's mind. The hawk swirled around him, making it impossible to leave the property. The nest must be somewhere in that direction. Christiaan headed the opposite way, past the drilling rig, toward the mountain.

The angry momma finally left him alone as he neared the rock face. He sat down on a boulder to noodle a way out of his predicament. Momma Hawk blocked his only known access point. Follow the old railroad bed into town? That would require knowing exactly where the old railroad bed was.

Mental note: Study the property maps a little more closely next time.

Christiaan shivered as his body started to cool down. *Great.* Getting sick would be par for the course. Cursing, he picked up a small rock and threw it into a near thicket.

"Mamma Mia, here I go again. My my, how can I resist you?" A woman's voice, singing at the top of her lungs—and dreadfully off key—echoed above him.

Christiaan looked up the rock face but couldn't see anything.

"Okay, Mr. Bear. I'm gonna just keep singing until you go away. Mamma Mia, does it show again? My, my just how much I've missed you."

Potverdomme! The woman couldn't carry a tune in a bucket with a lid on it across the street.

"Yes, I've been brokenhearted. Blue—"

"Mr. Bear promises to go away if you promise to stop

singing."

"Chr— Christiaan?"

"Vicky?"

A faint groan answered him.

"Vicky! Are you okay?"

Another groan, this one painful.

She's hurt! Christiaan pawed his way up the stones. He lost his footing several times and banged his knees, but finally managed to reach the ledge where she lay, covered in thick rock dust.

"You okay?" he asked.

Blood dripped from a cut above her eye. Bruised skin peeked out from a tear at the shoulder of her shirt. One arm looked scraped up pretty bad, and the other disappeared behind a large boulder.

"Just peachy."

That particular American quip was unfamiliar. Her tone hinted of irony. Her grimace, ashen cheeks, and quivering confirmed pain.

"How badly are you hurt?"

"Nothing serious..." Vicky shrugged her shoulders. "Except that this damn rock is squeezing the life from my hand!"

Christiaan squatted to get a better look. Her wrist was compressed to about half its normal thickness. Judging from the pale grayness of her hand, circulation had ceased. She was right. The rock was squeezing the life from her hand.

"Can you feel anything?" he asked.

Vicky took a deep breath, like she was gathering any remaining energy to answer. "Not now. It hurt like hell a couple hours ago. Now, nothing."

Christiaan slipped his hands under the boulder and tried lifting it. It didn't move. He repositioned himself and tried pushing the rock. It didn't even budge. The boulder was wedged under a five-inch shelf of granite right above Vicky's head.

Refusing to move.

Christiaan ground his teeth in frustration. Of all the times not have his phone to call for help.

"It's no use." Vicky tilted her head back against the rock face. "Unless you're carrying something in your running shorts that's long, hard, and strong enough to lift a rock, I'm screwed."

Christiaan arched an eyebrow. He hid something long and hard, but nothing strong enough for this particular situation.

"That's not what I meant." She tried to laugh, but managed only a weak smile.

Christiaan studied her. A single tear slipped down a beautiful cheek. He knew what had her worried. If circulation wasn't restored soon, she'd lose the hand.

He squatted down to cup her chin and brush away the tear with his thumb. A knot rose in his throat. He decided to do whatever possible to ensure not another one fell from those perfect platinum eyes.

"Everything's going to be okay."

The corner of her mouth twitched. She didn't believe him.

"What are you doing here?" Her brows rose skeptically.

"Planning my assault on the environmental degradation of the sacred, natural world, the destruction of wildlife habitats, and the despoliation of wild places. If I can somehow accelerate global warming, kudos to me." Christiaan grinned. "Actually, I was trying to work out my stress with a long run. Now I'm saving you. Something I seem to be doing a lot of lately."

"It's only fair..." Vicky eyes glazed over. "I saved you first." She began shivering.

Shock? He needed to free her... now.

"Hold on, Vicky. Hold on."

None of the branches or logs lying around would be strong enough to lift the rock. He eyed the axe in her free hand. Not long enough for leverage. Where, in the middle of these woods, would he find something strong enough to lift Vicky's jailer?

The drilling rig. Christiaan scrambled down the rocks and hit the ground running. He sprinted to the machinery. Come on, come on. There's got to be something laying around here that would work.

Yes! Propped against the rig was a long steel shaft. What it was used for, he had no idea. But, for now, it was a magic wand.

He grabbed the pole, raced back to the rock formation, and clambered up to Vicky.

Her face was as white as the clouds above, obviously on the verge of passing out. He needed to keep her awake and talking.

"Hey, you're still here," he said, trying to sound casual.

"Like I'm going anywhere."

Good sign. Sense of humor intact.

Christiaan thrust one end of the metal pole between the boulder and rock face and pushed on the other end with all his weight. The rock inched forward. Vicky's arm dropped free. He released the makeshift lever, and the boulder rolled back to its original spot.

The arm hung limply by her side. She hadn't even noticed it was free.

He kneeled down. Vicky seemed to be sleeping. He touched her face. The skin was cold and clammy.

"Vicky, you with me?" he asked.

"Always, Christiaan." Her eyes fluttered briefly. "Always."

He inspected the limb. No broken bones. No broken skin. Only two deep compression marks showing where she'd been pinned.

"Can you move the fingers?"

The hand remained motionless.

"N... n... no."

Hopefully, there was no permanent damage.

First obstacle overcome. Now, to get out of here.

"Is your truck nearby?" Christiaan asked.

"No... hiked... in."

Of course. Fate wouldn't want to make this any easier.

"I could run back into town, but I don't want to leave you like this."

"Radio," she whispered.

"What?"

"Radio... backpack... fell... somewhere." Vicky bobbed her head back and forth.

Christiaan looked around. A red backpack lay behind a bush below them. He retrieved the bag, found the radio, reported their location then scrambled back up to Vicky, now shivering.

He covered her with an emergency blanket from the backpack, sat down, and wrapped his arms around her.

"Hang in there. Help is on its way."

"I'm... sorry..." Vicky laid her head on his shoulder. The contact sent shivers up and down his body. "So... sorr... ry." Her voice trailed off.

"Stay with me, *mijn liefste*." The Dutch words for "my love" flowed off his tongue before he could stop them.

"Hmm..."

"Hey, let's sing your bear song until help arrives," Christiaan said. "How's it go?"

"What...?"

"Mamma Mia," he began singing. "Come on, I don't know the rest of the words."

"Here I... go... again. My, my..."

Christiaan hummed along.

CHAPTER 11

Vicky stood underneath the hot shower in her lodge, the pulsating spray kneading her sore muscles like the practiced hands of a masseuse.

If only the water could reach inside to soothe her troubled, confused heart.

Physically, she was fine. The ER doc had declared her lucky. No broken bones. No muscle or tissue damage. No lasting effects from shock. Just minor cuts and bad bruising. He'd sent her home with a shot of Demerol, a bottle of Vicodin, and a word of caution to take it easy for the next several days.

Mentally, she swam through a haze of feelings and desires that no amount of painkiller could clear. Annoyed Christiaan caught her trespassing. Grateful he'd found her. Furious he'd seen her so vulnerable.

Touched he'd stayed with her.

The problem was she didn't want to feel annoyed at him. Or grateful. Or furious. Or touched. She didn't want to feel anything for him.

Christiaan's concern for her safety had melted her defenses. He may see her as a stranger, but she saw him as the loving, gentle man she'd married fifteen years ago.

Vicky caressed her belly.

And conceived a son with.

She closed her eyes and let the water slip down her mature, lithe body. Hands slid across silken skin, and she shuddered in surprise. The touch was light and teasing. Heat rippled under her skin as she recognized the flush of desire she hadn't known in years.

Warm water flowed over her breasts, and Vicky leaned her body back until the spray hit her nipples. The stinging intensity made them harden.

Christiaan.

She leaned further against the cold tile and gave herself up to the moment. A small growl filled the small space.

Oh how I've missed you.

Her breath quickened as a finger traced the outline of her lower lips then found a home between them. The slow, gentle stroking sent intense sensations through her body.

Vicky's legs grew weak as the fingers thrust fast and deep. Waves of euphoria began to throb through her. Her hips bucked to meet the fingers, stroke for stroke.

Almost at once, moans of ecstasy escaped her throat as a burst of sensations filled her. The release was tormenting, yet pleasurable. Exhausting, yet invigorating. Everything she remembered.

Gradually, she regained her composure. Vicky turned off the shower and pushed open the glass door, shuddering as the cold air hit her warm skin.

A shadow darkened the bathroom. Christiaan stood there, holding a towel, and staring. A series of emotions played across his face. Shock. Curiosity. Lust.

He'd watched her! He'd seen everything! Her chest tightened, and a unwelcome blush crept into her cheeks.

Vicky tore the towel from his hand and wrapped it around her body. Embarrassment flashed to anger. "What are you doing here!"

His lips moved, but not a sound emerged. Total discomfort now covered his face.

"What are you doing here?" she repeated.

"I— I was worried. You were taking too… um… too long. I thought maybe something had happened."

"I'm *fine*." Vicky stepped out of the stall.

"I promised the emergency room doctor that I'd keep an eye on you for several hours. Just to make sure you're okay."

"Am I speaking English?" She took a step forward. "I'm fine!"

He retreated. "I'm only here because I wanted to see you're okay."

Vicky continued her advance and rant. "*You've* seen enough—way more than enough—to see that I'm okay. So instead of prancing around like you own the place, why don't you just go home?"

"I'm sorry but—"

"You will be if you don't get out of here." With a hard shove driving him backward then a slammed door, she ended the conversation.

"I'll be downstairs," he said. "But before I leave, let's make one thing very clear."

"What!"

"I've never pranced in my life."

Vicky couldn't help but laugh. Christiaan was certainly not a man who pranced. He might mosey. Maybe amble. But never prance.

She leaned forward and rested her forehead against the door. How much more could she take before her mind snapped like a taut rubber band?

How much had he seen? From the look on his face when she'd exited the shower, everything.

Vicky quickly dressed in a worn sweatshirt and jeans then padded down the stairs and into the main floor. Reflections from the fireplace danced off the polished stone floor, filling the main room with a warm, inviting glow.

Christiaan stood with his back to her. His palms braced against the mantel, he stared into the fire. The jeans and polo shirt someone at the hospital had loaned him clung to his frame like a second skin.

Her gaze drifted over her husband's thick dark hair, wide shoulders, and taut back. It took all her strength not to walk over and encircle his waist with her arms then drop a few strategically placed kisses on his neck to announce her presence.

Never would she have imagined him here, in this setting, with her.

"*Damn*," slipped out quietly.

Christiaan spun around to face her. Vicky's legs nearly buckled as she gazed at the strong, handsome face of her soul mate. The glow from the fire accentuated his high cheekbones. His tousled brown mane fell across his gorgeous blue eyes in the most sensual manner. His perfectly sculpted jaw shown lightly dusted with day-old beard. She ached to feel the stubble against her cheek as she kissed his soft, warm, inviting mouth.

"You need to go." *Before I do something I'll regret.*

"Not yet. The doctor said you needed to get something in your stomach before taking any more painkillers."

Vicky glanced at the stone sofa table. A silver sauce pan on a trivet between two place settings. On the right sat a basket of rolls. On the other side, her teapot and two cups.

"The table's set for two."

"I'm hungry."

"I'd rather eat alone."

"But I'd rather not."

"You know, you're bullheaded."

"My wife called me that many, many times."

Me.

He raised a hand. "Could we call a temporary truce? The sooner you eat, the sooner you'll feel better. The sooner you feel better, the sooner I leave."

Good point.

"Truce." She headed for the table.

Or tried to. Maybe she'd moved too fast. Maybe she was woozy from the Demerol. Maybe her mind had finally given up. Whatever the reason, she was falling. Forward. Toward the floor.

This is going to hurt.

Christiaan caught her.

"Whoa," he said. "You're not as fine as you think you are."

Hmm... He smelled tasty. Very tasty. Vicky held on, tightly.

The heat of his body seared her emotions. His nearness overwhelmed her. She steadied herself against his chest. The distinctive scent that was Christiaan permeated her senses.

"Allow me." He swooped her up into his arms. Vicky peered into her husband's eyes as he carried then gently eased her onto the couch. The electricity of his touch made her respond powerfully. The intense look in his eyes made her ache.

"Th-thanks," she offered with a smile. Fighting her undeniable need for him was getting harder by the minute.

Christiaan sat down in the highback chair opposite her then lifted the pan lid. A mouthwatering aroma caught her nose.

"Mix up some vegetables, brown rice, and curry powder and you've got what I believe you Americans call 'pot luck'," Christiaan explained. "Hope you like it."

He piled food on her plate and gestured to eat. "*Mevrouw*, dinner is served."

"Not bad," Vicky said after trying a mouthful. "When did you learn to cook?"

He laughed as he served himself. "Early in our marriage, Bri encouraged me to embrace the culinary arts after I set fire to the kitchen trying to make breakfast one day."

Vicky smiled at the memory. To prove he wasn't a spoiled rich boy, he'd vowed to make eggs and toast without the help of the estate's cook. Instead, he proved that bread burns when toasted at the highest setting and eggs don't cook when the burner is set on four hundred degrees.

"Well, I'm sure she would be impressed with tonight's

meal." *Quite impressed.*

"I bet she would." His face grew somber. "If she were here."

She is. Mijn liefste, she is.

They ate quietly, the crackling fire the only sound breaking the silence. Christiaan appeared visibly upset at the mention of Brianna.

Vicky shook her head. The Demerol was clouding her judgment. For a second, he sounded sincere. Like he'd cared for Brianna?

Not Astrid. *Me.*

"Does the Baroness share your newfound fondness for the culinary arts?" she asked.

"God, no." He laughed. "My stepmother's idea of cooking is 'Christiaan, dear, tell Cook they'll be twenty for dinner'."

"No, I meant your wife... the current Baroness."

"My stepmother *is* the current Baroness."

Vicky could barely breathe as the statement's truth permeated her mind and heart. She set her fork down before she dropped it. He was supposed to remarry. He was supposed to marry Astrid.

Wasn't that why he got rid of me?

Nevermind he was supposed to marry Astrid in the first place. Astrid was the one his stepmother said would carry the next van Laere heir. Astrid was the one he kissed on the balcony.

Astrid had left with Christiaan on his business trip the day after his birthday party. Astrid had answered the telephone in his hotel room. Astrid had stood next to him outside the Amsterdam police station when the TV news cameras ambushed him. They both smiled when a reporter asked, "Is it true Lady Astrid is the next Baroness van Laere?"

"You're... not... married?" Vicky asked.

"No. I've loved only one woman in my life," Christiaan answered, gaze locked on his plate. "And I lost her."

The raw emotion that bled from those words tore

through Vicky. The sincerity. The genuineness. The honesty. All a stark contrast to the monster she'd feared for the last eight years.

"But... the wedding band... on your finger..." Their rings were family heirlooms. She'd just assumed the band signified his remarriage to Astrid.

"I'll always be married to Bri... and only Bri."

No. No. No! You wanted me dead. I saw you. I heard you.

"So... you... didn't... murder..." Disbelief and shock made the words wedge in her throat.

"*Nee!* I did NOT murder my wife!" Christiaan's blue eyes darkened like angry thunderclouds. He jerked the gold chain out from under his shirt. Hanging from it was a small ring with white gold leaves intertwined around the band.

My wedding ring.

She'd left it in her car the day after their big fight. He'd refused to take her calls all day, making her so mad she'd yanked it off her finger and threw it in the cup holder. She'd thought about it later, but by then it was too late.

"Do you really think I could wear my wife's ring if I'd had her murdered?" Christiaan cried out, his voice strained with pain. "*Potverdomme*, it's all I have left of her."

The wind whooshed out of Vicky, like someone had kicked her in the stomach. This was a man very much in love with his wife. He missed her. He mourned her.

Her. *Me.*

Reality gripped her heart like a cold hand.

My God. What have I done?

"I loved Bri." Christiaan sighed then buried his head in his hands. "That damn explosion shredded all our dreams. For God sakes, we were starting a family!"

"What?" Vicky stared at him with disbelief. "What did you say?"

He raised his head and looked directly into her eyes.

"I was going to be a father!"

Christiaan's breath hitched as the emotional pain of losing his son mixed with the strange blessed relief to share a secret he hadn't shared with anyone. Not even Baz.

"You knew you were going to be a father?" Vicky asked, then began to nibble on her lower lip.

"Yes, I knew about the baby." Christiaan nodded. "The *politie*—police—told me. They explained it was routine in an investigation to review medical files." He expelled a slow exhale. "A doctor performed a pregnancy test shortly before her death. It was one of the few personal details I was able to keep out of the press."

Vicky sat perfectly still, her eyes darting left and right like searching for a way to put her thoughts into words.

She's trying to find a polite way to say "Enough! Now you're getting a little too personal."

And he was. Why, he couldn't understand. But telling these things to Vicky seemed.... right.

Christiaan stood and walked to the fireplace. "We'd been trying for years to have a baby." He stared into the dancing flames, the heat warming his cheeks. "Specialists, herbalists, acupuncture, everything. You name it, we tried it. By the time of the accident, I'd given up all hope." He paused to steady his voice. "She died carrying our child. Our son."

"So... it really was an accident, wasn't it?" Her voice faded as she pushed a hand through her hair.

"Yes. A plain... simple... devastating... accident." Tears stung his eyes. "A gasoline leak onto a hot exhaust. When they told me her car had exploded, I expected them to say she was all right. That she'd lent her Jag to someone. Then they found her body and her..." A jolt of grief ripped through him at the memory of identifying the only recognizable remains of Bri... her wedding band. He'd immediately had a gold chain made to match and wore both ever since.

"Her body?" Vicki said in a broken whisper.

"Not all of it." His mind burned at the thought of how

little of Bri he'd had to mourn with.

"Why did the press call it murder?"

Christiaan spun around, his back to the fire. "Because that's what they do," he shot at her. "Isn't that what you and your people counted on when you prompted that reporter to dig into Bri's death?"

"I'm so sorry," Vicky murmured, pressing her hands to her face. "I should have done something. I should have said something. I should have never believed you…"

Christiaan's stomach clenched watching her wilt. She didn't deserve the brunt of his anger. Her actions were motivated to protect something extremely precious to her. He had no room to talk. He'd been willing to steal her sobriety to save his company.

"No, I'm sorry. It's not your fault the press has no scruples. Eight years ago, they cried murder as soon as they learned the police had questioned me. Of course, the authorities talked to me. It was a formality. The police always ask the spouse questions, especially when that spouse has ties to the Dutch royal house."

"But the trouble in your marriage…," Vicky said, her voice low and somber. "That was real, wasn't it?"

She must sense my anguish. Christiaan sank down onto the warm hearth, his body slumped in despair.

"Yes," he answered, pain etched into every word. "We were going through a rough patch, but I didn't realize the depth until she was gone." He'd punished himself for the ignorance ever since. Bri had needed him, and he wasn't there.

"You loved her very much." Vicky tapered those smoking gray eyes on him.

"From the moment we met." He smiled at that memory. "I asked her to marry me only three days later." After much pleading, cajoling, and blatant begging.

"Why her? You were the most eligible bachelor in Europe."

Christiaan leaned forward, elbows on his knees, fingers

steepled against his chin. "Bri was beautiful, brilliant, and brassy. So different than the women usually throwing themselves at me because of my title and money. After we married, she gave up her job as a reporter to travel with me on business."

He studied Vicky's curious expression. She stared at him with such intensity, waiting for the next chapter of his tragic romantic tale. Sadness darkened her eyes. The emotion warmed his heart.

"I must sound like a real sappy—what do you Americans call it—chick flick?"

"Yeah," she answered, almost in a whisper.

Christiaan expelled a deep breath. "A chick flick with no happy ever after. Everything began to fall apart after we decided to try having a baby. The doctor advised Bri to stop traveling, so she spent more time at the estate... with my family. Big mistake."

Tears sparkled her cheeks.

"She tried fitting into the *hogere kringen*—high society— but she never had a chance. They were never going to accept her, especially when my family refused to. Bri was the complete opposite of the childhood friend they'd hoped I'd marry. My father and especially my stepmother never missed a chance to remind Brianna she was not 'our kind'."

His voice changed to a high, shrill female tone. "'Brianna, dear. One simply does not discuss politics or religion at dinner.' 'Brianna, dear. When one is in conversation, one's eyes should not dart around the room to see who else is there. One should give her undivided attention to the person.' 'Brianna, it's acceptable to be nice to the staff, but someone of our station never mixes with them.' 'Brianna, dear. Stop those tears. A van Laere does not show emotion.'" Christiaan's voice returned to normal. "She never had a chance."

"And turned to food for comfort," Vicky said, gazing past him into the fire. "And alcohol."

He weighed her with a critical squint. "How'd you know?"

"You mentioned it on the mountain," she explained.

"Ah... yeah." He nodded. "At the time, I didn't really get any of this. I couldn't understand why she overate, why she drank a lot. I didn't realize the pressure my family placed on her to fit in, to produce an heir, all the stuff they seemed to think was important. I was too busy with my own pressures like keeping the family business together. I was the fourth-generation van Laere at the helm. Conversion to a European Union economy hit us hard financially, but that didn't stop my father and stepmother from spending ridiculous amounts of money. It was all I could do to keep the company and my family's finances afloat."

"Really?" She glanced at him, then averted her eyes.

He shrugged his shoulders. "Nobody knew what was going on. That's the van Laere motto. 'Never complain. Never explain.' Bri and I fought... a lot. At first behind closed doors, then..."

"In public."

Christiaan nodded. He guessed she knew firsthand what he was talking about. She'd probably fought drunk in public with her loved ones.

"Bri created quite a scene at my last birthday party before she died," he explained. "I don't know where she got the alcohol because she'd instructed the staff not to serve her. But somehow, she managed to find a bottle of Scotch and drown herself in it."

"Sobriety is not something you can just turn on and off like a faucet."

Christiaan shivered as a sense of déjà vu nudged him. "Funny, that's what Bri said to me that night."

"It's... it's something we learn in AA," Vicky said. "That's how it is for an alcoholic."

"And a workaholic, too." He pointed to himself. "Only Bri didn't want to listen. She said I loved work more than her. The funny thing is, I'd already started cutting back.

We'd made a deal earlier that year. She'd stop drinking if I promised to stay home more. I was in the process of setting things up so I could stop traveling. I just needed to finish one last project. This one." Christiaan dropped his head to stare at the floor. "Then I lost her... and none of it mattered anymore."

He closed his eyes, concentrating on the sound of the crackling fire behind him. The memory of that last night haunted him. He could still hear the yelling, the accusations spewing from both their mouths. If only he could do it all over again, talk to Bri again, he'd make it right. He'd love her like he should have.

"I'm sorry Bri," he whispered to only himself. "I'm so sorry."

"Are you okay?"

Christiaan took deep breaths until he was ready to look at Vicky in the eye. Those depthless, smoky pools peered back at him with an intensity that surprised him. Intrigued him.

Scared him.

He'd just bared his soul to this woman. Why?

"I'm fine." He tried proving it by clearing up the dishes. As he lifted hers, he dropped a tea cup on the flagstone floor. Shattered pieces flew everywhere.

"*Potverdomme!*"

If he wasn't such a pragmatist, he'd have thought the mishap symbolic. Christiaan carefully carried the rest of the dishes into the kitchen and stacked them in the sink. He returned to the scene of the crime to find Vicky, broom in hand, rounding up the stray shards into a tiny pile.

"I sure hope that wasn't a family heirloom or something."

"It was."

Christiaan's heart sank.

"For somebody, I imagine." She smiled. "I bought it at a thrift shop."

He smiled right back. Wet droplets glistened on her

long dark lashes, making her eyes twinkle.

He wanted to reach over and finish the kiss they'd started on the dance floor. How odd. He'd met this woman less than a week ago, but felt like he'd know her his entire life.

Could he be falling in love with her? Why her? Why now?

Vicky grabbed a dustpan from a nearby closet. She knelt down and struggled to sweep the broken pieces into it.

"Here, let me help." Christiaan reached for the pan. His hand connected with hers and stayed there. The heat between them was palpable, burning hotter than the fire ten feet away.

Maybe it was the knight-in-shining-armor thing, saving her on the cliff. Maybe it was the peeping-tom bit, watching her pleasure herself in the shower. But right now, this knight would sell his soul to carry her upstairs and show her how much pleasure he could give her in the shower. The image of her wet, naked, and coming burned into his brain.

"But what about the divorce?"

H-e-l-l-o reality. "What?"

"Divorce." Vicky looked at him quizzically. "The press mentioned divorce."

"Some sleazy attorney said Bri had talked to him about one, but he never produced evidence to that fact. And the innuendo that I thought death was cheaper than divorce was just that... innuendo. They said the same thing about my father thirty-five years ago."

"When your mother died."

Damn the press. Christiaan tore his gaze and the broom away from Vicky and finished cleaning up. He emptied the dustpan into the garbage then returned everything to the closet.

Vicky sat in her chair, curled up like a cat, arms wrapped around her legs and rocking back and forth. Christiaan sat back down on the hearth.

"Christiaan... I'm so sorry. Your mother... I shouldn't

have brought her up."

He sighed. Over the years, he'd repeated the story so many times he could rattle the facts off like he was reading a newspaper account. "My mother's death was an accident, pure and simple. She was riding in the woods, was thrown or fell, and was dragged by her horse. She suffered severe head injuries. Unfortunately, she wasn't wearing a helmet."

"And you're certain it was an accident?"

Always the same question. "Yes. My father was devastated. He married my stepmother two months later. Before he died, he confessed to me the rebound marriage had been a mistake from the start. She was a close friend of my mother's. They didn't become involved until *after* my mother died, a fact my stepmother refused to refute in public. I'm sure that's where the murder idea surfaced."

"And you're certain she wasn't involved in your mother's death?"

Christiaan shook his head. "No. The Baroness doesn't have the stomach for it. That's where she and Astrid differ. Astrid would probably sell her soul to the devil if he promised her everything she ever wanted."

"The one you were *supposed* to marry."

"Marry, Astrid?" Christiaan laughed. "Never. All she's ever wanted was a title and the prestige and money that goes with it. I was just her first and—because we grew up together—the easiest target. Baz once said that if a genie gave Astrid three wishes, two of them would be to make her my wife and the next Baroness."

"And the third?"

"Erase all traces of Brianna from the face of the earth." Christiaan stood to toss more wood onto the fire. "Then again, Baz always has had a flair for the dramatic."

"He seems quite devoted to you."

Christiaan grabbed a log from the pile nearby and pitched it into the middle of the flames.

"We grew up together, so we're like brothers. But Baz has a chip on his shoulder because I'm a '*blauw bloed*', a blue blood, and he's not. For some reason, he has this tremendous need to prove to the world he's more than the gardener's son. Too bad Astrid wouldn't marry him. He's been in love with her since we were kids."

"But she wanted you."

Christiaan returned to his spot on the hearth. "Yes, and she never let Baz forget it. As she put it, she didn't mind slumming with the help for a little fun, but she deserved more than a boy born with dirt under his fingernails."

"What a bitch."

"Yes, a real *kutwijf*. Her attitude fueled Baz's need to prove himself. He did anything and everything he could to show he was more than that. One summer he spent with cousins living in Ireland he hung out with radicals. Baz came back with a stupid tattoo and an even bigger chip on his shoulder. He'd hoped all that would impress Astrid, but all she did was laugh at him."

"That must have pissed him off."

"Oh, yes." Christiaan nodded his head. "He ranted for days about how women enjoy screwing up men just for fun and how they're only good for one thing. He said a lot of nasty things, but Baz is all bark and no bite, isn't that how the American saying goes?"

"That's it." This time Vicky nodded. "You really do love him like a brother, don't you?"

"He's always been there when I need him. He supported me when I married Bri and even became good friends with her. He was devastated by her death. He's never really gotten over the fact that he was the last one to see her alive, to see her drive off before she..." Christiaan swallowed hard. "It should have been me."

"To be the last one to see her alive or to die in an accidental explosion?"

"Yes."

CHAPTER 12

Christiaan slowly paced in front of the fireplace. At every second turn, he stole a glance at Vicky. She'd stopped rocking in the chair several minutes ago, but remained silent. Curled up like that, she reminded him of a tired, worn-out child.

Yeah, tired and worn-out from listening to the Dutch idiot stealing her mountain ramble on about his life, his wife, and anything else that seemed to pop into his stupid little brain. Probably, at this very moment, she was working on a way to get him the hell out of her cabin.

And her life.

Christiaan stopped moving to stare into the fire. Its heat kindled something within him. Something he hadn't felt for an exceedingly long time.

His mind reeled with confusion. He should leave. Get back to doing what he came to America to do.

Save his company by any means possible.

Peering over his shoulder, he focused on the woman stopping him.

The crazy thing was, right now, he didn't want to do any of that.

Heat overwhelmed him, but it wasn't from the

fireplace. He wanted to walk right over, gather her in his arms, and carry her up to the bedroom where he'd make long, slow love to her until he knew her from the inside out. Images of a naked Vicky riding him in utter abandon assaulted his psyche.

Potverdomme! Christiaan focused on his feet to ensure they remained firmly attached to the floor. He adjusted his stance so she couldn't see the painful agony growing in his jeans.

What the hell was wrong with him? Only a few hours ago, the poor woman had been literally stuck between a rock and a hard place. Tired, medicated, and overwhelmed by a ridiculously eventful twenty-four hours, probably the only thing on her mind was how much she'd like this lunatic to get out of her house so she could get some rest.

And the only thing on his mind was how to get her into bed. Rest... optional.

He needed to get out of here before he did something he'd... they'd both regret.

Christiaan turned to go, but his legs refused to respond. He wasn't ready to leave. He couldn't. Not yet.

The fact was it wasn't just sex he wanted from Vicky. Yes, he was attracted to her. That *hard* truth was all too evident.

But, somehow, she'd gotten under his skin. From the moment he'd met her, she'd unknowingly penetrated his carefully constructed emotional walls. She'd touched parts of him he thought had died with Bri.

He wanted to know more about this woman. And not because he needed to find something to stop her or discredit her or harm her.

Because when you realize you've found someone that fills the long-empty space in your heart, you want to know everything there is to know about them.

Christiaan's gaze returned to Vicky.

"Who are you?"

Her head shot up like a bullet, and he realized he'd voiced his thought aloud. She opened her mouth to answer, but then closed it without making a sound. Biting her lip, she wound a hand in her short locks.

"Just who is Vicky Golden?" he asked, voice tight with emotion and curiosity.

"No one…" A sharp exhalation of breath escaped her lips. "No one in particular, really."

"Come now. *Iedere vogel prijst zijn nest.*"

"Meaning?"

"Literally, every bird likes its own nest." He folded his arms across his chest. "Figuratively, every bird loves to hear herself sing. Meaning, you're being too modest. You were intriguing enough for *Inc.* magazine to send a reporter to cover you."

"Not me." Vicky unfolded back into the chair. "The business. The idea was to feature Climbing for Singles. And *that madness* was not my idea."

Christiaan laughed. "Let me guess… the friendly, gregarious, never-met-a-story-I-didn't-want-to-tell-everyone-I-meet-whether-they-want-to-hear-it-or-not Dean? Bringing that bitch on the mountain was his idea?"

A small, weary smile danced across her face. "Let's just say no one can accuse my partner of not thinking big. As long as I've known him, he's always reached for the brass ring."

"You seem to work well together." A wave of jealously slammed through Christiaan. "Partners in every sense of the word?"

"No," she laughed. "No… no… just business partners."

Good. Christiaan sat down on the hearth, jealousy bridled, but not curiosity. "How long have you known Dean?"

"A few years."

Frustration blew through his mind. Getting information from her was like licking jelly from a sharp knife.

"When we were on the summit, Dean mentioned you were—how'd he put it—'a real gumby' when you first met. What were you doing before you decided to conquer mountains?"

Deep emotion clouded her face, but Christiaan couldn't peg the particular sentiment. Before he could internally hazard a guess to her state of mind, Vicky burst out laughing.

"I tell you what." She sat up straight in the chair and, for the first time since the conversation started, looked him in the eyes. "Let's play a little tit-for-tat."

"Tit for tat? I'm not familiar with that term."

"Information for information," she explained. "For every question I answer, you have to answer one of mine."

What's the harm? He'd already practically bared his soul to her. What more could she want to know about him?

"Deal." Placing elbows on knees, he leaned forward. "Now, answer my question. What was Vicky Golden doing before she became a mountain maven?"

"Oh, a little bit of everything. Waitressing in Maine… housecleaning in Nebraska… cashiering in Mississippi…"

"How interesting. Where are you originally from?"

"Ah, ah, ah." She wagged a finger at him. "That's not how the game is played. I answered your question. Now I get one."

He nodded.

"Why expand VL Holdings into the U.S. considering the majority of your holdings are in Europe, and why here at Shasta?"

Hmm… another woman that's been doing her homework. First, the reporter. Now this one.

"Ah, ah, ah." His turn to wag a finger. "That's two questions. I'll answer the first one. The greatest opportunity in renewable energy was here considering your government's recent approval of tax incentives as well as foreign investment incentives."

"Not to mention our easing of guidelines regarding granting power companies permits to develop alternative energy sources on Federal lands." Vicky sat ramrod straight, then pointed in his direction. "And that's why you chose Northern California, Shasta in particular."

The statement caught Christiaan off-guard. Gone was the tired, worn-out child. Here was the vibrant, driven, passionate woman he'd become enamored with only five short days ago.

"Actually, it was Baz who insisted on Shasta," he answered.

"Because the California Energy Commission pledged twenty million dollars over five years if your project was operational within eight." Her voice now a trifle petulant.

Like a dog with a bone. Christiaan shook his head. Wasn't that the expression Bri often used to describe what made a good reporter?

"Yes, that's one of the reasons why I came here. This project is extremely behind and getting extremely expensive."

"No doubt driven by the Department of Energy's Geowest Initiative calling for geothermal mining to meet ten percent of the West's electrical needs within twenty years." Burning, reproachful eyes glared at him. "Of course, no one cares to mention that support for that initiative diverts conservation efforts and cleaner energy alternatives such as solar."

Potverdomme. She knows her stuff.

"Neither does anyone mention the impact such a project would have on the beauty of the Shasta area as well as the destruction of numerous Native American cultural and sacred sites. My mountain deserves to be protected, and I'll do anything to make sure no one—I mean no one—takes her away from me."

And she's taking it personal. Very personal.

"The mitigation plan you submitted barely scratched the surface of issues such as…" Vicky began counting on one hand, a finger at a time. "… Hazardous material spills, wildlife, construction dust, noise, site decommissioning and reclamation…" Switching to the other hand, she continued her count and rant. "… Vegetation, emergency procedures, protection of Native American cultural interests, and visual impacts, not to mention odor compliance procedures... I've run out of fingers... notification of residents in case of a plant emergency, chemical spill procedures, fire—"

"Whoa." Christiaan held up his hands up to stop her. "Whoa! I'll admit our mitigation plan needs a few tweaks, but you're forgetting that we consulted with several local tribal elders on the historic preservation issues. They were willing to compromise, to accept some sacrifice in exchange for much needed employment for tribal members. What have *you* got against compromise?"

Vicky leaned back, her eyes unblinking. "Compromise is half defeat."

She's quoting me Sun Tzu? "You're forgetting the entire quote. 'If it becomes obvious that your current course of action will lead to defeat, then retreat and regroup. When your side is losing, there are only three choices remaining: surrender, compromise, or escape. Surrender is complete defeat, compromise is half defeat, but escape is not defeat'."

Christiaan's eyes clung to Vicky's, analyzing her reaction as he finished. "'As long as you are not defeated, you still have a chance.' Is that your plan? To escape? To retreat and regroup?"

"No." Vicky stirred a bit uneasily in her chair. "I did that once." She glanced toward a row of books on the right of the mantel. "Never again."

Christiaan regarded her quizzically for a moment. Were they still talking about the mountain? Or something else?

Or someone else?

"I believe it's my turn for a question," he said. "Ever been married?"

The instant the words left his lips, her head jerked back to stare at him. Hundreds of emotions seemed to pass over her face. She rose from the chair without a word and moved toward him. Her nearness rekindled his earlier lust.

He reached for her, but she breezed past him to stop near the far side of the mantel. As she reached for a book, her erotically stern profile teased his barely restrained self-control. Imagining her passion in bed as equal to her passion for her cause nearly set him off.

Christiaan studied her obliviousness to his desire. The answer to his earlier question had to be yes. Someone had married her, hurt her, and then let her go. What idiot would ever let such a beautiful and passionate woman get away from him?

"He was a fool for letting you go." Christiaan stood and stepped forward. Pulling her to him, he gently grasped her face. "I never would."

"Christiaan..." Tears filled her eyes. She uttered something, but it was lost to the sudden crackling of the fire. He clasped her body tightly to his. As her soft curves molded to the contours of his, his moans mixed with hers.

Potverdomme! This felt good. Very good.

Pressing his lips to hers, he caressed her mouth more than kissed it. She tasted like heaven. Then he raised his mouth from hers and gazed into her eyes. "You're better off without him."

Immediately, her body tensed. Christiaan hoped it was a sexual response, but the ardor he'd spied there only a moment ago drained from her face.

"We're both better off." Vicky pushed him away, moving to stand behind her chair. "My turn. Why so many truckloads of explosives?"

Great. Ice Princess was back. That cooled him off faster than if she'd tossed his butt into a cold shower.

She continued. "I thought your lease requirements called for passive seismic testing and magnetotellurics to map areas of increased temperatures. Pallets upon pallets upon pallets of explosive-making materials seems a bit excessive."

"You're mistaken." Christiaan sat back down on the hearth. "We're still in the initial phase of testing and mapping. Contrary to what you and your ShastaWatch buddies believe, I don't want any unnecessary harm to come to the mountain. That's why I pushed for passive exploration instead of traditional invasive drilling techniques."

"Passive? Really?" The Ice Princess remained standing, arms crossed defensively. "Then what are all the maps in the locked filing cabinet and hanging on the wall in the site trailer?"

"Locked filing cabinet? Site trailer?" He raised an eyebrow. "And you just happened to have a key to both?"

She colored fiercely and shook her head. "Sort of. It's a long story. The point is I saw several maps with all kinds of different colored dots connected by odd-shaped ovals. Another map had red and green plus signs all over it. And one that clearly shows you're actively drilling production wells. What's *that* all about?"

"You're jumping to conclusions. We're merely testing where to drill," Christiaan answered. "In fact, we're still waiting for meaningful data from the engineering group." *Wait.* Hadn't the seismologist said that he mentioned something to Baz "in my report"? Why hadn't Baz told Christiaan the data they'd been waiting for was available?

"I don't know." A suspicious line curved at the corners of Vicky's mouth. "Seems like a lot of equipment for passive testing."

"Honestly," he offered, emphasizing his words with a small shrug. "I'm a bit out of my element when it comes to job sites and mapping and numerous other stuff. Baz handles all that."

"Then why are you here?" She eyeballed him. "Why is the CEO of a Fortune International 600 company here?"

He may have opened his heart and spilled his soul to this woman, but his van Laere training wouldn't allow him to expose anything to her about his family's and company's finances. *Take a step back, and get a hold of yourself.*

He met her stare, and his heart turned over in response.

And your feelings.

"Because a pain-in-the-ass environmental group is dead set on thwarting my first project in the States."

She held his eyes without flinching.

"And still is."

In the background, the fire continued to crackle and pop. Neither said anything for what seemed like hours but was probably only minutes.

"Do you know what MEQ stands for?" Vicky asked.

"No, I'm not familiar with that. What is it?"

"I don't know either," she answered." "I saw it in the site trailer."

"We could Google it." Christiaan instinctively reached for his phone from his back pocket. Empty. "Oops, I still don't have my phone."

"Wouldn't matter. No cell coverage on this part of the mountain."

"Wifi?"

"Nope. No computer here either. I like my serenity and privacy."

"I guess you do," he commented, realizing he hadn't seen a radio or television anywhere in the lodge since his arrival. "You said you saw this acronym in the trailer?"

"Yes."

He didn't remember anything like what she described the last time he'd been in the trailer. Of course, he wasn't that familiar with what should be in a site trailer. Like his father before him, Christiaan was always in the periphery of a project.

But Vicky's observations made him curious. What could those maps be about? And what about that report the seismologist had mentioned?

Christiaan peered out the window. Luckily, the sun had yet to begin its descent into dusk. Enough time to drive back to the site and see what Vicky had stumbled across.

"I'd really like to see what's in that building. I'm heading back out there before it gets dark." He stood.

"Where are your truck keys?"

Vicky jumped to her feet. "I'm going along."

"No." Christian shook his head. "You need to rest."

"Yeah, but you need me more than I need rest."

"Really? Why's that?"

One side of her mouth lifted into a half-grin.

"Do Barons know how to pick locks?"

At any moment, Vicky expected to wake up and discover she'd been dreaming. That the events of the last eight years were simply an illusion brought on by exhaustion, stress, or too many jalapenos on her pizza.

That she hadn't wasted those years believing Christiaan capable of murder.

That the man she still loved wasn't sitting behind the wheel of her old pickup truck, grinding what gears remained on the long-past-worn-out transmission.

That her mental torment paled in comparison to the pain of treachery he'd feel if he realized his precious Bri's horrible error.

Guilt stabbed like a knife. Christiaan hadn't betrayed her. He hadn't had her killed. He hadn't married Astrid.

He'd known about the baby. He'd mourned his precious Bri.

He loved her. Still.

"My God," Vicky sighed, leaning her head against the passenger-side window. "What have I done?"

"Sorry?" Christiaan struggled with the stick shift. "I didn't catch that."

Her body stiffened. "I... I... said, 'Pick a gear. Any gear'."

The metallic sound of clutch plate grinding against flywheel answered her as Christiaan pulled onto the dirt road leading into the Mineral Springs property.

"You said you knew how to drive a stick." Vicky fought to keep her voice casual.

"I do." He laughed. "Just not one originally built by Henry Ford himself."

With what little humor she could manage, Vicky smiled.

"I could have driven," she said, grimacing as the truck whined and groaned. "And saved what's left of my transmission."

"Yes, you could have. But I'm not the one on painkillers."

"Good point." Leaning back into the worn seat, Vicky closed her eyes. Too bad said painkillers did nothing to dull the shocking realization that she had betrayed their love, not him. If she had trusted him, she wouldn't have lost the baby, and they'd have the family they'd always wanted.

"Hmm... that's interesting." Christiaan's voice pierced her torturous thoughts.

Vicky eyes shot open then followed to where he pointed. Parked next to the site office were a couple of pickup trucks.

"Gee, where were these guys when I was stuck earlier?" she said, peering around the rest of the clearing. Several pieces of equipment now sat next to the drilling rig. "And where was this stuff?"

"Definitely not here when I found you. It was just me and one crazy, dive-bombing hawk."

"Yeah, I've got a bone to pick with that bird, too." Vicky glanced past stacks of empty pallets towards the cliff where the hawk had attacked her. "So, this is Summit Energy back from a dinner break?"

"Can't be." Christiaan pulled up next to the pickup trucks and turned the engine off. "I told Baz to suspend all work until we could sort things out with your people."

"Then explain the unsecured gate we drove through at the entrance to this site."

"Actually, the rangers had to bust the lock when they came to help you." Christiaan reached for his back pocket.

"I'll text Baz and tell him to get it fix— *Potverdomme*! I keep forgetting I don't have my phone."

"And I forgot my backpack and walkie talkie." *'Cause I'm not thinking straight.* For a moment, she studied Christiaan intently. Her husband. Her loving husband.

Her loving husband she believed capable of murder. Pain squeezed her heart.

Christiaan stared back in waiting silence. A familiar shiver of awareness seemed to pass between them. Then he smiled. That irresistible, devastating smile she'd fallen in love with so many years ago.

If he knew what I've done, it would kill him. The thought stuck her like an avalanche. She'd killed Bri, not him. Vicky jammed a hand through her hair.

"You okay?" he asked, touching her lightly on the shoulder. Her heart almost stopped as she felt all the caring he was capable of surge through her body.

"Hey!" Christiaan shook her a bit. "Are. You. Okay?"

Chewing on her lower lip, she breathed deeply, trying to calm herself before answering. Exhaling slowly, she managed a simple, "Yes."

"Great," he answered before jumping out of the cab, obviously unaware of her inner turmoil. Vicky exited, too, slamming the door to her truck and her emotions closed. *Focus on the present, not the past.*

"*Potverdomme*! It's getting colder." Christiaan rubbed his arms.

"Yeah, we're running out of sun and daylight. There should be a couple of pullovers behind the seat."

Leaning back into the cab, he threw the bench seat forward and started rummaging.

"Dean's got an old blue one in there that should fit you," Vicky said. "I'll take the red one."

Christiaan tossed her the garment before slipping on Dean's, then closed the truck door.

Yanking the pullover over her head, she then stepped next to one of the other vehicles and scanned the inside.

Typical male fare. Old coffee cups on the seat. Past-due bills shoved between the dash and windshield. Empty beer cans on the floorboard. Bear claw and mini donut wrappers strewn everywhere. A rifle in the gun rack.

"Relic scavengers?" Christiaan asked, peering in from the other side of the truck.

"Possibly." She nodded. "But they're wasting their time. Most of this area has been picked clean for some time."

"Maybe they're hoping to lift a few things from here." Christiaan stepped over to the field office and looked into the window. "But I guess they couldn't get past the lock, unlike some people."

Vicky walked to the door. "Then they're complete idiots," she said, pointing to the unlatched lock.

Christiaan laughed as he approached. "I guess I didn't need you after all."

The painkillers must be screwing with her mind. She could have sworn she'd locked up when she left earlier.

Christiaan stepped up, swung the door open, and entered. Vicky slipped in behind him, wondering if she'd forgotten to turn the lights off, too.

"Anything seem to be missing?" As far as Vicky could tell, other than the lock and lights, everything seemed to be exactly as before.

"I wouldn't know." Christiaan shrugged his shoulders as he weaved around various equipment, crates, and boxes. "On-site is Baz's domain, not mine. I'm usually handling my end from the boardroom. But I am a bit surprised by the amount of stuff here considering we're only a month into this phase of the project."

"And you didn't notice this when you were here before because…?"

"Because Baz was merely giving me a site walk-through, familiarizing me with what's on the ground with what I'd seen on paper."

"You fly all the way from The Netherlands for a project that's…," she said, making air quotes.

"'...extremely behind and getting extremely expensive' and all you got was a cursory tour?"

Christiaan stiffened then turned to face her. "I was trying not to step on Baz's toes. He's been working on this project for over ten years."

And Baz's toes were easily injured. As Bri, she'd often remarked to Christiaan about his friend's thin skin, but he always defended Baz. *Een vriend achter je rug is een veilige brug.* A friend at one's back is a safe bridge.

"Still so protective."

"Still?" Christian looked puzzled.

Panic knotted in her throat. *Careful, girl. Don't give yourself away.* "I— I could tell during the summit climb that the two of you are close. The kind of close guys get after being friends for a really long time."

"Yeah, that happens when you grow up together." Christiaan nodded his head then grinned. "He's like the little brother I never had."

More like a big brother to her. Baz had been there for her after discovering Astrid answering Christiaan hotel room phone. The next day, she'd run into Baz and his friends exchanging gifts in a pub where she'd gone to soften the sting of her husband's affair. Too drunk to drive, she'd let Baz give her a lift back to the estate. The next morning, he'd graciously retrieved her car. That was the last time she saw him.

A warm hand brushing against her cheek brought her back to the present. Without thinking, Vicky closed her eyes and nuzzled against his touch.

"You sure you're okay?" Softly, his breath fanned her face.

Raising her lids, she gazed at him. His eyes brimmed with tenderness and concern. For a brief second, she was tempted to tell him everything. Who she was. What she'd done. How she'd screwed up the best thing that had ever happened to her.

"Vicky?"

Vicky? That's right. I'm Vicky. Brianna is dead. I killed her. I. Killed. Us. A suffocating sensation tightened her throat. If he knew the truth, he'd hate her.

He must never know. Ever.

"I'm fine, really." Looking away, she pulled out of his grasp and cleared her throat. "Um… what I wanted to show you is in the back." She led him into the small office.

Christiaan walked the perimeter, peering at the various items hanging from the walls. "Baz stepped me through some of this when I got here. Some he explained. Some he didn't. Mostly geoengineering stuff. Basic geological surveys. Some surface topographic maps. Some aerial photography."

"Where's the one with the funny green crosses?" Vicky pointed to the empty spot where the Forest Service map had been.

"Funny green crosses?" Christiaan snickered.

"Yeah, funny green crosses. Almost religious looking. Right next to it was a clipboard noting drilling depths. Depths that easily exceeded normal exploratory distances."

"Couldn't have. We're not drilling yet."

Vicky gritted her teeth and continued searching. "But according to both the map and the clipboard, you were. Five spots located all around the Mineral Springs area."

"Okay, show me." His condescending tone irked her. "Where's this incriminating evidence?"

Good question. Where was the damn thing?

"What about the maps you were talking about with the weird ovals and colored dots?" Christiaan asked. "Where are they?"

"In here." She headed over to the two filing cabinets, popped the lock on one, and opened the bottom drawer. "In a cardboard tube."

"You're quite the criminal." Christiaan closed the space between them to take a closer look at the contents.

Vicky ignored his comment but couldn't ignore his smell. *Delicious.* A rich, intoxicating mix of man, sweat, and sandalwood. Falling asleep next to it in her former life was intoxicating. Waking up to it... provocative.

And tasting it during sex... better than any chocolate made on earth.

"There's nothing here." Christiaan's sharp tone startled her.

Damn. The drawer was empty. Completely empty. Nothing but air.

"They were right here," she said. "Rolled up in two cardboard tubes."

"Are you sure?"

"Yes!" She ground the word out between clenched teeth. "I pulled the maps out and laid them on that table to look at." She'd put them back. She was sure of it.

"Could you have laid them somewhere else?" he asked quietly, but with a slight edge to his voice.

"No! I put them back exactly where I'd found them." With her foot, she slammed the drawer shut while she opened another with her hand. It, too, was empty. She tried another. Empty. Another. The same. "There were file folders in every single one of these," she stammered in disbelief and anger.

"Well, they aren't now, Miss Golden." His return to formality wasn't lost on her. She recognized her husband's attempt to tether a smoldering anger. She'd experienced it many times in her previous life. Christiaan stood, turned, and then leaned against the cabinet. Even before she looked up, she guessed the muscle on the right side of his jaw pulsed.

Vicky inhaled deeply. *Focus.* You're your own woman. Not the one that got pushed around.

Maybe she had the wrong cabinet. Popping the lock on the second one, she jerked every drawer open. Empty, too.

"I'm telling you there were all kinds of stuff in here from pictures to computer printouts to—" Vicky spun around. *Computer.* Rushing over to the machine, she leaned forward to boot it up. "Maybe we can find something in here."

"You broke into the computer, too?" Christiaan asked, coming to stand next to her.

"Not exactly. There are quite a few files here, but I couldn't get past the passwords. Perhaps you can help with that."

He leaned over her shoulder to peer at the screen. "Depends on the file." She shuddered as his breath tickled her neck. *Focus, girl. Focus.*

The Summit Energies logo appeared on-screen as she rattled off the names she could remember. "Costs to Date, Marketing Strategy, Proposals, etc."

"I wouldn't mind taking a look at Costs to Date myself. My admin password should get us into those."

"Great. And there were a few in Dutch and one in a language I didn't recognize. *Di— diord fi… fionn*, I think."

"That's not Dutch. Sounds Irish."

Vicky clicked to the file management area. *Damn.* As empty as the filing cabinets.

"What the hell?" She closed the file and reopened it, hoping somehow the effort would make a difference.

It didn't. Everything was gone.

"Miss Golden." Christiaan's stare drilled into her. "I don't know exactly what you're trying to pull here but—"

"Pull here?" Vicky shot straight up. "Pull here? Are you suggesting that somehow I made everything up?"

His blue eyes darkened as he held her gaze without answering. Typical van Laere argument tactic. Let a long silence prey on your opponent.

Well, she wasn't a van Laere anymore. She was a Golden. And Goldens prefer in-your-face tactics.

She lifted her chin and met his glare with one of her own. "You think I stole it."

"No," he answered in a voice so low and so slow the condescension conveyed by it pissed her off even more. "I think you helped your ShastaWatch cohorts steal it."

"Are you kidding me? Why would we do that?"

"For the same reason you've done everything until now... to stop this project. For all I know, that's what you were finishing up when you got trapped on that cliff."

"Did you find anything on me? Were there any maps or paperwork or anything in my backpack when you got the walkie talkie out to call for help?"

Christiaan shook his head. "No, but your ShastaWatch buddies could have taken it."

"And left me as bear food. Not likely."

"If you and your friends didn't steal it, then where is it?"

"Then you admit the information exists?" Vicky couldn't stop the smug smile crossing her face. "That Summit Energy was drilling despite your lease restrictions?"

"I've already told you we're not."

"Despite the drilling rig sitting in the clearing."

"That isn't drilling because I've put this project on hold."

"But was drilling before?"

"No." He paused, his face creased with an odd expression. "It wasn't drilling before."

"Despite what the map and clipboard showed?"

He cocked his head toward the hole where map and clipboard had been. "What map and clipboard, Ms. Golden?"

They stood in silence for a minute then broke into ironic laughter.

"This circle of argument could go on for hours," Vicky admitted.

"Look, it's possible that Baz *could* have removed everything." Christiaan stood, turned, and then leaned against the table. "Obviously, he cleared out the filing cabinets, pulled important documents from the walls, and dropped everything from the computer on a thumb drive."

"But why would he do that?"

"Because I told him I wanted to put this project on hold until we could come to some mutual agreement with

ShastaWatch." The corner of Christiaan's lip twisted. "Considering what I just witnessed with the filing cabinet locks, I'm glad he did."

Vicky ignored the later comment to focus on the former one. "So Mineral Springs is definitely on hold?"

"Maybe." Christiaan's voice dropped to a threatening octave. "But if I see one word about it on the Internet, I'll push forward at twice the pace."

The Internet. Vicky quickly brought up the browser and accessed the History file. Empty. *Of course.*

"No trash mag sites. No porn links." Frustrated, she slouched back into the chair. "No cool YouTube videos."

"Trash mags and porn sounds like Baz. YouTube? What was so interesting there?"

"Well, it was a really cool animation by the group Die Frackers Die on how injecting high-pressure fluids into the ground could contribute to earthquakes."

"Die Frackers Die?" Christiaan commented, raising an eyebrow. "Really?"

"I know. The name sounds like they're a little out there—"

"A little?"

She shook her head. "But the animation was incredible. It showed how if several fluid injections are accidentally placed near mapped as well as unmapped fault zones, it could cause a major problem."

"Hmm." Christiaan crossed his arms and frowned.

"I get it. You're skeptical." Wait! Maybe she could find the video herself. Vicky typed "Die Frackers Die Earthquake YouTube Video" into the browser and pressed Enter.

Unable to connect to the Internet.

Argh! So much for noticing the big old red X over the Internet connection indicator in the right-hand corner of the screen.

"Well, the point of it all had something to do with things called tectonic plates and seismic threats, i.e., earthquakes that could level entire regions. I didn't pay as much attention as I should have. I'd planned on googling and studying it later at the office."

"Interesting." He simply nodded.

"I know. You don't believe me."

"No, it's just that—" The sound of a door slamming shut cut him off. Too far away to be the site office one. Vicky jumped up to peek out the window. Christiaan followed right behind her.

For a second, nothing looked any different from when they'd arrived. Then, two workers came out of the storage building, the heavy door banging behind them. Wheeling a hand truck, they headed toward the pallets. There, they loaded up six bags before stopping to drink from a flask.

"What do you think they're doing?" Vicky pressed her face against the window.

"Other than drinking on the job? I don't know. Let's ask." He headed outside with her hot on his heels.

"Hey! You there!" Christiaan yelled.

Both men startled, turned to see who called, and then started running.

"Wait!" Christiaan called out. "I'd like to talk to you!"

Without a look back, the men made a beeline for the ridge.

"*Potverdomme!*" Christiaan stopped short next to the hand truck. "What's wrong with them?"

"My... guess..." Vicky stopped talking long enough to catch her breath. So much for the ER doc's suggestion to take it easy. "They think... you're somebody... important and... you'll either fire... them for the... alcohol or for stealing..." She nodded toward the stack of blasting caps.

"For all I know, they don't even work for me. And considering this site is supposed to be closed, then they are stealing. Come on. Let's see if we can get some answers."

Christiaan broke into a sprint while Vicky struggled to keep up. *Demerol and running do not mix.* Reaching the edge of the tree line, he stopped to let her catch her breath.

"We lost them." He turned a three-sixty. "Where could they have gone?"

"Any number... of places." With one arm, Vicky made a sweeping gesture. "There are some... natural hot springs dotted... around here as well as... a few old steam caves."

"Steam caves?"

"Groundwater   heated   by   underground   lava chambers... becomes steam. It's the same natural process that... produces the hot springs around here. Geothermal energy. There's a whole network of caves and tunnels throughout the property. A wide web that darts in and out of the ridge and up and down from the ground." She stood tall and crossed her arms defensively. "You know, the whole reason you're trying to turn this beautiful, natural place into your renewable energy extravaganza."

"Is it safe?"

"Your plan to wreak havoc on the ecosystem and displace thousands of species? No, but I thought I already told you how I feel about that."

"Yes." Christiaan nodded and laughed. "You've made yourself quite clear on that particular subject. No, I meant the steam in the caves. Is it safe?"

"Quite safe. The steam is from groundwater, not lava. So no poisonous gases."

A piercing squawk nearly drowned out the end of Vicky's answer. The hawk that had plagued them both earlier circled overhead.

"Let's find one of those caves before Mama Bird here attacks." He extended his arm in an invitation to go ahead of him. "Point me in the right direction, guide lady."

"I believe there's one not too far from here." Vicky headed out, keeping parallel to the ridgeline. Within minutes, she spotted the entrance as well as footprints indicating someone had recently been there. "This might be where your workers went."

"Lead on."

Entering the dark cave, Vicky reached for her backpack

to grab a flashlight. Damn.

"Remember? You forgot your backpack."

Wait! She unzipped the kangaroo pocket on her pullover, dug out two emergency glowsticks, and handed one to Christiaan. *Thank God I'm not a complete idiot.* Tearing open the outer wrapper, Vicky snapped then shook the stick. Christiaan mimicked her actions with his. In seconds, warm yellow light pushed at the darkness. Not luminous, but better than nothing.

Hooking the glowsticks onto their zipper pulls, they headed further into the black and steam. "Stay close." Without thinking, she reached behind her to grab her husband's hand. Her heart jolted the moment they touched. The instinctive response to him was so powerful her legs almost buckled. She reveled in the singular sensation of his touch.

Then he dropped her hand like a hot potato.

"Sorry." Vicky cleared her throat, hoping he didn't notice her emotional unbalance.

"No problem. I'll just stay close behind you, okay?"

Ahhh… So close she could feel the heat from his body.

"Su—" She swallowed tightly. "Sure." *Focus, girl. Focus!*

A significant feat considering they were now far enough into the cave that all outside light had disappeared. Ahead, a faint trail of steam indicated the source might be down a narrow passageway.

"Do you really think those guys went down this way?" he asked as they headed that direction.

Muffled voices—or something that sounded like muffled voices—echoed down the corridor.

"Obviously," Vicky answered.

"Hello?" Christiaan called out. "Is anyone in here?"

A low rumble answered. Suddenly, the ceiling caved in.

"Come on!" Christiaan grabbed her hand and started running back towards the main entrance, rocks raining down from all sides. Dust flew everywhere, getting in their eyes, their hair, and their mouths.

A boulder rolled into their path, knocking Vicky off her feet. Christiaan stopped to pull her back up. The effort seemed hopeless as the surrounding walls appeared to be caving in on top of them. Sharp stone edges dug into her shoulders and arms as she bounced off the sides, struggling to keep up. A small rock bit into her cheek, and she licked the metallic taste of blood off her upper lip.

The closer they got to the main cave, the less dust and steam there was. As suddenly as it began, the rumbling ceased. Vicky aimed the glowstick miraculously still attached to her pullover toward the entrance.

Or what should have been the entrance.

But it was gone. Rocks jammed together like puzzle pieces now barred their escape. Christiaan pulled up short.

"*Potverdomme*!" he managed to grunt out before having a coughing fit.

Vicky tried lifting one of the boulders out of the way. It didn't move.

Christiaan pushed against the rocks. "Nothing!"

"Maybe together," Vicky said before knocking a few coughs—and tons of dust—from her lungs. On reflex, she reached for the ice axe hanging from her hip. Nothing. *Damn, I forgot that, too.*

They both struggled to move a rock… any rock… a few inches, but failed.

"Maybe there's another way out." Christiaan retreated back down the narrow passageway. Obviously not far because the light from his glowstick didn't completely disappear.

"See anything?" she called after him.

"Lots of rocks. Lots and lots of rocks."

"Any openings?"

"Nothing. Not even a crack." He reappeared and sat down next to her on a boulder.

They remained quiet for a bit, each contemplating their situation.

Christiaan broke the silence first. "No one knows we're

here."

"Not a soul." She shook her head in the negative, then took a deep breath. "And I stupidly forgot all my gear, and you stupidly forgot your phone."

"Thanks for stating the obvious," he muttered. "*We zijn de lul.*"

"Yep," Vicky concurred. "We're screwed."

Totally.

CHAPTER 13

What a difference five days makes.

Vicky wiped a bead of sweat from her forehead.

Five days ago, she'd woken up in her lodge, ready for another uneventful day.

Five days ago, she'd headed up the mountain, ready for another uneventful rescue.

She peered over at her husband, seated near her on one of the many boulders the rockslide... the seismic tremor... the... the... the *whatever* had knocked loose.

Five days ago, she'd so-o-o-o not been ready for all of this.

Another bead of sweat formed on her brow. At least the cold wasn't on her growing list of worries. Heated air blowing through the cave from the geothermic wells offered them warmth as well as oxygen.

Christiaan yanked off his pullover to reveal an already-taut, drenched-in-sweat polo shirt that clung to his body like Vicky had wanted to for days. The painkillers might be screwing with her memory, but she swore he was sexier now than when they were married. *And he'd been Brad Pitt/Channing Tatum/Adam Levine sexy then*!

She bit her lip to stop the sexual growl forming in her throat. Tilting his head, Christiaan peered at her strangely, his piercing blue eyes boring straight into her. It unnerved her that he still had this kind of hold on her body. She shifted her seat on the rock to stop the sexual growl forming between her celibate-for-too-damn-long legs.

Argh! If I had any sense left, I'd get as far away from him as I could. Even if that meant only to the other side of the cave.

He leaned over and brushed away a sweat bead headed down her face. Inches from his, her mouth went ferociously dry as she battled the urge to lick perspiration from his upper lip. She leaned in two seconds before Christiaan rocked back and ran a hand over his face.

Obviously, sense was on vacation.

Vicky stood and hurried over to the blocked entrance a few feet away. Five days ago, she'd believed this man capable of lying, cheating, and murder. But everything she'd learned since then proved one irrefutable thing… she'd been a complete fool to believe him capable of any of that. How could she have been so wrong? How could she have overreacted so badly?

Because you were a low-self-esteem drunk willing to believe what everyone else said about you, your husband, and your marriage.

She sighed. Baz had suggested that very thing when she'd cried on his shoulder her last day in The Netherlands, before she'd headed to the airport. He'd handed her the keys to her car and told her not to worry about anything. He'd take care of everything.

Then all hell broke loose. *And Brianna ceased to exist.*

"So, what happened?" Christiaan's soothing voice slid over Vicky like silk.

"I don't know." She ran a trembling hand through her hair. "One minute, I was a woman on a mission, and the next, I no longer existed."

"One minute you were… what?" Christiaan's laugh pierced her thoughts.

"What?"

"Earth to Vicky. I said, 'What just happened?'." He shrugged his shoulders and gestured around the cave.

"Oh... *Oh!*" The too-damn-close personal revelation sent her mind reeling. "You... uh... you meant the tremor." She shoved one of the boulders at the entrance with her foot and tried to refocus her attention. Of course, it didn't move. "I... I have no... no idea. They occur on a semi-regular basis on Shasta, just like the one that trapped my arm earlier. Last I read, California has something like thirty-seven-thousand a year. Some tremors barely register. Others cause minor rock slides. Not surprising considering three-hundred fault lines run beneath the entire state."

Brushing aside some loose rock from the entrance, she hoped some... any... outside light might reach through. No such luck. "Caves appear and disappear all the time." She pushed against another stone. Again, not a budge. "Guess my timing with rocks isn't very good today."

"First rule of crisis management... assess your situation." Christiaan rose and began pacing. "We're stuck in a small cave with no water, no food, and no source of communication. Two sticks of light are our only source of illumination, and no one has any idea where we are. Does that sound like a fair assessment?"

Ever the pragmatist. There's the man I fell in love with. Vicky leaned against the blocked entrance to watch him in action. "What's the next rule?"

"Gather all the facts. Fact one... the rocks blocking our escape are immovable."

Vicky chimed in. "Fact two... geothermic warm air is reaching us from the tunnels so we won't suffocate and freeze to death."

"Hot, geothermic energy at its best." Christiaan pulled his soaked shirt away from his chest, fanning.

Vicky stepped toward him then caught herself. A sharp intake of air followed by a long, slow groan out barely tamped down the involuntary urge to rip off that soaked shirt and cover his chest with hers. "Hot. Yes, very hot."

As usual, he was oblivious to her physical response. "Fact three... not only does no one know where we are, but no one has any reason to come look for us."

Somebody please find us. Her gaze trailed down the length of his long, lean body. *And save me from myself.*

Christiaan stopped pacing directly in front of her, his face a strange study of quiet concentration and relentless purpose mixed with intense desire. His eyes burned into hers. A ripple of excitement spread through her and settled between her legs. She moved toward him, and his ragged breath confirmed her suspicion. He wanted her just as much as she wanted him.

But he wanted Vicky. She wanted him to want Bri.

Don't I? No. He'd never forgive Bri for what you've done. Bri. Is. Dead.

"Third rule?" She leaned closer.

"Develop a plan of action." The smile in his eyes was downright sinful.

"Which, in our case, means wait."

"With fingers crossed. But for how long?"

Long enough to make love? Vicky chuckled. Buried alive in a cave with no immediate means of escape and all she could think about was sex. Wow, Rainbow would have a field day with this.

Rainbow!

"Wait!" Vicky brushed past him to the other side of the cave. "It's a long shot, but I usually have breakfast with the ShastaWatch crew on Thursday mornings. Rainbow will worry if I don't show up."

He answered with a pained grunt followed by, "Enough to look for you?"

"Yeah, she'll show up here eventually, especially if she talks to Duff. I ran into him earlier today not too far from here. Hopefully, when she sees my truck parked by the trailer, she'll look around, maybe find our tracks…" Vicky tilted her head and shrugged her shoulders.

"Definitely a long shot, but it's all we've got." Christiaan headed toward the opposite side of the cave.

"I guess it's a good thing we ate earlier. That should

hold us through the night." All night... together. She stared at the floor, irritated at the conflicting emotions spinning within her. With all her being, she wanted to make love to her husband. But would that be fair to him? To her? To them?

"What's this?" Christiaan's voice saved her from the turmoil.

She looked up to see him staring at something on one of cave walls. Carved into the rock were two human figures running away from a bird toward a mountain. Christiaan pointed to the creature and laughed.

"Obviously, we're not the first people to be tortured by a hawk."

"Neat." Vicky walked over, then traced the drawing with her finger. "Old Indian petroglyphs. Chief Running Bear once told me there were lots of drawings in the caves, but I've never seen any of them until now."

"Chief Running Bear?"

"Yes, he's the spiritual leader of the Shasta Indians." She sighed. "*Was* the spiritual leader of the Shasta Indians. I met him when I first moved here."

"Sounds like you really miss him."

She nodded. "I do. He taught me all about Mother Shasta and how she and the people are interconnected." He'd helped her let go of the past and begin anew. To say goodbye to Brianna and embrace Vicky.

She pointed to another petroglyph a few inches below. The etching showed a line of figures coming out of a mountain and walking down the side. "See, the Shasta Indians believe that they and the mountain are one in the same. That their strength comes directly from Mother Shasta."

"You say that with such reverence. I noticed that when you were talking to the reporter at the beginning of our summit climb. The chief must have really fired you up."

"He did." Vicky teared up at the memory of the man who meant so much to her rebirth. "He really did."

Christiaan followed the curve of the wall. "Wow, look at this one." He gestured toward a drawing of a couple holding hands, standing in front of a blazing sun. He snorted. "This one reminds me of some pictures Bri and I saw on our honeymoon. Somewhere we were hiking in Sweden had a spot that supposedly used to be an ancient Norse honeymoon spot. Bri insisted we hike miles and miles up a mountain to see the spot because local folklore said newlyweds viewing the drawings there would be ensured good luck throughout their marriage." He snorted again. "A lot of good it did us."

Vicky dropped her head so he couldn't see her smile. Actually, the folklore said that a couple that *made love* under the drawings was guaranteed good luck. She and Christiaan had done it twice, but the double insurance hadn't translated into extra good luck.

And whose fault was that? Mine. All mine.

Christiaan walked over to the opposite wall. "Hmm… look at this one."

She followed him to a much larger petroglyph. This one illustrated the mountain with wavy lines around it and many figures lying down.

"This one must be about the great earthquake in the late 18th century that killed thousands of Shasta Indians. Until then, they'd lived in these caves. But after that, they never did again."

"Yeah, well, that's a once-in-lifetime kind of thing, right?"

"Are you kidding me?" Vicky gave him an incredulous glare, the fire to protect her mountain flared. "This entire area sits on a plethora of mapped and unmapped fault lines that string out throughout the western part of North America. Why do you think environmentalists were able to hold back the government and people like you for so long?"

Christiaan simply stared at her.

She continued. "Mapped faults that intersect with the Pacific, Juan de Fuca, and North American plates cause minor ground fluctuations all the time and, occasionally, a big one. But it's the hundreds of minor, unmapped faults that could cause the really big one everyone has been predicting."

"Yeah…" Christiaan's eyebrows furrowed. "I think someone told me something about that once. But it's not a problem because we're using vibration trucks to test potential drilling sites."

She crossed her arms. "Vibration trucks don't use blasting caps."

"No, no they don't. But if we don't get any decent readings, we may need to do some old-fashioned blast testing. Baz assures me the risk will be minimal."

"Yeah, well, he assured Rainbow that you guys hadn't started drilling," Vicky snapped. "Yet the maps in your office said otherwise."

"Again with the maps." He shook his head.

"They were there! I saw them! Undeniable proof that you're forging ahead with this project, environmentalists be damned! Why here? Why this project? What's your *damn* hurry?"

"Vicky, let's not do this again." His voice was low, but full of intensity. Despite herself, she found the inflection arousing. She tried to shake the feeling off.

"Why not? We're not going anywhere any time soon."

"And neither is the project. I already told you, it's on hold."

"On hold, but not abandoned, right?"

He let out a long sigh and merely stared at her. Again, the long-silence tactic.

She forged ahead, unfazed. "But not abandoned, *right*?"

Again, that infuriating-yet-seductive silence.

"How long, Christiaan? How long until you decide that there's more to life than business? That money isn't everything—"

"*Potverdomme*!" His face twisted as he rubbed the back of his neck. "I don't have time for this right now."

"Time?" Vicky leaned in, literally and fugitively. "You

don't have *time* to do everything within your power to ensure that a landscape and a people that have been here for eons remain safe?"

"No, I don't!" He shoved his face to within an inch of hers. "I'm broke!"

She blinked, stunned as the reality of his words soaked in. A van Laere? Broke? How could that be? They had more money than God.

Christiaan stepped back, took a long breath, and slumped down onto the closest boulder. "If I don't get this project moving within a year, I can kiss millions of government incentive money goodbye. I need that money to shore up my company and, in turn, my family."

"Oh, my God. What happened?"

"I really don't feel like going into all the details," he answered with staid calmness. "Let's just say my golden business touch never fully recovered after Bri's death."

Her chest tightened as the array of emotions she'd sifted through in the last twelve hours all hit her like the rocks that had fallen in the cave earlier. He'd suffered, too. In the last eight years, he'd suffered.

They'd both suffered. *Because of me.*

"Shortly after Bri died, I lost some business over the whole 'he's a murderer' thing. But that was peanuts compared to the millions I lost in the ethanol futures market. Usually, that wouldn't be a problem. I've lost money on speculation before. But then shortly after getting the Mineral Springs project moving, it started bleeding money like crazy. Add to that my father's and stepmother's usual crazy spending, and before I knew it..." He steepled his fingers under his chin. His face bleak with despair. "My family... my employees... my company depends on me. And I've failed them." He took a deep, pained breath. "Just like I failed Bri."

Her eyes blurred with tears. No wonder he was balls to the wall to get the project moving. The weight of the world rested on his shoulders. Everything he'd ever cared about was falling apart.

Thanks to me.

The full impact of her mistake hit Vicky like an avalanche. Because she hadn't trusted him or their love, she'd… he'd… they'd lost everything. Her shortsightedness had created a miserable situation for the man she vowed to love "'til death us do part".

Worse yet, somehow he blamed himself for her death.

"I'm so sorry, Christiaan." She moved next to him, and he dipped his head forward to rest it on her belly. "So very… very… sorry."

She brushed her fingers through his hair in a clumsy effort to comfort him. He responded by wrapping an arm around her legs and nuzzling deeper. The spot below her belly clenched, and her breath become short and sharp. A savage moan escaped her throat before she could stop it.

Christiaan stood to his full height and gazed down into her eyes. A muscle ticked in his jaw. Vicky smiled, remembering the first time she'd seen that involuntary sexual tell. Six hours after meeting for the first time.

He'd talked her into joining him for dinner in Paris while they were still sixteen-hundred miles away in Stockholm. On his private jet, she'd spied that tick after they'd had several glasses of champagne and before he'd kissed her then initiated them both into the mile-high club.

She swallowed hard, remembering that first time.

In the cave, Christiaan dropped his head to nuzzle at her neck. Another moan—this one bordering pornographic—erupted from her.

"You're so beautiful," he whispered in her ear, his hot breath making her even wetter. "So beautiful."

Vicky arched against him, yearning to get as close as two people can. She was back on that plane to Paris. She was back in her husband's arms. She was back—

He stopped, and she gasped. Before she could beg him to continue, he slid a hand to each side of her face and forced her to look deep into his eyes.

"Do you want this?"

Her heart hammered against her ribs as she breathed in deep his familiar scent. *Yes!*

"*Mijn minnares,*" he purred, then softly kissed her lips before repeating the question. "Do you want this?"

Breathless, all she could manage was to nod yes.

Christiaan kissed her deeply, as if he wanted them to share the same breath. His tongue pushed through her lips to dance an exotic ballet with hers. Desire stronger than anything she'd ever felt before flared from a place she didn't even know existed. Catching his bottom lip between her teeth, she tugged gently. The bulge in his pants jumped a bit, and he began to grind his hips against hers.

Her breasts tingled against his chest, the nipples hardening and screaming for escape from their confinement. Like a child at Christmas, Vicky tore off her pullover and sweatshirt. Christiaan slipped a hand behind her back and unhooked her bra. The garment fell to the ground, and he took a step back.

"Beautiful. Absolutely beautiful."

She reached for him and jerked his shirt up. Spreading her hands across his naked chest, she savored the texture of hard muscles and hot flesh. When her fingers brushed the wedding band hanging from his neck, Christiaan moved to remove the chain, but she shook her head no. For this brief interlude, let the symbol of their love remain between them.

Teasing his nipples first with her hands, then her tongue, Vicky then slowly followed the soft patch of hair leading down to his manhood. A primal sound escaped Christiaan's lips. Kicking away some rocks, he retrieved the abandoned clothes and carefully placed them on the cave floor. He then stretched out and reached for her, pulling Vicky down next to him on the makeshift bed.

Lying on her back, she watched his face while he rolled over and savored her nude breasts with his teeth. His eyes never left hers, and the power she felt knowing that the raw passion she saw in those blue pools because of her was intoxicating… shameless…. empowering.

Vicky ran a hand along his bare arm, tracing the peaks and valleys of his muscles, remembering how it felt once to have them wrapped around her nakedness. Her body leapt at the memory. He must have sensed her growing hunger and placed his hand between her legs. She drowned in the sensation, moving so her body bucked against his palm, the seam of her jeans rubbing perfectly against her clitoris. *Damn these jeans!*

"Move your hand," she pleaded. "Please."

"Not yet, *mijn minnares*." Christiaan nipped at a painfully hard nipple. "Not yet."

"Yes! Now!"

"Not. Yet." He removed his hand, and Vicky gasped for air. *No!* Before she could breathe out another protest, he'd tore off her jeans and panties and plunged a finger deep into her. She clenched around it and cried out.

"Already so wet. For me," he whispered before dropping his head to her crotch.

Oh. My. God! She sucked in a breath then shifted her hips to press hard against him. His tongue drove deep inside while his lips sucked on her clit. Over and over, she bucked against the erotic onslaught. Just as she was about to go over the tantalizing edge, Christiaan stopped and peered up.

No… No!

"Not. Yet." He grinned and slowly licked his glistening lips.

Vicky stared, wordlessly. Sex had never been like this between them. The Christiaan she'd married enjoyed lovemaking, but bed play had always been relaxed… traditional… basic. No talking. No teasing. Just two people simply sharing a bond and enjoying one another.

This Christiaan was like a man possessed, eager to have her, willing to tell her, and determined to make her his own.

Eagerness seized her body, and in one swift movement, she sat up and rolled Christiaan onto his back. An expression somewhere between surprise and desire crossed his face. He reached for her breasts, and she pushed his hands away.

"Not. Yet." She teased then palmed his crotch. *Two can play this game.*

The muscles in his belly drew up, and sweat dotted his forehead. Vicky rubbed until a pitiful whimper escaped his lips. Pulling him free from the bindings of his jeans, his moan mirrored hers as she took him into her mouth. He tasted of salt, musk, and man.

Just like she remembered. Like licking a melting ice cream cone, she worked her tongue around his shaft. The quick intake of breath told her he enjoyed being her special treat.

But he wasn't going to have all the fun. She straddled his leg and rubbed herself against his thigh, letting her body move in unison with the movement of her mouth. Then she shifted her weight enough to make direct contact with his knee.

Yeah, that's it.

Eight years without sex had turned her into a brazen hussy. Each moan, each cascade of pleasure pushed her past previous barriers of acceptable behavior.

Damn! It felt good to let go.

Christiaan whimpered like a lost boy when she stopped stroking him to remove his pants. He tried to pull her forward, on top of him, but she shook her head, mouthed no, and returned to driving him—and herself—crazy.

Her power was intoxicating. His powerlessness, an aphrodisiac.

Her lips slipped up and down. Repeatedly she welcomed him to feel the back of her throat, slowly increasing the pressure and rhythm of her lips on his shaft. Christiaan lifted his hips to meet her. His panting told her he was near. But as much as she wanted that, she wanted more to hear him beg. She stopped everything.

"*Potverdomme!* You're killing me!"

She grinned. He was hers... once again.

With a primal howl, he hauled her on top of him and

sank into her. She tried riding him, but he held her hips fast. A whimper escaped her lips.

He grinned. "My turn, again."

Vicky shrieked with pleasure as Christiaan rubbed her swollen clit with his thumb, drawing tight, hard circles around it. She arched her back and pressed against his fingers. Did he really expect her to remain still with him already deep inside of her?

Sweat beaded between her breasts as she struggled to maintain her sanity.

"Dammit, Christiaan! You're killing me!"

He shook his head, mouthed no, and returned to driving her crazy with each penetrating thrust.

She gritted her teeth, unable to take any more of this sweet, maddening torture. Vicky bucked against her husband, her body begging for release. Christiaan matched her pace with his own, and together they found their familiar rhythm. Separation hadn't doused their bond.

Both cried out as simultaneous orgasms rocked their bodies and souls to the core. They clung to each other for what seemed like eternity until their breathing returned to normal.

Then they did it again. And again.

Christiaan didn't know it, but they had years to make up for, and Vicky refused to waste another second. For hours, they made love, stopping only long enough to gather strength for another round.

Eventually, both exhausted, they began to doze off. Lying warm and satiated in her husband's arms, Vicky's thoughts on the consequences of what had just happened barely registered.

Tomorrow. She yawned. *I'll worry... about... that... to...mor...row...*

"Je hoort bij mij en mij alleen, mijn minnares," Christiaan mumbled as he nuzzled her ear.

Hmmm... Vicky entwined her leg with his and settled into his shoulder. *"Welterusten, mijn liefste. Spreek je morgen."*

Christiaan's body seizing like he'd been electrocuted jerked her awake. "*Potverdomme*!" He pushed her away, pain and recognition etched sharply in his face. "*Potverdomme*!"

Damn.

"You're alive!"

Christiaan couldn't breathe. He couldn't move.

His precious Bri was alive?

The first thing he thought of every morning and the last thing he hoped for every night.

She was alive?

The reason he'd punished himself for eight years with long hours, long runs, and celibacy.

She *was* alive?

He'd lost her. He'd buried her. He'd mourned her.

She was *alive*?

Welterusten, mijn liefste. Spreek je morgen. One of the first Dutch phrasings he'd taught her. She'd gotten into the habit of telling him that every night right before they fell asleep. Even when he traveled, Bri would leave him a voice message in Dutch saying, "Good night, my love. Talk to you tomorrow."

When she was still alive.

Is she?

Hands shaking, Christiaan gently reached for her head. At a young age, Bri had had her protruding ears pinned back. She'd been worried their child would inherit the same trait and that his father and stepmother would insist on the same painful surgery. Tenderly, he folded one of Vicky's ears forward to reveal a thin white scar. Just like his precious Bri.

Potverdomme!

Bits and pieces of the last several days washed over him like a tsunami. Her reluctant confession to being a recovering alcoholic... Dean's slip of the tongue regarding her former fear of heights... The undeniable and inexplicable connection Christiaan had felt from the moment they met.

Bri was alive!

How could he have not known? Cupping her chin with his hand, he stared at her. How could he have not seen it?

Because she looked different.

She sounded different.

And she was supposed to be dead.

Tears welling in his eyes, Christiaan enveloped her into his arms. His precious Bri was alive. Alive and in his arms.

"Bri... where have you been? Why didn't you contact me? What happened to you?" The questions came so fast he could barely breathe.

"I... I..."

"Oh my God, you don't know how many times I've dreamed you'd turn up alive." He hugged her tighter, if that was even possible. "That somehow, some way you had escaped the explosion and were back safe in my arms." This... Christiaan glanced around the cave and laughed. *This* had never entered his mind.

"I mfmfmfmf brmfmf."

Her warm breath on his chest caressed him like a lover. His lover. *Mijn minnares.* "What, my love?"

"I mfmfmfmf brmfmf."

"What?" He carefully laid her back onto the pallet of pullovers.

"I can't breathe."

Christiaan chuckled. Oh, the irony. Discover your wife alive after eight years only to smother her to death with pure joy.

"I'm sorry, Bri, but I'm just so... so..." He struggled to find the right word to describe his emotions. Nothing in English or Dutch suited. "I don't know what to say! Tell me everything! I want to know everything! Where have you been? What have you been doing?"

She wiped a hand through her hair and bit her bottom lip.

"The hair thing! How did I not see that before?" *You*

did see it. You just didn't make the connection. She was dead, remember? "Don't cry, *mijn minnares.*" He brushed a thumb across her cheek to catch the moisture. "*Alles zal goed komen.* Everything will be all right. You're alive, and we're together again. "

"It's not what you think." She shook her head sharply. "I'm not... I'm not..."

"*Potverdomme!* You don't know who you really are, do you, Bri? You must have *geheugenverlies*... um... in English, that's... um... um... amnesia! Yes, that's the word!"

"No, that's not it—"

"You don't realize it, but you're my wife, Brianna Stokman, Lady van Laere. No, wait, now you're Brianna Stokman, *Baroness* van Laere. That... *that* will upset my stepmother."

"Christiaan... please..."

"I know. I know, Bri." He cupped her chin in his hand. "This is all so difficult for you to understand. But eight years ago, you were taken from me, and now I've found you."

"No, that's—"

"Yes, that's what happened." He brushed his palm across her cheek and buried his fingers in her hair. "Obviously... miraculously... you didn't die, Bri. We all thought you had. " He couldn't stop touching her and saying her name. Bri was here. Bri was alive!

"Please, you don't understand. I—"

"Somehow... some way, you escaped and ended up here." Tracing his thumb across her lips, he could barely contain his emotions. His heart hammered against his ribs. "Obviously, the trauma of it all caused you to lose your memory. Somewhere along the way, you became Vicky Golden. But you are—and always will be—my precious Bri." Replacing his thumb with his lips, Christiaan crushed her to him.

Or tried to.

"Christiaan!" She drew back. "Stop!"

He did, suddenly realizing that she was probably as

overwhelmed and confused by the situation as he was.

"I'm sorry, Bri, but I can't help myself." Propping himself on an elbow, he let out a short snort. "All this time, you had no idea who you were."

Her eyes darkened, and her face stilled.

"Right, Bri?"

He recognized the expression. She usually wore it when she had something to say she knew would upset him.

"Right... Bri?"

She slowly shook her head then looked away. That gesture generally meant he wouldn't just be upset... he'd be furious. Her refusal to answer and agitated body language confirmed his suspicion.

"Oh, Bri..." He swallowed hard as reality slammed into him like a wrecking ball. "You know who you are, don't you?"

She refused to answer. Finally, she nodded.

"You let me think you were dead." Christiaan grabbed her, and they locked eyes like sabers.

Slowly her lips moved. "Yes."

"Why? *Potverdomme*, why would you do that to me?" He couldn't think. He could barely breathe. What could she possibly say that could make any sense of this?

"I... I..." She cleared her throat. "I thought you had me killed."

What?! Christiaan gasped. Had he heard her wrong? He must have. He struggled to take long, deep breaths. "You thought what?"

"That you had me killed. That you paid someone to blow me up."

"It was an accident!" Christiaan's temples pounded. His stomach clenched. Bri believed him capable of murder? Capable of murdering *her*? Tight-jawed and trembling, he suddenly realized he was staring between her legs.

Warm nutmeg. Bri's natural hair color. Not Vicky's deep auburn. His cheeks burned remembering what he'd done with that warm nutmeg spot most of the night.

Tearing his gaze away, Christiaan refocused on the face of the woman who'd just torn his heart out.

"*Alsjeblieft*, Christiaan, *het spijt me zo.*" She leaned toward him, continuing in still-surprisingly correct and fluent Dutch. "*In die tijd wist ik niet—*"

"Stop it. Stop it!" He didn't want to hear an apology, in his native language or English. "And put something on… please." Coming to terms with his wife's unexpected resurrection was one thing, talking to her about it while naked was another.

Bri scrambled to find and pull on her pants and shirt, then handed him his. Christiaan stood and methodically took his time redressing, needing every second to sort out the roller coaster of emotions fighting for center stage.

Joy that she was alive.

Shock that she was here.

Anguish that she'd abandoned him.

Disbelief that she thought he'd had her murdered.

"How could you… why would you even… when did you…" Carving his hands through his hair, he struggled with what question to ask first.

Bri sat cross-legged on the pallet of pullovers. Arms wrapped around herself, she exhaled gently. "It all happened so fast. At the time, we weren't doing so well, remember? Our once idyllic marriage was falling apart. I drowned my sorrows in food and Scotch, and you drowned yours in work. Neither of us was happy."

Christiaan nodded. He'd taken to scheduling eighteen-hour days to avoid their daily fights.

"The pressure to fit into your high-and-mighty crowd as well as produce the requisite van Laere heir was overwhelming. Trying to control my eating and my drinking was near impossible. And your stepmother…" Her brows flickered a little.

"Never passed up a chance to verbally knock you around." He sat down on the nearest rock, his pulse racing as fast as if he'd just finished a marathon. "I knew that was happening but never did anything about it."

Bri bobbed her head. "She was never happy about me as the next Baroness. She totally fed into my insecurities, always alluding to the fact that Astrid would make the more suitable daughter-in-law."

He grit his teeth. "I already explained my feelings about Astrid to you… yesterday as well as eight years ago."

"I know. I know. But back then, I was an overweight, alcoholic, insecure woman raging with trying-to-get-pregnant hormones and dealing with a husband that was never home and his family that was never kind."

Guilt squeezed out some of the raw emotions warring within him. He'd defied his family to marry her, then left her to the wolves while he focused on saving the company his father had run into the ground. Not his finest hour.

Bri continued. "That night, at your birthday dinner, Astrid had your undivided attention, and—"

"*Potverdomme!*" Christiaan jerked forward. "I told you before, she'd just lost her father, I was—" Bri's raised hand cut him short.

"Please, let me finish." With a deep breath, she struggled to compose herself before continuing. "That night, shortly after dinner, I overheard the Baroness tell someone that you and Astrid were sleeping together and that you were planning to get rid of me one way or another." Bri pursed her lips.

"And you assumed that meant…" A few seconds passed as Christiaan made the mental jump. "Ahh… my mother."

Bri nodded. "I tried not to believe what your stepmother said, but I couldn't. After three Scotches, I wasn't in the right frame of mind. Then I saw you and Astrid kissing on the balcony… and then we fought… man, we fought… and… and…" Bri choked back a sob.

"And you yelled, 'Your life would be so much better if I were dead, wouldn't it?'." Profound pain from that night washed over him like a bucket of ice water. Over the years, he'd replayed that scene over and over, each time wishing he could change his answer.

A single tear slipped down her cheek. "And you said… 'Yes'."

Silence enveloped the cave. Christiaan studied her face. The sting was still as fresh as it had been than night.

When he chose to punish his wife for his failings as a husband.

"It… it…" He struggled to compose himself. "It was just something stupid said in a fit of anger. You actually can't believe that I…"

She shook her head.

Obviously she did.

"I didn't want to believe any of it," Bri answered. "What you said… what your stepmother said… what Astrid said—"

"What? When did you talk with Astrid? What did she say?"

"Remember that next morning? When you flew out early on yet another business trip? This one to Spain?"

"Yes." Christiaan sat back and leaned against the cave wall. "And you were going to some expensive spa in Switzerland and weren't to be bothered."

"Actually, I changed my mind and arranged to go to an exclusive alcoholic treatment center here in the States under an assumed name to protect the family from scandal. Baz helped me get a fake passport, and I wired cash for the airfare and treatment center."

"What. Did. Astrid. Say!"

Bri took a deep breath. "At the airport, right before I left, I called your hotel room. I wanted to tell you I was sorry about everything that had happened. Astrid answered and explained that you'd just jumped into the shower. She made it *quite clear* that you weren't planning on bathing alone."

Christiaan knew exactly what Bri was talking about. After Astrid had flung herself on him on the balcony at the party the night before, she'd surprised him by showing up at his Madrid hotel. Like so many times before, he made it clear that he loved Brianna and had no intentions of ever being with Astrid, no matter what she or his stepmother had in mind. And, as usual, Astrid paid absolutely no attention to his warning, showing up later, after he'd lost Bri.

He drew a quick breath of utter astonishment. "You actually believed I was with Astrid? And that I was willing to kill for her?"

"I didn't want to," Bri answered, hands knotted in her lap. "I didn't want to believe any of it. Then, later, I saw news coverage of the two of you coming out of the police station and a reporter asking if Lady Astrid was going to be the next Baroness and..." Bri's voice trailed off.

"And you thought she was," Christiaan finished. "And that I had done what everyone had accused my father of doing to my mother." Everyone, including Astrid, had thought she would be the next Baroness. The pressure he'd felt to remarry had nearly severed the already-tenuous ties with his family. After a while, Astrid reluctantly moved on and shortly thereafter married some crazy prince from a defunct European throne.

"When you spoke to the reporters about me, you sounded so cold, like you'd just simply lost a business deal, not your wife. Then someone asked you if you thought you could get away with murder because you were so rich and so well connected. You made this face, this emotionless... distant... stoic face, grabbed Astrid's arm, and got into a limo." Bri smirked. "Happily ever after."

Christiaan stood and began pacing to control his seesawing emotions. "The only way I could keep it together was to act emotionless... distant... stoic. *Potverdomme!* I'd just lost the love of my life to a horrible accident! People were tossing accusations left and right. I had to turn my feelings off. It hurt too much to feel!"

"I guess Astrid helped you out with that." Bri leaned forward, pursed her lips, and crossed her arms defiantly.

He stopped moving right in front of her. "She just

showed up at the station. I jumped into her waiting limo because all I wanted to do was get out of there. My wife was gone. Life as I knew it was over."

"I thought you'd done it. That you finally succumbed to your family's pressure." Her shoulders stiffened. "You really did look better off without me, just like you said that night. So…" She took a deep breath. "… to protect myself, Brianna stayed dead and buried."

"To protect yourself…" He sighed heavily, his voice filled with anguish. His wife thought her only option was to hide from him. From *him*! "Then it must have been quite a surprise when I showed up here."

"Yes, but you didn't seem to recognize me, so I thought I was safe. But, then, during the singles climb, you were behind me on the summit descent—"

"You thought I'd pushed you?" Shock almost choked him. Oh, this just gets better and better. "Of course you did. If I was capable of murdering my wife, I was certainly capable of murdering some bitch standing between me and my geothermal project. Sorry to disappoint you, but Baz was behind you, not me. You fell all on your own, Mighty Miss Golden. All on your own."

Christiaan stepped back to give them both some literal and figurative breathing room. He rubbed a hand across his mouth, then down his neck. Absorbing everything she said overwhelmed him. Sorting it all out was next to impossible. He reached for the ring hanging from his neck. Mourning Bri had been the hardest thing he'd ever done. He stared at the band, then at her.

"But this ring—*your* ring—was found in the wreckage."

"I was so angry at your betrayal that I took it off and threw it in the cup holder. I didn't realize I didn't have it until I was already on the plane to the States."

An innocent-enough explanation. Christiaan fingered the wedding band. The only thing that remained of his precious Bri.

Until now.

His brow furrowed. "But there was a body. I had your remains—what meager amount there was—cremated. If it wasn't you, then who was in your car?"

"I don't know." She shrugged her shoulders. "I honestly don't know."

Slipping his pinky finger through the ring, he replayed the drama created when he'd told his father Bri wouldn't be laid to rest in the van Laere vault. Once again, the Baron had been unhappy with his son's breech of protocol. Instead, Christiaan had helped Baz's father—the estate gardener—plant tulip beds near that main house, mixing Bri's ashes into the soil. Christiaan smiled. Two tulip beds. One for Bri, and one for their unborn son.

"The baby!" He flinched as if slapped. "Our baby! Where's our son?"

A heavy gasp escaped as she placed a hand on her belly. "I... I... lost him. I miscarried, shortly after arriving at the treatment center. The doctors said it was probably chromosomal abnormalities. I'm sure my drinking and the stress of thinking you had me mur— taken care of didn't help." Tears blinded her eyes as she turned away. "Christiaan, I'm sorry. I'm so... so... sorry."

His heart ached at the sight of her grief. She'd been alone when she lost the baby. All alone.

Of course, he'd been alone when he lost them both.

Warring feelings tumbled through him. He wanted to hug her. He wanted to strangle her. Christiaan stomped aimlessly around the cave. They'd kissed. They'd danced.

They'd made love.

He and Vicky. No, he and Bri.

A ripple of ironic mirth escaped him. What a strange *ménage à trois*. He'd given himself to a new woman last night while at the same time reaffirming his bond with another.

The emotional mixture threatened to crush him. He slumped onto the nearest boulder and cradled his head. Bri was alive but had hid from him. She believed him capable of infidelity and murder. She'd survived. She'd started a new life.

Without him.

"So, you got sober and started a new life." He paused to regain control of his growing anger. "That's when Vicky Golden was born?"

"Yes."

"And the stuff you said earlier... waitressing in Maine... housecleaning in Nebraska... cashiering in Mississippi... that was all true?"

"Yes."

"And along the way you dyed and cut your hair, lost your Texas twang and a bunch of weight, and did something with your... your..."

"Boobs?" She laughed. "Yes, and my nose. Thanks to a plastic surgeon hoping to avoid an auto-accident lawsuit."

Christiaan lifted his head to study her, but said nothing. He pursed his lips, hoping to contain the bitter remarks struggling to leave his mouth.

"The hair?" She touched the top of her head. "Just seemed like the thing to do. New name. New hairdo. The twang? Lost it as I worked all over the country, trying to fit in. The weight? Lack of funds and physical labor makes for a great diet program."

"Your name. How did you come up with that?"

"Well, the first name is from my childhood friend Vicky Boxler, and the last is from the phrase 'Silence is Golden'." She snickered. "I know. Not very creative."

"A new name... a new life..." He snorted. "Well, isn't that just peachy."

"Christiaan, I—"

"Ran off to another country... Believed your husband had you murdered..." His nostrils flared. *Potverdomme* controlling his opinion and his anger. "... *And* left him at the mercy of a headline-hungry media that thrives on international scandal."

"I'm sorry. It was just a huge misunderstanding. If I

knew then what—"

"Then, when I 'run into' my wife, she pretends not to know me." He let loose a sardonic laugh. "All while I'm trying desperately to save my company that's struggling because of what she did to me and my family and my company eight years ago when she 'died'!"

"Christiaan, I'm sorry for that. I mean it!" Bri jumped to her feet and headed toward him. "But you have to understand, I was a different woman then."

He stood and backed away from her, his shoulders brushing against the blocked entrance. "You basically left the world to believe that I'd had you murdered, that my freedom was more important to me than my marriage." Another bitter chuckle left his lips. "But I didn't do any of that. I may have failed my marriage by not giving it the priority it deserved, but what you did was much, much worse."

"What I did?" Bri bridled.

"You failed our love."

She bit her lower lip, teeth sinking into the wet pink flesh.

"You chose to believe others instead of your husband."

Wetness filled the big, beautiful eyes clinging to his.

Behind him, the sound of something tapping against rock tore his focus away. Tapping turned into heavy knocking, and small stones from the blocked entrance began falling to the ground.

"Sweetie? You in there?" A muffled voice passed through.

"Rainbow?" Bri ran to the sound and answered. "Rainbow! You found us!"

Suddenly, a small patch of sunlight broke through. "Us?" snaked through the opening. "Who else is in there?"

"Myself and… and… Ms. Golden." Christiaan answered. "Thank God you found us."

"Baron von Rat Face? How weird to find you in there." Rainbow laughed. "Now that's an interesting turn of events. Okay, guys. Hang tight. We'll have you out of there in a jiffy."

"Christiaan," Bri's voice dropped an octave. She placed a hand on his forearm. "Before they break through, I need you to understand that I never meant to hurt you. Then or now. I never expected any of this to happen. Over the last several days, I've learned so much about you and about us. Us from before, and us today. If I'd have known then what I know now, I'd have done everything differently."

"Well, Ms. Golden. You can forget it all. I know I will." He clenched his jaw. "I'm going to forget the last twenty-four hours ever existed." He yanked his arm away from her hand. "In fact, I'm going to forget that the last several days ever existed." Peeling off the ring and chain hanging from his neck, he dropped them at her feet. "*Potverdomme*, I'm going to forget that Mt. Shasta and Mineral Springs and ShastaWatch even existed."

For a long while, only the sound of rescuers struggling to move boulders filled the cave.

"Let me guess," Bri said, her voice tight with emotion. "Your life would be so much better if I were dead, wouldn't it?"

Leaning forward, he peered into Bri's sparkling platinum eyes.

"Yes."

CHAPTER 14

Vicky was Bri. Bri was Vicky.

And Christiaan was out of here.

Zipping up the garment bag laying on the penthouse bed, he slid it over to the edge to make room for his suitcase.

Back home. Back to The Netherlands. Back to the only place that made sense to him.

Bri's pained face from earlier this morning crossed his mind. *"Let me guess, your life would be so much better if I were dead, wouldn't it?"*

"Yes." The answer had flowed from his lips as easily as it had eight years ago. The ease of its second utterance shook him to the center of his being.

How could she have done this to him? To *him*? The man she'd promised to love, honor, and cherish? Hadn't they added that American touch to their wedding vows just for her?

Events from the last twenty-four hours kept running through his head. Making love to Vicky. Realizing she was Bri. Discovering he never really knew her.

That... *woman* wasn't the precious Bri he remembered. His precious Bri loved him. His precious Bri never lied.

His precious Bri would never have considered him capable of murder.

Christiaan shook his head. Was he remembering someone different? Obviously, because his precious Bri *hadn't* loved him. His precious Bri *had* lied to him *for eight years*. His precious Bri *had* allowed him to believe she was dead while she built a brand new life for herself as a totally different woman.

Then made love to him without ever planning on telling him the truth.

Grabbing the suitcase from the closet, Christiaan slammed it down onto the bed so hard the garment bag bounced off the side.

"*Potverdomme!*" Temples pounding, he kicked the suitcase off the bed, too. It struck the wall, leaving a fist-sized hole. "*Potverdomme! Potverdomme! Potverdomme!*"

He stared at the damage, his throat tight and hot. Unnerved by the physical evidence of his anger, Christiaan sat down on the bed to get a hold of himself. The erotic picture of Vicky's mouth working him like an ice cream cone flashed into his mind, tempering his anger and heating his ardor. He replayed exactly what had followed after that. How could he have not known he was making love to his wife? Wouldn't a man know such a thing?

He and Bri had made love hundreds of times during their marriage. But it had never been like this. Bri had always been interested, responsive, and engaging. But in the cave, as Vicky, she'd been aggressive, strong, and fearless. Christiaan snorted at the cruel irony. He'd experienced every married man's dream, hadn't he? Making love to another woman without cheating on the wife.

The wife. His wife.

But he had cheated on his wife because Bri was alive. *No!* He hadn't cheated on his wife because Vicky was Bri. *And Bri is my wife.*

"*Potverdomme!*" *Was* his wife. *She's not Bri anymore. And she's not the wife I remember.*

Christiaan jerked upright then rescued the garment bag and suitcase from the floor. At least he didn't have to worry about waking Baz with these antics. When he'd gotten back earlier, his friend's bed was still made. Christiaan checked the alarm clock. 10:45 AM. Obviously, the tryst with the waitress was lasting a good, long time.

Good for him. At least one of us is having fun with a woman.

Christiaan yanked open a dresser drawer, scooped up his socks, and flung them into the suitcase.

Home. He just needed to get back home. With an ocean between them, he'd forget about Bri. *She wants to be dead? Let her stay dead.* He slammed the drawer shut with his foot.

First, he'd contact his personal attorney. They'd need to be prepared to threaten her with fraud or abandonment or something should she decide down the road to reclaim her position and title.

Christiaan jerked open another drawer, grabbed everything, and added it to the mess growing in his suitcase.

Next, he'd need to talk to his finance people. Abandoning and selling Mineral Springs was possibly going to bankrupt him and the company. He'd probably have to settle for pennies on the dollar. But at this point, he and his business needed to get as far away as possible from Bri.

Vicky. Vicky! Stop calling her Bri!

Soon, running shirts and shorts were hurled into the suitcase. The sound of a door opening and closing stopped him from focusing his anger—and foot—on another drawer.

"I'm feeling fine, just fine as wine." Baz's slightly off-key rendition of Blackberry Smoke's "Ain't Got The Blues" filtered into Christiaan. "I can't frown for grinning, I can't lose for winning. I ain't got the blues anymore."

Christiaan let the drawer have it anyway. The entire dresser slammed hard enough to rattle the open Scotch bottle and almost-empty glass he'd placed there earlier.

"Wh— who's there?" Baz yelled.

"Who the hell do you think it is?"

"Bro? Is that you?"

"You were expecting someone else?" Christiaan let out a short snort before grabbing the snifter and downing the contents. "Perhaps the maid that's been wanting to turn down your sheets since we got here?"

Silence answered him.

"Things must have gone well with Phoebe, huh?"

More silence.

"Phoebe... the waitress... right?"

Shirt flipped over one shoulder, a bare-chested Baz appeared in the bedroom doorway, face white as a sheet.

"Wow." Christiaan laughed. "She must have really taken you for a ride, so to speak. You look like hell."

"I... ah... I ah..." He looked away hastily then paced around the room.

"Obviously haven't had a cup of coffee yet. Me, neither." Christiaan nodded toward the Scotch. "You're welcome to partake if you think you need a bigger morning wake up. Grab something to put it in from the living room."

"I just wasn't expecting you..." Baz walked off then returned with an empty glass. "... I was just headed into the shower." Hands shaking, Baz poured two fingers of the Scotch, downed it, and poured another two before leaning against the wall.

"I didn't mean to scare you." Christiaan poured himself another drink.

"No... no problem. I just wasn't expecting you to be... um... um... drinking this early."

Before today, Christiaan would never have considered imbibing in alcohol before evening. However, after everything that had happened, he could appreciate why Bri had turned to Scotch to ease her life as a van Laere. Tipping his head back, he savored the crisp, liquid amber kiss that joined the others he'd taken over the last hour or so to dull the painful reality of his situation.

He gestured for his friend to empty his glass so Christiaan could pour another. Baz was going to need it. "Look, I have something incredible to tell you." Christiaan snorted. "Something you absolutely won't believe."

"You're leaving?" Baz nodded toward the suitcase and garment bag on the bed. "Today?"

"Yes, but that's not what I need to tell you." He poured another drink for both of them.

"Am I leaving?"

"No." Christiaan shook his head.

"So I'm staying to get the Mineral Springs project moving again…"

"No, but that—"

"Because I think you're making a mistake, bro, putting this important project on hold. Just let me—"

"Baz, STOP!" Christiaan held up his hands to emphasize the point, then put his Scotch down on the dresser. He gestured for Baz to sit, and his friend dropped to the edge of the bed. Christiaan leaned against the opposite wall.

"Bri is alive." Even aloud, the fact still sounded surreal. A vague, disquieting feeling tugged at him. A lot of questions about her disappearance still needed answered, but Christiaan wasn't sure he was ready for that.

He studied his friend. Baz's face was an amalgam of a hundred different expressions. Peering around the room, Baz seemed to search for the correct response to Christiaan's revelation. Christiaan could appreciate the emotional confusion. He'd been on an emotional roller coaster since this morning. For a long while, the only sound in the bedroom was the gentle hum of the electric alarm clock on the dresser.

Christiaan's gaze dropped to the dark tattoo on Baz's upper right chest. Funny. He'd noticed the heart-shaped graphic before but never the tiny little words written below the ring.

"What do you mean 'Bri is alive'?" Baz murmured.

Focus. "Vicky is Bri. Bri is Vicky."

"Vicky…" Baz licked his lips in confusion. "The hot guide that saved our asses on the mountain then ran our asses back up the mountain on that stupid singles climb you made me go on is really Brianna?"

"Yes." Christiaan nodded.

"Vicky…" Baz's voice raised slightly. "The pain-in-the-ass ShastaWatch witch whose persistent meddling turned my dream project into a nightmare is really Brianna?"

"One in the same." Christiaan poured a few more fingers of whiskey for both of them. They were going to need it.

"Vicky…" This time, Baz ground the name out between his teeth. "The recovering alcoholic that should have relapsed in the bar the other night but was saved by you is really Brianna?"

"Yep." Christiaan tapped his glass against Baz's. "That's her. That's Bri."

"She's… alive?"

"Always has been."

Baz shook his head. "How did I not see it?"

"You did but couldn't believe it. I couldn't either. Not when Bri is supposed to be dead."

"And you're sure?" Baz's brow furrowed.

Muscles leapt in Christiaan's jaw, followed by every other muscle in his body—including the one between his legs—as he quickly replayed last night's and this morning's events. He needed to do less of that.

Or drink more.

He threw back the Scotch. "I'm not going into the details, but suffice it to say she's definitely Bri."

"That bitch!" Baz's eyes flashed anger as he jumped up from the bed.

"Yeah. Couldn't have said it better myself."

"Alive?" Baz paced around the room, head shaking. "This whole time? How did she… then who was in the car… why didn't she tell me… us…?" He tossed back what was in his glass. "Ah, shit. Shit... shit... shit!"

Christiaan didn't know what exactly to say. Baz had a right to be mad. Bri had lied to him, too. And Vicky had made both their lives a living hell for the last several months. Baz stormed into the living room.

"She played us both like a piano," Christiaan called after him. Confused on so many levels, he was certain about two things. One, that he didn't want to relive and relay the details about Bri's return to life to Baz. And, two, that he wanted to get as far away as possible from Mt. Shasta as soon as possible.

Jeans. Bottom drawer. He grabbed them and flung them into the suitcase. Toiletry bag from the bathroom. He tossed it into his luggage and flipped the top closed. Zipping the suitcase shut, Christiaan dropped it on the floor next to the bed then poured another drink.

"That fucking bitch!" Glass shattering against the fireplace in the living room startled Christiaan. The memory of dropping the teacup at Vicky's lodge and touching her hand flashed across his mind.

"That fucking, fucking bitch!"

Baz certainly has picked up the American vernacular. Thanks MTV.

"This whole time... this whole time Brianna has been jerking my chain. I should have fucking known."

The anger was understandable. Baz had been working on the Mineral Springs project since before Bri's "death". But the rage did seem a little irrational. Then again, he'd been under a lot of pressure lately, was short of cash, and never took the I'm-not-a-blue-blood chip off his shoulder. That and he probably hadn't slept much last night. Christiaan nodded. In reality, this was the hotheaded, irrational Baz he'd known since birth.

Christiaan carried his suitcase and garment bag into the living room. The sound of broken glass cracking under Baz's pacing feet grated on what remained of Christiaan's nerves.

"So..." His friend stopped to look at the luggage then

at Christiaan. "... you're leaving. Where exactly does that leave the Mineral Springs project? Where exactly does that leave me? And what do I do about *her*?"

Christiaan pointed for Baz to take a seat then headed back into the bedroom to grab the whiskey bottle and snifter. Returning to the living room, he retrieved another glass from the wet bar, poured them each a few more fingers, and handed the Scotch to Baz before sitting down across from him.

"I'm done here." Christiaan studied his friend's face. "I'd like you to stay and see if you can find another buyer for the project. I'm going to head back home, hire some incredible accounting consultants, and see if there's anything I missed that could save the company."

"But, bro, you don't understand. You can't—"

"Look. I know. You've poured your heart and soul into this project for the last ten years." Christiaan took a long swig of Scotch. Bri's face on the last night he saw her alive as his wife ran across his memory, quickly followed by her face this morning when he stormed out of the cave after the rescuers had finally freed them. "But this project is over."

"You can't let that bitch—"

"Enough. My decision isn't up for discussion. I'm sorry you're upset. I'm sorry you're feeling like the world is handing you shit, but we're done here."

"No! I refuse to let you screw—" A knock at the door cut Baz off. "I'll get that." He slammed his glass onto the coffee table and bolted.

Christiaan stared at the now-empty snifter in his hand, contemplating whether it would be smart for him to pour another one. His fifth? Sixth? Shrugging his shoulders, he poured another one. Why not? He wouldn't be flying the plane.

Plane. That's right. He needed to call the pilot and let him know they were to head home ASAP. Now, where had Baz put Christiaan's phone? He peered around the living room. Desk? No. Coffee table? No. Fireplace mantel? No.

Muffled voices drifted in from the entryway.

"Who's at the door?" Christiaan called out.

"Me, Baron Boy," a familiar thick Irish voice called out.

"Irishman!" Christiaan called out. "Come on in. Have a drink with us."

"No!" Baz countered. "He doesn't need to be here."

"Come on, now. What's a drink among friends, right?"

Duff entered the main room, with a frowning-like-a-toddler-told-no Baz on his heels, now with his shirt on. The Irishman peered at Christiaan with a raised eyebrow. "'Tis a bit early fer a drop of whiske', eh?" He sat down across from Christiaan.

Christiaan laughed. "Now that's not something I ever thought I'd hear an Irishman say." Snagging another glass from the wet bar, he poured it halfway with Scotch then added some to both his and Baz's snifters.

"What ar' we toastin' to?"

"*De toekomst.*" Christiaan raised his glass. "The future." He wasn't exactly sure what tomorrow held for him, his company, or his family, but as long as his feet weren't on American soil, he'd take that as progress. He nodded to Baz.

Baz touched his Scotch to Christiaan's. "The future." Then he knocked Duff's glass. "*De toekomst.*"

"Thet future. *An todhchaí.*" The Irishman grinned as he met their toasts with tremendous vigor. Whiskey from all their glasses splashed onto his left hand and dripped over a faded heart band tattooed on Duff's ring finger.

"So, Irishman? What brings you here?"

"He...ah... he was... um..." Baz started then buried his face into his Scotch.

Duff smacked him on the back then smiled at Christiaan. "Well, I'm finally gettn' me arse around to take me lucky jacket back."

"I think it's hanging in my closet." Baz jumped up and made a beeline to the other side of the penthouse.

"Maybe   you   need   to   rename   your   jacket,

considering…" Christiaan nodded toward Duff's colorful cast. "How's the arm doing by the way?" Two words— *Diord Fionn*—caught his eye. Where had he heard something like that? Probably from the Irishman during one of their aerial tours.

"*Ach! Ni bhionn an rath ach mar a mbionn an smacht.*" Duff leaned over and grabbed the Scotch bottle. "'Tis no luck except where 'tis discipline."

Running back into the room, Baz stumbled over Christiaan's suitcase.

"Calm down, Dutchie. Look at thet puss on you. What's thet story?"

"I'm closing the project." Christiaan pushed his empty glass toward Duff. "And Dutchie here isn't very happy about it."

The Irishman peered over at Baz. "'Tis so?" Then he turned his attention to Christiaan. "I tot ye were hell bent to be up an' runnin' in a year or two, ShastaWatch an' all?"

Christiaan smiled but said nothing. He wasn't about to share anything with Duff.

"Oh, tha' ought to make me Victoria as 'appy as a clam." The Irishman refilled everyone's glasses.

"Yeah." Christiaan laughed. "That should make Victoria one very happy clam." And him too poor to pay attention.

"Who gives a fuck what Victoria thinks!" Baz raised his glass and aimed for the fireplace.

Duff caught his hand mid-throw. "Calm down, Dutchie. No need to fly off thet 'andle like ye do. All 'tis well."

Christiaan laughed harder. "For someone who only met Baz a few weeks ago, you sure seem to know him well."

The Irishman just laughed and emptied his glass. Leaning forward to retrieve his next drink, Christiaan felt the room shift slightly. *Hmm…* maybe it was time to reconsider his self-medication. At this rate, he wouldn't be in any shape to get home. And he certainly wasn't going to stay another hour in the same country as Vicky. Christiaan slapped his hands against his thighs.

"That's it, boys. I'm done. As much as I'd love to have another…" He slowly pushed himself to standing. "One more, and I won't be able to climb the airstairs. Which reminds me… Baz, where's my phone? I need to call the flight crew."

"It's a… It's a…" Baz fidgeted then leaned over to the small garbage can next to the couch and retrieved Christiaan's phone. "Um… here." Pulling off a candy wrapper stuck to the back, Baz handed the device to his boss.

Christiaan peered down at it. Something sticky coated the screen. Frowning, he rubbed the front of the phone against his pant leg to clean it. Hitting the on button, the device started its boot-up cycle.

"Where's tha' leave ye, Dutchie, thet boss headin' back an' all?" Duff poured himself and Baz another drink.

"Looking for a buyer." Baz downed the Scotch in one swig. "ASAP."

"Really? Ye're sellin' thet place, Baron Boy?"

"Yes." Christiaan paged through his contact list for the pilot's number. "Know anybody who'd want to buy it?"

"Me? No." The Irishman laughed. "Nice piece of property an' all. Lots of potential thar, right, Dutchie?"

Baz didn't seem to enjoy the lighthearted banter. "Baron Boy is headed home to take a closer look at the corporate financials."

"Really?" Duff laughed.

"Yes, and the sooner the better." Christiaan touched the number and waited for his pilot to answer. "If you'll excuse me, gentlemen, I've got to contact my flight crew about getting me home as well as a taxi operator about getting me to the airport." He headed toward his bedroom.

"I'd be 'appy to get ye on yer way," Duff offered.

Christiaan stopped and turned around. "I thought you were grounded."

"From flying, but not driving. Wadda ye say you let me get ye to thet airport. Me way of sayin' I'm sorry for all thet trouble I've put ye thou'. Besides, it will give me a chance to see tha' fine air chariot ye people love to gallivant 'round thet world in."

Ahh, hatred of the rich. That must be the common thread Baz and Duff had bonded over. But, hey, a ride's a ride.

Christiaan nodded. "Okay, Irishman. Let me just finish packing, and I'll be ready to go."

"Don't ye worry, Baron Boy. I'll take care of everything."

"Your life would be so much better if I were dead, wouldn't it?"

"Yes."

The words reverberated inside Vicky's head like an echo on Everest.

Staring at the flames dancing in the fireplace, she sat curled up in her favorite chair, hands encircling a cup of Chamomile. The tea had long since gone cold as she replayed those awful words—and their emotional impact—again and again.

"Your life would be so much better if I were dead, wouldn't it?"

"Yes."

Another crashing wave of regret washed over her. She tried to shrug it off, but the emotion clung to her like a shroud. Tears threatened to spill. She shook them away. Christiaan's life would be better without her.

This time.

Her chest tightened. Now that she'd spent time with him again... connected with him again... fell in love with him again... the thought of him living without her again was almost too much to bear.

An ironic chuckle escaped her lips. Only a week ago, she'd relished the fact that her husband was living his life without her.

Today, she was dying inside because he would continue to do exactly that.

Vicky glanced at the highback he'd sat in last night, then at the sofa table where they'd shared the meal he'd cooked. Right after he'd spied her masturbating in the shower. Her face flushed at the memory of both their embarrassment.

She burrowed deeper into her chair. The same position she'd assumed last night after realizing the horrible mistake she'd made eight years ago. Christiaan professing his undying love for his late wife... wearing both their wedding rings... expressing excitement then profound anguish regarding their baby... displaying devastating grief at the accident that took her life... showing sheer disgust at idea of marrying Astrid... The telling moments replayed in her head and her heart.

Hmm. Maybe she should have taken Rainbow up on that offer to stay at her place. Sitting here, alone with her thoughts, wasn't doing Vicky any good. She bit her lip until it throbbed like her pulse. Good thing there wasn't any alcohol within twenty miles because her chances of blowing off eight years of sobriety were significant. She'd already flushed the Vicodin down the toilet to eliminate all chemical mind-altering temptation.

Suddenly, Christiaan's face as he realized who she really was seized her thoughts. *"Welterusten, mijn liefste. Spreek je morgen."* What had compelled her to say that? What had she been thinking?

She hadn't.

She'd just made love to her husband, rolling in emotions she hadn't felt since the early part of their marriage. Caught in a blissful after-sex haze and what was left of the Demerol shot, she'd forgotten who she was, where she was, and what she was supposed to be doing.

You were Bri once again. You said exactly what Bri would have said.

What Bri did say. No, what Vicky said.

Damn! Now she was forgetting who she was!

Face it. You haven't been Bri for a very long time.

Placing the teacup on the coffee table, Vicky stood and tightened the belt on her fuzzy robe before stepping over to the fireplace. She sat down on the warm raised hearth and wiggled her fingers through shower-damp hair. Too bad she couldn't as easily manipulate her thoughts.

"You failed our love."

Christiaan was right. She had. Instead of believing in the bond they'd forged, she'd allowed her doubts, insecurities, and fears to creep into her mind, to cloud her judgment, and—worst of all—harden her heart. To keep her from seeing the truth. To poison their relationship.

To fail our love.

Vicky shivered despite the blazing fire. The emotional chaos raging inside of her because of all the pain she'd caused him refused to ease.

And like trying to unscramble eggs. Couldn't be done.

But she could do something... anything... to avoid feeling this way.

Like brewing fresh tea. Vicky grabbed the pot from the table and padded into the kitchen. Filling the kettle from the sink, she then put it on the stove to boil. She'd just settled against the counter to wait when the phone rang. Leaning back, she read the Caller ID on the back of the handset.

"Rainbow Cell."

Although she didn't feel like talking to anybody, Vicky couldn't ignore her best friend. Both she and Christiaan would still be stuck in that cave if it weren't for Rainbow and her tenacity. Besides, Vicky had promised her friend that she'd call as soon as she'd gotten out of the shower and, of course, with current life as tranquil as a cyclone, Vicky had forgotten.

Steeling herself to sound perky, she answered after the next ring. "I'm sorry, girl. I totally forgot to call."

Rainbow laughed. "Yeah, I knew you would. No prob. You doing okay, sweetie?"

No. But how could Vicky ever explain that to Rainbow?

"Yes," Vicky answered instead.

"Okay," Rainbow crooned. "Now, I know you said you didn't want to talk about what happened. But, sweetie, you looked so upset, and Baron von Rat Face was so pissed that I can't help but be worried about you. Are you sure you're okay? Are you sure you don't want to talk about it?"

Only one person existed that Vicky could talk to about this, and he wasn't about to listen to anything more from her.

"Really, Rainbow. I'm okay. I promise."

"O...k...a...y..." Her friend didn't sound convinced. "Do me a favor anyway. Got any dried Chamomile flowers?"

"Yes. In fact, I'm getting ready to brew a fresh pot of tea as we speak."

"Great! Chamomile is just the ticket to calm your nerves, relieve your stress, and help you sleep. Before you drink your next cup, take some deep breaths and let the soothing aroma fill your nose and relax your body and soul."

Vicky snickered. Easier said than done. "Sounds like a plan."

"Okay, well, I'll be by later with some dinner, sweetie."

"Let me guess... beetroot soup with spinach/lentil balls."

"Nope." Rainbow laughed. "After your adventure, I'd say you're entitled to some pizza."

After this adventure, I'm entitled to some eighteen-year-old, single-malt Scotch. "Large thick crust with pepperoni and extra cheese?"

"Large thick cauliflower crust with artichokes, spinach, polenta, and extra goat cheese."

Of course. Vicky chuckled. "I'm looking forward to it. See you then. And Rainbow?"

"Yeah, sweetie?"

"Thanks..." She cleared her throat, suddenly tight with emotion. "Thanks for finding me... finding us."

When Vicky didn't show up for the regular Thursday morning ShastaWatch breakfast, Rainbow and the crew had gone on a tear looking for her, even enlisting Dean to help. When Vicky didn't turn up anywhere, they decided on a lark to check the Mineral Springs property. Spying her truck, her business partner then recognized her boot prints leading to the cave. Fresh sand and scratch marks meant a recent cave-in. With their bare hands and a hot-wired Bobcat, the ShastaWatch crew dug them out.

"Hey, what are friends for, right?" Rainbow answered. "*Ciao!*"

Vicky put the handset back onto the holder. Staring at the phone, she fought the sudden and ridiculous urge to call Christiaan. And say what? That she's sorry? So very sorry? So. Very. Very. Sorry?

So very, very sorry for what?

For becoming an alcoholic?

For running away?

For losing their baby?

For letting him think she was dead?

For not trusting their love?

Her hand came to rest on the handset. *That's a lot of sorrys, sister.*

The hot kettle singing pulled Vicky out of her thoughts. For the next several minutes, she occupied herself and her mind with the calming ritual of tea making. Then she headed back into the living room with the fresh pot. Filling her cup, she returned to her spot on the hearth.

Rainbow was right. Take some relaxing breaths and put all this crap behind you. Let the soothing aroma stop your thinking.

Especially about him.

Wrapping both hands around the teacup, she closed her eyes and took a long, deep breath. The soothing Chamomile aroma filled her, draping her worried mind in a calming haze. For a few blissful minutes, there was nothing in the world except her, her tea, and the soft crackling of the fire next to her. No Christiaan. No Bri. No Vicky.

No nothing. *Hmm… nice.*

Taking another deep breath, Vicky opened her eyes. She spied the blue pullover Christiaan had worn earlier, draped on the highback. Once freed from the cave, he'd stomped away from her so fast he didn't notice or care that he'd left it. She'd scooped it up before anyone else had.

He'd looked so damn sexy in the garment. A flush of arousal rushed through her body. He'd looked so damn sexy out of it, too.

Before she could stop herself, she put down the teacup, picked up the pullover, and held it to her nose. It smelled of his distinctive male scent. The ache between her legs intensified. With one hand, she untied the belt to her robe and let it fall to the floor. Pulling his garment on, she savored the sensual feel of the soft material brushing over her bare body. Hugging herself and breathing in Christiaan's erotic smell was almost like being with the man himself.

Almost. But not quite.

But the closest she was ever going to get again.

Vicky unzipped the chest pocket on the pullover and reached in to retrieve that other item Christiaan had left behind in the cave... her wedding band. Slipping the gold chain around her neck, the ring came to rest between her breasts. With one hand, she pressed the ring against her chest and then took a deep breath. The idea that he had worn this since her death was touching. A tear ticked one eye. The memory of his bitterness as he stormed out of the cave was heartbreaking.

They had once been so happy. *Once.*

Before she realized it, Vicky retrieved that worn manila envelope from behind the books on the mantel and dumped everything—photos, marriage license, articles—onto the hearth beside her. Their wedding portrait landed on top. She traced the image with her finger. Fifteen years ago, they'd joined together to take on the world as a couple.

For better... for worse... 'til death us do part...

She wiped a tear from her cheek. He'd fulfilled his end of the bargain. He'd loved her. Not perfectly, but honestly and completely.

What a fool she'd been. From the moment the

honeymoon had ended, she'd allowed her anxieties about herself and her vulnerabilities about her marriage take control of her life. She'd bought into his family's lies about her suitability and Astrid's deceit about her relationship with Christiaan.

"You failed our love."

Yes I did. Horribly.

She'd lost her marriage because she refused to believe Christiaan loved her.

She'd lost her son because she refused to stop drinking the pain away.

She'd lost her "life" because she refused to gut it out and make her marriage work.

And because of all that, she'd lost the only man she ever loved.

Christiaan.

And now she'd lost him… for the last time.

Vicky tried tossing the picture into the fire, but her fingers wouldn't let go. The flames blurred as her tears flowed freely. Rocking back and forth, she waited for the anguish to somehow ease.

The phone ringing from the kitchen pulled her out of her lament.

Nope. Not answering it.

Three more rings, then the machine picked up. After a short pause, her business partner's voice played through the speaker.

"Yo, Vic. It's Dean. Just wanted to let you know I just dropped your truck off."

Her truck. Vicky laughed despite her mood, remembering Christiaan killing her clutch on the way to Mineral Springs. *Pick a gear. Any gear.*

"I figured you were probably sleeping considering everything that happened, so I slipped the keys under the back door mat."

Her keys! Her heart lifted. She could drive into town, find Christiaan, and try to explain everything. Try to make him understand why she did what she did.

"I'm glad we found you. I don't know what I'd have done if you'd have wound up dead, Vic." Dean stopped to clear his throat.

Dead. Brianna was dead. Not Vicky. Brianna.

"But you didn't die... so... yeah! Well, can't wait to hear how the hell you ended up stuck in a cave. In the meantime, take care. Bye!"

And, with Brianna "dead", Christiaan would be better off.

Just like he said. Then and now.

Closing her eyes, Vicky gave herself into the moment. Resistance melted away as clarity regarding her situation evolved. Nothing she could say and nothing she could do could ever make up for eight years of lying... eight years of believing your husband capable of murder... eight years of letting a man that clearly loved you believe you were dead.

Vicky dropped her head to stare at the picture.

For better... for worse... 'til death us do part...

Christiaan was better off without her.

For several minutes, Vicky sat, absorbing her decision, then calmly tossed the wedding photo into the fire. Brianna Stokman, Lady van Laere. No, Brianna Stokman, *Baroness* van Laere, was gone. *Forever.*

Watching the image burn into nothingness, Vicky suddenly felt very tired. *Great, the Chamomile is working.* She went to close the fireplace screen and head up to bed when a color graphic from one of her old articles on the pile still lying on the hearth caught her eye. The small visual was with the expose she'd written on power companies developing alternative energy sources on Federal lands. When she was a reporter, she rarely paid attention to ancillary items added to her pieces by her editor. In fact, she couldn't remember ever really seeing this one.

The graphic showed a gridded map of the United States with red and green plus signs dotted throughout the country.

Like I saw in the trailer!

The caption read "Current existing microearthquake (MEQ) data sites of proposed geothermal sites show seismic evidence of potential cataclysmic, tectonic chain reactions affecting fault lines throughout North America. Energy proponents—both in government and the private sector— vow the risk is infinitesimal." Vicky snickered. Definitely not a reader-friendly explanation she'd have written.

She'd just poured herself another cup of tea and settled down to study the map closer when the phone rang again.

Let the machine get it. She focused on the high number of red plus signs in the western section of the United States, especially in California, Nevada, and Arizona.

A familiar Dutch accent coming from the answering machine speaker wound its way into her brain.

Christiaan?

Vicky dropped everything, her earlier decision to let things well enough alone forgotten at the sound of his voice. Rushing across the slate floor, she grabbed the handset and answered, "Hello?"

"Hey, it's Baz."

"Oh." She frowned in disappointment.

"Wow. You sound down in the dumps. You were expecting Christiaan perhaps?"

With all my heart and soul.

"Yes. No." Vicky hesitated, blinking with bafflement. She didn't know what to say. She didn't know what to do. Had Christiaan told Baz who she was? What had happened in the cave? "I... I..." Still wearing Christiaan's pullover, she took a deep breath to calm herself. Thankful, his scent had faded some. Soon, it would disappear entirely, and life would go on. Vicky Golden would go on.

Baz laughed. "You're speechless! That's so unlike you."

"Yes." She managed to chuckle. "Look, it's been a long several days. I'd really like to get some sleep. So, if you don't mind, I'd just like—"

"Look, it's Christiaan. He'd really like to talk to you."

A soft gasp escaped her. "He would?"

"Yes. He really doesn't want to leave things the way they are between the two of you."

Really? Vicky touched the gold band hanging from her neck. *"Your life would be so much better if I were dead, wouldn't it?" "Yes."* "I'm sorry, Baz, but I think Christiaan and I said all there is to say. Goodbye."

"Wait!" Baz's voice was low, but full of intensity. "He loves you."

His words stopped her. "What?" was all she could manage to say.

"Look, I'm not exactly sure what happened between you two in the cave, but whatever it was it must have been incredible. I haven't seen him this excited about a woman since his wedding day."

Our wedding day.

"In fact," Baz continued. "He's already on his way up to Serenity Rock. He said something about that being a special place for you."

Christiaan wanted to see her! At Serenity Rock!

Letting out a huge breath, Vicky pressed the gold band to her heart. Christiaan still loved her! He'd obviously calmed down and had heard everything she'd said. Now he was willing to talk it out with her.

She shot a glance at the clock on the stove. She wasn't exactly sure what had caused her husband's change of heart, but she wasn't going to waste any time thinking about. If she got dressed right now, she could take a shortcut to Serenity Rock and arrive about the same time as he did. They might not fix everything or even get back together, but at least they'd have this one chance to talk calmly and rationally about everything.

"If I'm going to meet him, Baz, I've got to get going."

"Okay. Good luck."

"Thanks for everything."

"My pleasure."

Vicky hung up the phone and raced up the stairs to dress. *For better… for worse… 'til death us do part…*

CHAPTER 15

The towering majesty of Mt. Shasta loomed at Christiaan from the windshield. If someone had told him less than a week ago that stepping into this behemoth's shadow would have turned his life upside down and all around, he'd have called them crazy.

"*Potverdomme* crazy." He leaned back into the front passenger seat.

"What's tha', Baron Boy?" Duff grunted from behind the wheel of his luxury Land Rover. Christiaan had expected the Irishman to drive an old, beat-up Jeep, not a brand-new, top-of-the-line compact SUV. Soft-grain leather seats, black lacquer dashboard, and surround-sound audio system blaring Blackberry Smoke's "Sleeping Dogs" made for quite a sweet ride. *Isn't that the expression Baz picked up from MTV?*

"Nothing, Irishman. Just me growling about life." Scotch, the passage of time, and the decision to head home had tempered Christiaan's anger, but now he couldn't shake an unsettled feeling as they headed to the airport. No matter how many times he reviewed his decision to leave Mt. Shasta behind and everything that had happened here, it didn't feel right.

He sighed and rolled his cell phone over and over in his right hand. Why was he questioning his decision? He never questioned his decisions. Correction. He never questioned his *business* decisions. Those were cut and dried. Either they made sense or they didn't.

But affairs of the heart. Those... those were much harder to deal with.

Business. Yeah, business. That's what he needed to focus on from now on. How to save his company.

As Duff slowed for a stop sign, a hawk circled overhead. *The same one that tormented me earlier?* Him and Vicky? Christiaan chuckled, realizing that for the first time today he'd thought of her as Vicky, not Bri. As he watched the bird soar off toward the mountain, reality slowly engraved itself on his mind. *Because that's who she is now. Vicky Golden. My precious Bri is gone.*

Duff accelerated from the stop onto a different rough-paved road. Passing yet-another green valley pasture filled with horses and other livestock, Christiaan could see why she liked it here. Beautiful. Relaxing. Compelling.

Just like her.

"Wouldn't the freeway have been faster?"

"Jaysus, dis route is prettier, wouldn't ye say?" Duff gestured to the countryside with his cast. "Besides, what's yer hurry? 'Tis not like ye have to catch a regular flight like us ordinary folk do. Ye're *special*, aren't ye? Ye've yer own private air chariot. Thet best ye oul' fancy-pants money can buy. I mean, 'tis not like thet plane will leave without ye. Ye're thet boss, right?"

"That's me. 'Thet boss'." Of a practically bankrupt company. Christiaan dragged a hand through his hair. Hopefully, whatever he could sell the project permits, leases, related equipment, and real estate for would be enough to save everything. Otherwise, he'd have to start all over again.

A chuckle escaped his lips. Maybe he could move to a new country, change his name, and start another career. For a brief second, the idea sounded great. *It worked for Bri, right?*

He stared out the side window at Mt. Shasta. What could Vicky be up to right now? Heading to the summit with another group of singles? Hiking up to her "spot" at Serenity Rock? Hanging around her beautiful lodge, curled up in a chair in front of the fireplace?

Maybe taking a shower? A nice... long... hot shower. Christiaan's breath hitched as the memory of Vicky masturbating as water cascaded down her naked body filled his mind.

And crotch.

He shifted in his seat, trying to alleviate the growing pressure. The flashback was equal parts pleasant and torturous. Her hands skimming her wet, naked body. Her hips rocking in sweet, slow motion. Her face writhing in pure, absolute ecstasy. A shiver rippled through him.

Then her face had twisted in sudden, intense anger as she accused him of being a voyeur.

Christiaan shook his head. Another misunderstanding. Just like their entire marriage. One big misunderstanding after another, provoked by the people around them and each of their selfish, conceited needs.

His father... who wanted a blue-blooded heir to carry on the van Laere dynasty and the fortune to match... whatever it took.

His stepmother... who wanted money, prestige, and power... whatever it took.

Astrid... who wanted a title and riches... whatever it took.

Baz... who wanted Astrid and someone to atone for his low birth... whatever it took.

Himself... who wanted his father's approval via business success... whatever it took.

Guilt knotted Christiaan's stomach. "Whatever it took" turned out to be Bri's physical stability, emotional sanity and, eventually, her "life". He sighed and leaned his head against the passenger window with a thump.

"Good Lord, Baron Boy. Why thet long face?"

"Tough couple of days, Irishman. Tough couple of days."

"Ye know what ye need?"

A chance to redo the last fifteen years of my life? "What?" Christiaan answered instead.

"More of dis." From under the driver's seat, Duff pulled a half-full Scotch bottle he'd obviously snagged from the penthouse.

Christiaan shook his head and waved a hand. "No, thanks. I've had enough. Of course, as your passenger, I'd appreciate you not partaking either."

Propping his cast against the steering wheel, the Irishman tilted the container toward his free hand and twisted the lid off. He smirked at Christiaan. "Then me guess 'tis a good thing ye'r just me passenger an' not me boss, eh?" Duff pulled a long swallow then settled the open bottle between his legs.

The cynicism of the remark grated. Christiaan liked the Irishman, but his obvious resentment for the rich and titled bordered on contempt. No wonder Duff and Baz had become friends. Baz's bitterness fed off the Irishman's animosity.

Christiaan returned his focus to Mt. Shasta, still looming in the distance. Baz had always had a chip on his shoulder about being the estate gardener's son, but his anger hadn't hit high gear until Astrid had broken his heart.

Potverdomme, Astrid, for rejecting Baz's love and being such a bitch about it!

She'd known since they were all children playing together on the estate that Baz was in love with her. She'd toyed with his affections, pretending to care, even sleeping with him although Christiaan had begged her not to so as to protect his best friend's fragile feelings. Then, shortly after Christiaan got his MBA and Baz finally finished university, Baz proposed to Astrid.

And she laughed in his face.

Baz had taken her to a nice restaurant in Amsterdam,

where he'd invited all their family and friends to a surprise engagement party. Astrid humiliated Baz in front of everyone when he offered her a beautiful diamond ring Christiaan knew had cost both his friend and his friend's father most of their savings. Laughing hysterically, Astrid tossed the bauble into the canal, explained she was meant for more than a lowly gardener's son, and walked off. The pain of his friend's public disgrace still echoed in Christiaan's memory.

Baz spent that summer licking his wounds with cousins living in Ireland. When he came back home, his skin for the rich and privileged was even thinner than before.

"So," Duff interrupted Christiaan's thoughts. "Ye'r headed back home to take a closer look at thet money end of things, eh?"

"Yes." Christiaan peered over at the Irishman, driving with his cast propped on the steering wheel. Once again, *Diord Fionn* written in black caught his eye. *Where have I seen that before?*

"Things tha' bad?"

"Don't worry, Irishman. I'll make sure the bill for your services is paid."

Duff laughed heartily then took another swig of Scotch. "Oh, don't ye worry, Baron Boy. I'll make sure thet bill 'tis paid. Paid in full."

Christiaan twisted the corner of his lip up and returned to watching the passing countryside. Was the Irishman terribly drunk or insanely weird?

Or both?

For several miles, they drove in silence before Duff spoke up. "I'm curious. Does Victoria know ye're giving up?"

"Not exactly," Christiaan answered. "She knows the Mineral Springs project is on hold. What she doesn't know is that I plan to sell everything off as soon as possible."

"Well, Victoria 'tis sure to be dancing thet jig when she find out tha' news. I've never met a woman tha' could yap so much crap about renewable energy an' climate change an' other stupid stuff like tha'."

Christiaan laughed. She'd been an environmental reporter after all. On a lark, he hit the Internet browser button on his phone and Googled her maiden name—Brianna Beabes. A long list of articles popped up. Scrolling through, he stopped to pull up one with a headline that mentioned alternative energy sources on Federal lands. He skimmed it and recognized several passages Vicky had quoted on various occasions over the last week.

From the corner of his eye, he could see Duff raise the Scotch bottle in a toast. "'Ere's to Victoria gettin' everything she deserves."

Christiaan stopped reading the caption about microearthquake data and looked up. "My turn to be curious. Why do you call Vicky 'Victoria'?"

"Nothing, really." Duff chuckled then shrugged a shoulder. "Just a poor oul' Irishman's way of showing a fine thing some respect."

A jealous pinch jabbed Christiaan. Tapping the photos icon on his phone, he pulled up the scanned copy of Bri on the picnic blanket. A gentle melancholy settled over him as he stared at the picture taken a week after they met.

They'd started out with such love and promise with and for each other. His bride-to-be's eyes bored into him from fifteen years ago, wreaking havoc with his already splintered heart. Regret for all he'd done—and didn't do—hit him like a wrecking ball.

He'd failed her. He and his superficial world of appearances and proprietary. His pride and van Laere upbringing had gotten in the way. Guilt burned in his chest. He'd failed Bri. He'd failed their love.

The SUV lurching into a tight curve pulled Christiaan's attention from his pity party. Outside the passenger window, Mt. Shasta still towered in the distance.

Bri had gotten a second chance at life and took it for all it was worth. She'd gone to AA and stayed clean for eight years. Lost weight. Learned to climb. Got strong...

mentally and physically.

A gentle smile touched his face. She'd found herself again. As Vicky, Brianna had rediscovered the incredible woman she'd once been.

He peered back at the picture. The incredible woman he'd fallen in love with.

Fifteen years ago.

And all over again six days ago.

He reached for the wedding band hanging from his neck. *Potverdomme*! He'd dropped it at her feet in the cave.

And now he wanted it back.

Her, too.

Like a lightning bolt to the head, the revelation shocked Christiaan. He refocused his attention on the mountains in the distance. Vicky was there, somewhere. And right now, he wanted to talk to her. He wasn't sure she'd want to talk to him, but he had to at least try.

"Irishman, turn the car around. I need to take care of something. I need to go to Vicky's lodge. Do you know how to get there?"

"Seriously?" Duff looked at him like he'd gone crazy.

"Yes." As serious as a heart attack. *Another MTV/Baz expression.*

"Can me ask why?"

"You can ask, Irishman, but I won't tell you."

Frowning, Duff shrugged his shoulders and took another swig of Scotch. "'Cause I'm just the lowly chauffeur, right?"

Christiaan started to reply when Blackberry Smoke's "Good One Comin' On" blared from his phone. Bri's picture disappeared as the screen read "Lou Cell". Christiaan hit the answer button and put the device to his ear.

"Hey, Lou!" he answered then gestured to the Irishman with an index finger circling in the air to turn the car around. Duff nodded as he turned down the music. Christiaan refocused on the call.

"Where the hell have you been, Boss?" Lou yelled.

"I've been leaving you message after message!"

"Yeah, well, I've—"

"It doesn't matter now that I have you. Those fingerprints. The ones on the photograph you sent over. Are you ready for this? They're your wife's. Can you believe it? The mountain guide is your wife!"

Christiaan threw his head back and laughed hard. "Too late. I already know."

"You do? How?"

A brief replay of this morning's cave scene raced through Christiaan's mind. "It's a long story…" He looked at Duff. "… that I don't care to go into right now. Suffice it to say I'm certain. Beyond a shadow of doubt."

"And we're happy about this?" Lou asked.

"We're still figuring that all out."

"Does Vicky know who she really is?"

"Yes." Christiaan nodded, watching the Irishman take another drink and thinking he ought to take the bottle away for both their sakes. "Yes, she does. Look, Lou, at some point, I'll fill you in on all the details. But right now, I need you to keep this to yourself. Can I count on you to do that?"

"Of course. That goes without saying. But do you at least know if she planned this accident so she could disappear or was she simply one hell-of-a lucky victim?"

"What does it matter at this point?" Christiaan asked.

"Well." Lou cleared his throat. "Based on the revelation that your wife is alive and well and living under an assumed name, I decided to take a closer look at the file on her supposed death."

As Duff finally pulled off the side of the road to turn around, Christiaan noticed the "lucky" Celtic jacket lying in the backseat.

Lou continued. "The description of the accident reminded me of the bomb signature of a radical IRA splinter group of the *Saor Eire* I dealt with when I was stationed in Europe for the Agency."

Christiaan smiled. Lou's "fishing trips".

"Unlike most IRA groups that liked to make big splashes and immediately claim credit, these guys specialized in bombings made to look like accidents. The group usually went after big-money targets and aristocrats like yourself."

"Bombers for hire?"

"Unfortunately, there's no real evidence what their motivation was since they never claimed credit for anything. The only reason we know anything about them at all is because we had someone undercover in the organization for a while…" Lou's voice grew unsteady then dropped off for a few seconds before continuing. "… for a while before she… um… she… she disappeared."

How close to this "she" had Lou been? "And you think maybe this group had something to do with Bri's accident?"

Duff shoved the Scotch bottle at Christiaan, but he shook his head "no". The Irishman grimaced, shrugged his shoulders, and took another drink.

"The head dude was a real, real bad ass, Boss. Went by the name *Croi Dubh* or Black Heart."

Christiaan's heart skipped a beat. "Say that again, Lou. *Croi* what?"

"*Croi Dubh.* Pardon my rusty Irish accent. It's been awhile."

"Dubb?"

"No, *dubh,*" Lou corrected the pronunciation. "It kind of sounds like rough… *dubh.*"

Christiaan peered over at his driver. "*Dubh.*"

The Irishman nodded then began humming some pop tune.

"That's right," Lou continued. "Now, I haven't dealt with this shit for a while, so I had to do a little digging into my old files. The guy's name—this Black Heart—was Sean Dean. Former helicopter pilot that got tossed out of the Irish military for his IRA leanings. He was one scary dude 'cause he looked and acted like a cool cucumber whenever necessary. But heaven help anyone that got in his way 'cause he was willing to do anything to achieve his goals. Hence the nickname Black Heart."

As Lou rambled on, Christiaan looked out the window at Mt. Shasta. Wait. Shouldn't the mountain be on the other side of the car if Duff had turned around?

"*Croi Dubh* fell off the grid about the same time I left the Agency. I figured he'd either blown himself up or one of his lesser commands had taken him out."

Christiaan peeked at Duff's free hand, the one with the heart ring tattoo he'd noticed at the penthouse earlier when they'd toasted to the future. The heart had a crown on top.

And the heart was black.

"So," Lou continued. "I talked to a few of my buddies still with the Agency. Word is that Black Heart is in the US, possibly laundering European funds through American companies, and planning something big. Really big."

A paralyzing moment of sudden insight struck Christiaan. He hadn't read the Ethanol market wrong. Not. At. All.

Pulling his gaze away from Duff's tattoo, Christiaan found himself staring into the Irishman's smiling face. Then Duff drained the Scotch bottle and tossed it into the back. Reaching under the driver's seat, he pulled out a gun and gestured with it for Christiaan to hang up the phone.

A spasm of fear gripped him, and Christiaan slowly nodded in acknowledgment. "Lou… I have to go—"

"Wait, there's more—"

"Lou, what's d-i-o-r-d-f-i-o-n-n?"

"*Diord fionn*?"

"Yes, *diord fionn*."

"I don't recognize *diord*, but *fionn* means fair or blond, Boss, what's—"

Christiaan ended the call and suddenly recognized the tune Duff hummed. The same one Vicky sang while trapped by the rock at Mineral Springs. All at once, the back of his neck prickled. Baz had been humming it, too, at the diner.

"Good, Baron Boy," Duff cooed, his 190-proof breath wafting through Christiaan's nose. "Now, roll down thet window an' toss thet squawk box out."

Christiaan complied.

"For yer information, *Diord Fionn* was thet war cry of thet *Fianna*, a mythical group of Celtic warriors. '*Glaine ar gcroi. Neart ar ngeag. Beart de reir ar mbriathar.*' Truth in our hearts. Strength in our hands. Action to match our speech."

"And the name of a file on the computer in the Mineral Springs site trailer." Mental connections clicked into place for Christiaan.

"*Used* to be on thet computer in thet Mineral Springs trailer," Duff corrected. "Tha' fecking Dutchie of yours tot he was being clever an' sentimental naming it tha'. Jaysus, what an idiot."

Fecking Dutchie… heart ring… diord fionn… "Baz's tattoo."

"Aye, thet tattoo." The Irishman laughed. "Yes, allow me to be thet first to inform ye tha' yer closest an' dearest friend works fer me an' me modern-day *Fianna*."

Christiaan struggled to register the significance of those words. Baz had betrayed him? Vicky had told the truth? As Christiaan tried to sort everything out, he spied the yellow sunburst with two upside-down Fs on Duff's cast. The Irishman noticed Christiaan's stare.

"Thet sunburst is an oul' Irish symbol fer divine strength."

"And the two green Fs in the middle?"

"An ironic play on *Fianna Fail*, thet Irish Republican Party. They've failed to secure thet world's support fer a free Ireland, so I'm gonna demand it."

"Demand it?"

Duff gave a cold, hard smile. "Aye, demand it."

The look on the Irishman's face chilled Christiaan to

the bone and sent his mind into overdrive trying to make sense of everything. His thoughts jumped to things Vicky said she'd seen at the Mineral Springs trailer.

"*An todhchaí*," Christiaan said. "That was another file on the computer. You said '*an todhchaí*' during your toast at the penthouse. You said it meant 'the future'. What's the future doing on my company's computer?"

Duff broke into a hardy laugh. "Me future has been thet future fer a very long time, Baron Boy. Fer a very... long... time."

Christiaan's breath caught as more things clicked into place. Baz's summer in Ireland. His demands to have a bigger role in the company. His push for the Mineral Springs project. His insistence on Christiaan staying hands off.

The money... or lack thereof.

"I can see thet wheels turning in yer head. Allow me to connect some of thet dots fer ye."

"Please do." Christiaan tried to stay calm, but the gun pointed at his chest made the effort difficult.

"Yer boy has been workin' fer me fer a very long time. I met him in Dublin just after thet snooty bitch tossed his sorry bollocks aside."

Damn you, Astrid.

"Jaysus, he was all full of anger an' hate about being a nobody. I showed him tha' he wasn't a nobody in me world. Tha' he could be a somebody. A bigger somebody than he could ever dream of."

Poor Baz. Christiaan let out a heavy sigh. This sociopath had done something he'd failed to do... recognize how much his friend had been hurting. *Just like I missed how much Bri had been hurting.*

"I'd been lookin' fer a way to gain legitimate access to thet States as well as some easy cash, an' thet Dutchie an' yer company was me ticket."

Like a punch in the gut, the confirmation of what Christiaan had suspected a few minutes ago stung like hell. Unraveling the conspiracy was easy now that he knew where the weak link was.

"Let me guess, Baz created fake vendors and authorized payments for non-existent services." His friend's reluctance to let Christiaan see costs-to-date and status rundowns explained that. "Millions and millions of dollars for you and your cause." An ironic laugh slipped out. "I'm guessing I bought you this car."

"Yes, ye did." Duff nodded at Christiaan and laughed. "I an' me cause thank ye very much."

Relief that his financial idiocy wasn't what caused his company to fail wasn't enough to overshadow the fact that Christiaan had blindly placed his trust in Baz, and, in turn, this obvious maniac.

Duff started humming that song again. The gun dipped up and down to the beat. Looking out the passenger window, Christiaan spied the hawk overhead.

A sensation of utter chaos ripped through him as everything he'd learned in the last ten minutes mixed with the events of the last fifteen years. His mind whirled like a cyclone. Taking a deep breath, he willed himself to respond to a mental trick his father had taught him to use when business negotiations were crazy and at a breaking point.

Focus your thoughts. Untangle the web of intertwining ideas. Evaluate each piece of data. Assemble the information together like a jigsaw puzzle until the entire picture is clear.

The bird circled as Christiaan slowly put the puzzle together. He just needed a few more pieces.

"Why kill Bri eight years ago?"

Duff laughed. "Aye, ye figured tha' out. Because she was gettin' in the way, pressuring ye to abandon Mineral Springs an' spend more time with her. Dutchie tot he had her under control until she stumbled across us meetin' in a local pub. Tha' was da final straw for me. She had to go. Baz took care of it, or so we all tot."

Christiaan choked down the sour taste rising in his throat. Baz had killed Bri! The man he considered his brother had murdered the woman he loved!

"Why so much importance to this project here?" Christiaan turned his attention back to Duff, forcing himself to focus on learning every last thing he could about the events of the last decade and half. "But this isn't just a way to get some big cash. You could have raised money doing what you've always done. Bombings made to look like accidents. There's something more going on at Mineral Springs, isn't there? The pallets of explosive materials. Drilling reports for a site that's not drilling. What's going on there?"

Again with the cold, hard smile. "Can't hurt to tell ye."

Another piece slid into place. "Because I'll be dead anyway, right? Here. On this county road. With no witnesses." Christiaan let out a sharp exhalation. "That's why you offered to drive me to the airport. That's why you picked this route. That's why you didn't turn around to go to Vicky's like I asked you to."

More chilling laughter from the sociopath drew Christiaan's attention back into the car. "But at least yer demise will be quick an' easy," Duff taunted. "Unlike thet rest of thet continent's, who have been sentenced to death."

This guy really is a freak. "And what crime are you charging this continent with?"

"Doing absolutely nothing while me Irish brothers an' sisters die needlessly at thet hands of British bourgeois nationalists. English rule is an' always has been based on force an' fraud an' maintained by military occupation against thet declared will of thet people. No more two Irelands! No more violation of Irish national sovereignty! No more 'normalizing' of Northern Ireland. Me actions will ensure thet will of thet Irish people prevails. Me actions will serve as true retribution fer dis side of thet world sitting on their arses an' letting Easter Week an' Bloody Sunday an' Thet Troubles happen. Only after North America has been annihilated will thet rest of thet world understand tha' a united Ireland is inevitable."

Diatribe over, Duff finally took a deep breath and smiled. A thin trickle of saliva dribbled from a corner of his mouth.

The words and passionate sentiment sent cold fear through Christiaan. The Irishman was nuts. Certifiably.

"So, your plan is to destroy all of North America and everyone in it?"

Duff's grin widened. "In. One. Fatal. Swoop."

With a new part of the puzzle to solve, Christiaan began sorting through the pieces running around his mind.

"The explosives. The drilling depths. The green crosses. Vicky was right. There was more than just testing going on at Mineral Springs."

"And tis' all me…" The Irishman let out a short snort. "…fault."

Fault? Fault. "*Unmapped fault zones.*" What little Christiaan could remember from the fractured phone conversation with the seismologist yesterday suddenly came screaming to his attention. "*… rupture of a main strike-slip fault could infer… significant seismic threat for the surrounding continent… cautioned Mr. Yager against the use of explosives…*" *Potverdomme*! He should have paid better attention!

Wait! Vicky said something about an Internet video she'd watched at the site trailer. Something about tectonic plates and seismic threats and earthquakes that could level entire regions. And her article. Christiaan struggled to remember what little he'd just read on his phone. "Microearthquake… proposed geothermal sites show seismic evidence of potential cataclysmic, tectonic chain reactions affecting fault line throughout North America…"

"Have you figured it out yet, Baron Boy?" Duff sneered.

Christiaan ignored the Irishman and the acute danger slowly suffocating him as he continued to sort through the evidence. Pallets… explosives… workers with hand trucks… footprints around cave entrances… people disappearing down passageways… muffled voices… *What had Vicky said about the network of caves and tunnels?* A wide web that darts in and out of the ridge and up and down from the ground.

The last piece of the puzzle slid into place. *This nut case is using Mineral Springs to cause a "cataclysmic, tectonic chain reaction"!*

Dread must have covered his face because Duff suddenly laughed. "Tha's right. Thar's gonna be wan big fecking earthquake."

"Vicky." Christiaan shook his head and forced his gaze away from the lunatic and back out the passenger window at Mt. Shasta far off in the distance. "You were definitely on to something." The hawk circled overhead. "I should have listened."

"Don't worry about thet precious Victoria Golden. She won't suffer. She'll be long gone by thet time this place shakes apart."

Christiaan whipped his head around. "What the hell are you talking about?"

"As we speak, stupid Dutchie is taking care of thet snoopy bitch."

"Baz is going to kill Vicky?" Christiaan's heartbeat thundered in his ears.

"Yes, up at thet stupid rock of hers. Let's hope he gets it right dis time."

Panic threatened to overwhelm him, and Christiaan fought to keep his mind clear. He needed to stop Baz.

First rule of crisis management… assess your situation. Gun pointed at chest. Moving car. Crazy Irishman at the wheel. Drunk crazy Irishman at the wheel.

Second rule… gather all the facts. Only one mattered… *Vicky will die if I don't get my ass up to Serenity Rock as soon as possible.*

Third rule… develop a plan of action. I need to get out of the car now. I'll figure out the rest as I go along.

Slowing the car for a tight curve, Duff relaxed his focus for a second. Enough time for Christiaan to unfasten the seat belt with his left hand, punch open the passenger door with his right, and roll out onto the road. Quickly jumping to his feet, he spied the Irishman looking at him through the rear window, gun aimed point blank. Suddenly, the Land Rover ran off the side of the road into a deep ditch, and the sound of a single gunshot echoed across the countryside.

Christiaan waited until he was certain no sign of movement came from the vehicle. Approaching the SUV, now resting on its side against a fence row, he spied a steady flow of blood coming from the back of Duff's head. Obviously drinking, driving, and handguns don't mix. Blank eyes stared at him, and Christiaan couldn't help but offer the Irishman the same cold hard smile he'd focused on "Baron Boy" earlier.

Vicky. He needed to get to her.

Christiaan shoved the lightweight vehicle back onto its wheels. Next, he opened the driver's door, unhooked Duff's seatbelt, and dragged the body into the ditch. Dropping into the bloody, wet, sticky driver's seat, Christiaan prayed that Land Rover's Above and Beyond marketing was true then started the SUV. He hesitated before slamming the car into gear. Reaching over the backseat, he grabbed the Irishman's lucky jacket, rolled down the window, and tossed it onto the body.

"Diord Fionn, you crazy bastard. Diord Fionn."

Rocking back and forth like a granny on steroids, Vicky tried to calm herself by reciting a Zen walking poem. How ironic! Normally, she was relaxed and at ease when perched on Serenity Rock. But today... today was a whole different ballgame. "Antsy" best described her emotions while sitting here, waiting for her husband to stumble up the trail.

Thank God for her little-known shortcut. She'd beaten Christiaan here, giving her a chance to think.

Vicky breathed deep. When he finally arrived, what would he say? Baz told her on the phone that Christiaan wasn't angry anymore. Maybe he simply wanted to apologize. For their previous life. For the last week. For... everything.

Drawing her legs up to her chest, she wrapped her arms around her knees. Would he want to pick up where they left off eight years ago? This morning?

Both?

Would he expect her to go back to being Bri in The Netherlands? Could she hope to retain her life as Vicky here?

So damn many questions. So little answers. If she thought the emotional chaos she'd dealt with earlier was confusing, this was down right... *argh*!

She didn't want to get her hopes up. Whether they found a compromise or not, as long as he forgave her for giving up on them eight years ago and everything since, she'd be happy.

Alone, but happy.

A loud squawk overhead pulled her attention to the sky where a hawk slowly circled. *The same one that tormented me earlier?* That dove at her on the cliff, right before all those rocks gave way and trapped her? That chased her and Christiaan into the cave, right before everything gave way and trapped them?

Unexpectedly... Sure a lot of unexpected rock action going on around here. The caption she'd read earlier popped into her head. The mention of MEQ data of proposed geothermal sites affecting fault lines kept sticking in her head.

MEQ... That was one of the acronyms she saw in the trailer, right next to the clipboard with the drill sites sheet. *Hmm... drilling...* The Die Frackers Die video rushed to mind. Could Christiaan's drilling have caused some unexpected rock action? Otherwise known as microearthquakes? Could there be more? Could they be worse? And, more importantly, is the risk of a cataclysmic chain reaction really as infinitesimal as the "energy proponents" say?

The bird rode the wind a bit more, then flew off toward the countryside. Just then, a baritone voice rose from the main trail. "Mamma Mia, here I go again. My my, how can I resist you?"

He remembered! A girlish, tingly feeling rushed from her head to her toes as Vicky joined in. "Mamma Mia, does it show again? My, my just how much I've missed you."

Now it was a duet. "Yes, I've been brokenhearted. Blue since the day we parted. Why, why did I ever let you go?" She cut the last syllable off abruptly as the owner of the baritone voice came into view.

"Baz? What are you doing here? I thought you said Christiaan was meeting me?"

"I lied." Baz smiled with a starched stiffness then shrugged his shoulders. "I lied. I told a dirty rotten little lie. I should be spanked. I should be punished." He turned around, aimed his butt at her, and smacked it with a open palm. Then he turned back around and started giggling like a little girl with a secret.

Is he drunk? Her nose searched the air for the smell of alcohol. Nothing.

"Vicky... Vicky... Vicky." He trailed a finger down her arm, then began giggling again.

That's... weird? Her skin began to crawl. Baz had always been funny and light-hearted, but this... this... bordered on creepy.

The giggling suddenly stopped. "So. Yeah. I lied." His expression stilled then darkened. "Then again, so did you. Right, Brianna?"

Vicky unlocked her arms from around her legs and shifted her seat on the boulder. Christiaan had told him her secret. Not surprising. They were like brothers.

"So..." She bit into her bottom lip and dragged a hand through her hair. "You know."

"Argh!" Baz jerked both hands into the air and turned

around in a circle. "The hair thing! You did it all the time *then*. You do it all the time *now*. Damn! How could I have not gotten that?" Yanking his arms back down, he gently folded them across his chest then leaned forward, his face inches from hers. "How? Because. You're. Supposed. To. Be. Dead."

The strange intensity burning in his eyes unnerved her even more. She couldn't remember ever seeing him this... this... volatile was the word that came to mind.

"You're supposed to be dead, Brianna. Dead. Dead. Dead." His sing-song tone frightened her. A bead of sweat rolled down the nape of her neck.

They'd always been friends. In fact, Baz had been the one there for her when Christiaan wasn't. But now... Vicky swallowed thickly. She'd never been afraid of Baz before.

Before today.

"So—" She choked before the rest of the sentence left her mouth. Clearing her throat, she tried again. "So, Christiaan's not coming?"

Stepping back, Baz began walking around the rock and Vicky. "Christiaan... Christiaan... Christiaan—" He accidentally stumbled over the gearbag she'd dropped upon her arrival earlier. He grunted in anger then kicked the offending object into some nearby bushes. "No. Christiaan is not coming. Hopefully, by now, the great Baron van Laere is out... of... the... way."

What did that mean? Out of the way? Vicky tried to read Baz's cold, congested expression. Christiaan was on his way to the airport? On his way back home? She swallowed hard again. Something worse? A loud squawk overhead told Vicky the red-tailed hawk had returned.

"You know... he was never supposed to come here." Baz continued to circle her. "This...Mineral Springs... was my project. My baby. *An todhchaí*. The future."

An todhchaí. The file on the trailer computer. The future? Whose?

"But... no. Some crazy bitch decided she knew better.

That she knew what was best for this world. Then and now. You know… I'm really getting tired of crazy bitches thinking they know better than anyone else." He stopped moving right in front of Vicky, spread his legs out, and rested his wrapped arms on his chest.

An apprehensive shiver chased down her back.

He let out a short snort. "You're pathetic. Do you know that? Vicky or Brianna or whatever you're gonna call yourself now that your secret is out. I mean, I tell you the great Baron van Laere wants to talk to you, and you practically come in my hands." Baz laughed and pretended to hold a phone to his ear. "It's Christiaan. He'd really like to talk to you." Changing his voice to falsetto, he continued. "He would?" Back to his regular tone. "Yes. He really doesn't want to leave things the way they are between the two of you. He loves you." Baz dropped his hand. "Pathetic bitch."

Christiaan had never wanted to speak with her. He wasn't worried about how things were between them. He didn't love her.

I really am pathetic.

"But then again, that's what women like you do, right?" Baz returned to circling the rock. "Whatever the men with titles and money and power want you to do."

Vicky relaxed a little. This rant wasn't about her. It was about Astrid.

"You just couldn't stay dead, could you, Brianna?"

Or maybe not. She needed an exit strategy. Fast. Unfortunately, Baz's circling made escape nearly impossible. Wait. *What?* "Stay dead?"

Baz started waving his hands and arms around. "First, you couldn't stay out of my business back in Enschede. I'd been working on this project for years. Then, Christiaan decides he wants to cut back on work because you're too tired or too stressed or too drunk or too stupid or too whatever to get pregnant. That means he doesn't want to jump into another industry, into another country. That…

that my dear Brianna, didn't make *Croi dubh* happy."

Croi dubh? Dubh? Duff?

Baz continued to ramble. "Then, like an idiot, you stumble on us meeting at the pub in town. Luckily for him, you didn't see him there. Unluckily for you, he thought you were too big a wrench in his plans. So, you had to die."

Duff? My Duff?

"Remember?" Baz nods his head. "You were too drunk to drive home so I brought your car home for you the next morning?

"Duff?"

"Yes!" Baz stomped his feet like a two-year-old having a temper tantrum. "Duff! *Croi dubh*. Black heart! The boss. Him!" Baz stopped and seemed to calm down immediately. "Now, back to my story."

She shook her head and listened with bewilderment. Duff? That devilishly handsome, somewhat arrogant Irishman? Who'd cautioned her a few days ago to be more careful on the mountain? Who happened to be at Mineral Springs at the same time she was and warned her off the caves? The caves she'd ended up trapped in.

"Duff?" She repeated.

"Yes! Duff!"

Oh. My. God. "He had Brianna killed?"

"*He* ordered it," Baz harrumphed. "But *I* made the arrangements."

"*You* arranged to have me blown up?" The shock of his brutal truth hit her full force. Staring at him, tongue-tied, she opened and closed her mouth like she had something to say but didn't know what.

She didn't want to believe anything Baz was telling her, but deep down his histrionics made strange sense. Memories from eight years ago surfaced. His surprise at running into her at the pub. His anger at the news that Astrid and Christiaan were having an affair. His insistence he drive her home that day. His delivery of her car to her the next morning, right before she left for the airport.

The hawk squawked again. Vicky looked up in time to see it swoop down over Baz's head. He didn't even notice.

"Blowing a car up and making it look like an accident is actually fairly simple. First, you ask your local IRA bombmaker to build a simple explosive device the size of a soda can. Then, you—" He shook his head. "Oh... never mind. You're not interested in the details. The point is, by the end of the day, you were dead. Problem solved."

"But I'm not dead." Her body began to shake as the fearful images of what could have happened taunted her. "So who was in the car?"

"Hmm..." Scrunching his face up in thought, Baz put a finger to his lips "You know, I've been noodling on that since Christiaan told me you were alive. The only thing I can come up with is that some poor idiot with the world's worst luck stole your loaded luxury Jaguar at the worst possible time."

"That's the only explanation," she whispered, feeling a little disembodied discussing her close brush with death. "I parked at the airport, and my car exploded on the motorway."

"Hmm... mystery solved." He placed his hands on Vicky's shoulders and squeezed... hard. "But you didn't die, did you?"

"No, I didn't." She nodded complacently, hoping the tears welling up in her eyes weren't evident to him.

Baz released her and started strutting around the rock again. "Which would have been fine, too, except for some reason God has a patent dislike for me because he has you causing shit again for me. I mean... what are the chances?"

Better than the ones of my getting away from you.

"First, you're just a simple thorn in my side as some random crazy environmental bitch hiding behind ShastaWatch. Then, Christiaan shows up and can't get enough of you. Insists I go along on some crazy mountain climb so he 'can get to know you better'. Now I'm right back where I started eight years ago..." Stopping directly in front of Vicky, he leaned in so close that spittle from his angry words sprayed her face. "… with a pathetic bitch fucking up my plans. So, this time I took care of business myself."

Something clicked in her mind. "You pushed me down the mountain."

"Yeah. That was me." He stepped back, put his hand on his stomach, and laughed hard. "You should have seen yourself. After Dean's big talk about how surefooted you were on Mt. McKinley and everybody was so, 'Oh my God, Vicky, you're so fucking wonderful,' all I had to do was slip a foot in front of yours as we got started, and you tumbled down the mountain like a rag doll in a washing machine."

I knew it wasn't an accident. But she'd blamed Christiaan. Not this… this… lunatic.

"But… of course… as usual… You. Didn't. Die!"

"Sorry to disappoint you." She didn't bother to hide her sarcasm.

Baz chuckled. "Oh Bri… Oh Vicky… a disappointment is all you've ever been to me. Like on the cliff."

"You had something to do with that?"

He laughed again. "Well, Duff and I saw you poking around the trailer and stuff, so we waited until you'd headed back up the cliffside trail and had the boys set off a test earthquake."

The boys. That explains the men she and Christiaan chased into the cave.

"But, again, much to my chagrin, you didn't die." He looked up into the sky. "Again, God fucking me over." Baz returned his attention to Vicky. "But you were so cute, trying to keep yourself safe from Mr. Nasty Old Bear." He reared his hands and acted like a bear.

You bastard. "That was you in the bushes."

"Yeah. I figured at some point a bear would get you, and my problems would be solved."

She snickered. "If it weren't for bad luck, you'd have no luck at all."

Baz stared at her. His jaw clenched. His eyes narrowed. Vicky's false bravado faded as she realized this freak had no intentions of letting her leave here alive.

Suddenly, he resumed his good-natured banter. "Yes, you certainly do have nine lives."

Another thought crashed into her. "The cave. That was you."

"Yes!" Baz laughed that crazy, maniacal laugh again. "You and Christiaan stumbled into earthquake central. Finally, FINALLY..." Baz peered up into the sky before finishing. "I think God is ready to answer my prayers. So I had some of the boys set off another MEQ."

Test earthquake. *MEQ... seismic evidence... tectonic chain reactions... Shit! These guys are playing with fire.*

"You'd be surprised what a few pieces of well-placed explosives in one of the many steam caves and tunnels around here can do."

His remark triggered memories of the maps she'd viewed in the trailer. "Earthquake central?" slipped from her lips.

Unexpectedly, Baz turned sentimental. "Look, Bri... Vicky..." He shook his head. "You were always my friend. You always treated me nice, not like everyone else. Then... then... you got in the way, and you had to go. Now I have to do something more permanent." Pulling a pistol from his coat pocket, he pointed it at her. "Besides, you should thank me. This will be a much better and faster way to die than what's planned."

Sweat rivered down the back of her neck. Don't panic! "What's planned, Baz?" She touched his arm, hoping she had the balls to grab the gun at the right moment. "What's planned?"

The unrelenting, harsh squawk of the hawk almost stole her focus.

Instead, her husband's voice startled her.

"Yes, Baz. Tell us what's planned."

CHAPTER 16

Relief at the sight of a living, breathing, and uninjured
Vicky gave Christiaan some peace. However, the pistol
pointed at her—and now at them both—gave him pause.
Potverdomme! Why didn't I grab Duff's gun from the car?

Baz's face was an odd mix of stark disbelief and bitter
hatred. Without warning, he stomped his feet like a little
boy told no and looked into the sky. "Are you kidding me?
Are you fucking kidding me, God?" Baz's focus dropped
to Christiaan. "You're supposed to be gone. Gone. Done.
Finished. Out. Of. The. Way."

Christiaan ignored the rant to peer at Vicky. She'd
managed to step back and put distance between her and
the obviously unstable traitor. Running a hand through her
hair, she bit her lower lip.

There's my girl.

"You okay?" he asked, feeling as defenseless as a
declawed cat.

"Shut up!" Baz's maniacal voice boomed.

She flinched. Her expression changed from hope she
wasn't alone to face this indescribable situation to fear
there wasn't any way out. Peering at Christiaan, she
struggled to put on a brave face and slowly nodded an

affirmative answer to his question.

The need to comfort and protect his wife took over, and he moved toward her. The sound of a gunshot whizzing past his ear stopped him cold.

"No... no... no," Baz's maniacal voice soothed. "No sweet reunions here, my friends."

Mental note: The gun is loaded, and he isn't afraid to use it.

Christiaan fought the urge to smack the twisted, mocking smile right off his former friend's face. He contemplated his next move.

"Where's Duff, bro?" Baz asked like they were simply holding a normal conversation. "He was supposed to have taken care of you. Me do Vicky. Him do you. That was the plan."

Christiaan breathed deep and played along. "Well, plans change, *bro*. Right now, the Irishman is gathering flies in a drainage ditch about ten miles from here. *Diord fionn*, bro."

Brows furrowed, Baz stared blankly. "Duff... Duff is dead?" The gun barrel dropped slightly. "Duff... dead. Hmm..." Christiaan saw the opportunity and moved toward the weapon. He stopped short when the lunatic began giggling like a little kid getting to stay up past his bedtime.

"Duff's dead! That puts me in charge now, right? Finally. I'm in charge. *I'm* in fucking charge. Whoo-hoo!" Baz shook his head then looked directly at Christiaan, a satanic smile spread across his thin lips. "No Irishman to tell me what to do, and..." He leveled the gun directly at Christiaan's chest. "No Baron to tell me what to do... *ever again*!"

"Come on, Baz. You don't want to do this."

"You know, bro, you think you're so fucking wonderful." He rocked his head back and forth, from one shoulder to another. "The great Baron von Laere. All hail the blue blood. All hail the clean, perfect noble. Fuck the dirty gardener's son."

Potverdomme! All this because of that. "Come on. It was never like that."

"Shut up! Yes, it was!" Baz's nostrils flared. "All my life, I've been stuck in your fucking shadow. Growing up, you got everything, and I got nothing but hand-me downs. At school, everybody wanted to be your friend. They only tolerated me because you insisted. At work, you could do no wrong. I couldn't do anything right. All because you were the golden boy and I wasn't."

"Baz, I never saw you that way."

"Shut... up!" He shook his head violently. "How could anyone see what I had to offer when all they could see was you? Perfect, perfect you. Astrid couldn't see. Even you couldn't see. But Duff did. He saw what I had to offer and gave me a chance to shine." Baz's mouth twitched with amusement.

"He didn't care about you." Christiaan took a small step forward. Maybe, just maybe, if he could got closer, he could grab the pistol. "The Irishman was just using you."

Baz's maniacal smile deepened into maniacal laughter. "No, we were just using you. You... your company... your mone—"

"Save it. Duff filled me in on the all details." Another step. "But he's gone now. There's no reason for any of this craziness to go any further, right?"

Baz shrugged his shoulders. "What do I care what happens after I take care of you two? With Duff gone, I'm the only one with access to the funds we stole. So, by this time tomorrow, I'll be starting a new life of luxury in Cabo or Dubai or the Caymans or wherever I decide to have the company plane take me."

"You're willing to let millions of innocent people die?" Vicky offered in a voice calmer than Christiaan thought possible considering the situation. "All because you're one crazy, insane, self-absorbed, adolescent, jealous bastard?"

Umm... mijn minnares ... he has a gun.

Baz's grin hardened for a second, and his eyes brimmed with genuine hatred. Then he chuckled and gave her a soothing smile. "Who cares if this half of the world disappears? Not me. Look at it this way, Vicky darling. At least you'll have succeeded in stopping the geothermal project. You can go to your grave knowing that you achieved that. Isn't that nice, hmm?"

Christiaan inched forward.

"But, before my new life begins, I have a few things to take care of. First you..." Baz nodded at Christiaan then winked at Vicky. "... then you." Slowly, he aimed the pistol at Christiaan.

From the corner of his eye, Christiaan watched her pick up a fist-sized rock and hurl it. The projectile nailed Baz directly in the chest as he pulled the trigger, and the gun flew from his hand.

"Run, Christiaan. Run!"

He turned to do that exact thing when he saw her jerk upright, clap a hand to her leg, and fall to the ground.

She's hit! Racing to her side, he struggled with what to do next. Baz ended the indecision by rushing them. Christiaan crouched and prepared his best Rugby dump tackle. Aiming a shoulder for Baz's stomach, he nailed it then picked up the maniac's legs and lifted them to the side. Baz grunted as he hit the ground hard.

Grabbing Vicky's arm and wrapping it around his neck, Christiaan pulled her to her feet and tore up the trail, hoping to get as much distance between them and Baz as possible. Christiaan stole a look at her leg, where a large stain appeared mid-thigh. All the distance in the world wouldn't help if she bled to death. Dragging her behind some bushes, he sat her down and quickly assessed her condition.

"Don't stop," her voice strained and wavered. "We need to keep moving. Get to higher ground. He doesn't know the snowfields like I do. Come on!" She tried to stand, but Christiaan held her down.

"First, let me take a quick look at that scratch of yours." Blood now trickled to the ground. From where they sat, he could see a trail of red drops that even a blind man could follow.

She was right. They needed to get moving... soon.

Yanking his handkerchief from a back pocket, he pressed the fabric hard against her thigh.

"Argh!"

"Sorry." If he could endure the pain for her, he would. But he couldn't. All he could do was try to keep her safe until they could find help. Ripping the belt off his pants, he placed it around the makeshift battle dressing, tightening the leather enough to stop the bleeding but not so much to cut off circulation. She'd need that leg to climb more mountains.

"Vicky... Bri... *mijn minnares*... I'm sorry for all of this. I need you to know that however this turns out, I never stopped loving you... ever."

"Christiaan..." She peered up at him with those gorgeous gray eyes. "I never stopped... loving you either... I'm so... sorry I ever doubted... you or us or—"

He brushed her lips with a soft kiss. She moaned and opened her mouth. His tongue accepted the invitation. A rush of heat shot through his core. Overhead, the red hawk squawked. Christiaan pulled away.

"Come on... Let's go." Vicky gestured for him to stand and help her up. Wrapping an arm around her waist, he pulled her against him and squeezed through the bushes. They'd just cleared the greenery when bark from a tree near their heads splintered.

"Great. He... he found the... the damn gun." Vicky pushed Christiaan to the left. "Hurry. Maybe... maybe... maybe we can... lose him... him... in the grove... up... here." A second shot. The splinter shower forced them to the right.

"*Potverdomme*! Now what?"

Vicky pointed off trail. "I... I... I know a shortcut. We... we just... just have to be careful—" She stopped talking long enough to catch her breath. Misgivings swarmed his mind. Her injury and the effort to keep moving were taking a toll. "When we hit snow... lots of hidden dangers." She stumbled and grunted. "Look for... look for sagging... sagging snow bridges or... or... lots of ripples in the snow... must watch... must watch for cre... crevasses. Hopefully... if we can get far enough... ahead of him, we can cut... cut down toward Bunny Flat. There's... there's always somebody on that trail... He wouldn't... he wouldn't risk shooting... shooting... shooting us in front of other people... would... would he?"

"At this point, my guess is as good as yours." Christiaan looked over his shoulder. Baz was a kilometer or two back. Out in the open like this, they'd need to start zigzagging to make it harder for Baz to land a shot.

Christiaan's focus returned to the front. Snow lay ahead. It would impede their progress somewhat, but the white stuff would delay Baz's, too.

For what seemed like forever, they sloshed through rising snow levels, the red hawk circling overhead. But the dropping temperature, lack of proper weather gear, and Vicky's steady decline worked against them. Christiaan tried to focus on the positive.

I found her, and I'm not going to lose her again.

"How soon to the shortcut?"

"Not... not far, but gotta... gotta watch for—" A shot ricocheting off a boulder inches from their heads cut her answer off.

Potverdomme! Christiaan dashed to the left.

"—for that crevasse."

Too late. Christiaan pulled up short of the opening, but Vicky's injured leg couldn't control her forward momentum. Time slowed to a snail's pace as he watched her tumble out of his arms and disappear over the edge.

"No! Vicky!" He stared at where she'd disappeared. Dropping to his stomach, he low-crawled to the cavity. "Vicky! Vicky!" *Please be okay. Potverdomme! Please be okay.*

His heart sank as deep as the crevasse in front of him. The chasm must be at least a full rugby-field deep.

Wait! There! Was that something sprawled on a ledge? About twenty meters down? "Vicky? Can you hear me?" It moved. She moved? "Vicky? Vicky? Are you okay?"

"Aww... did you lose something, Baron van Laere?" Baz's voice cooed from behind. "No problem, bro. You got along just fine the first time she died. You can do it again." He laughed that stupid... grating... maniacal laugh. "Of course, this time, you'll only be a widower for a few short minutes."

"Crime of passion" was a defense Christiaan had never understood. But today, the meaning was crystal clear. *This crazy maniac... this raving lunatic... this evil son of a bitch ruined my company... betrayed our friendship...*

And killed my wife.

Once. Possibly twice.

"The good news?" Baz sneered. "Maybe you'll find each other again in heaven."

Without another thought, Christiaan sprang to his feet with a growl. Like a man possessed, he tackled Baz and heaved him five meters back into the snow. The gun flew. Pinning him to the ground, Christiaan vised his hands around Baz's neck. Overhead, the hawk continued her piercing squawk.

"*Potverdomme*, you lousy piece of shit!" He squeezed tighter. "You had everything. More than you could have ever achieved on your own. Because of me! Me! And this is how you repay me? By taking the only thing that ever really mattered to me?"

"Gave... me? Gave... me?" Baz struggled to release Christiaan's grip. "You... gave... me... nothing... but... grief."

"I loved you like a brother!"

"I... didn't... want... a... brother... I... wanted... to... be... you."

Emotions swarmed Christiaan like angry bees. He'd known from the first time Baz had shoved him into one of the estate canals during their early childhood. And each time he'd endured punishment for something his "friend" had blamed on him. And each time he'd taken a test or written a paper in school to help his "brother" stay on track. And every time he'd bailed Baz out of jail or debt. The truth of everything Christiaan had forced himself to ignore for more than forty years boiled to the surface. He'd always known Baz resented him for his title and his status. But hate him enough to kill not only Bri but half the United States? *Potverdomme!*

"*Watje,*" Baz said.

Pussy? My hands are around his neck, squeezing the life from his body, and he's calling me pussy?

"Go... ahead... try... Baron... van... loser... you... don't... have... the... guts... to... do... it."

"The hell I don't." Christiaan closed his eyes and focused all his strength—mentally and physically—into his hands. The sound of Baz's short, gurgling breath filled Christiaan with laughter. A maniacal one. *This feels so good...*

"Christiaan... don't."

Both men froze at the sound of Vicky's voice.

"He's not... not... not... worth it."

Christiaan and Baz turned to the spot where she'd disappeared a few minutes earlier. There she stood. Alive, but not well. Her chest heaved, and she appeared ready to pass out.

Potverdomme!

"What... the... fuck?" Baz gasped.

"How'd you...?" The euphoria of her resurrection loosened Christiaan's grip.

She smiled and held up her ice axe. "Never leave... leave home... without it."

He laughed again, only this time it sounded and felt like a kid on Christmas day.

Taking a deep breath, she smiled at him then her face turned as white as the snow beneath them.

Suddenly, something slammed his head to one side, and he tumbled off of Baz. The shadow of another blow ready to strike appeared above, and Christiaan rolled away before it could connect. With a foot, he knocked the rock from Baz's hand then scrambled to stand. Baz nailed a cheap shot to the kidney area, and Christiaan fought the urge to roll up in a ball from the intense pain.

Must find gun. Must. Find. Gun.

Collecting his strength, he staggered back onto his feet, prepared to beat the lunatic to the pistol.

Too late. The weapon was once again in Baz's hands, pointed directly at Vicky's temple.

"Looking for this?" Baz jeered.

Violent emotion churned inside. It took everything Christiaan had not to rush the idiot. But said idiot was gripping Vicky, so any attempt at ending his life would end hers, too.

"Vicky... Bri... I'm so sorry..." The sheer weight of his guilt at causing her so much pain rested like a mountain on his soul. "For everything."

She nodded. "I'm sorry, too. For everything."

He shuddered. How could it end this way? All their hopes and dreams dying on top of a cold mountain. Her face blurred as his gaze clouded with tears.

"Baz?" Vicky said. "I'm so sorry, too."

"For what?"

"This." A quick elbow to the chest, and Baz tumbling backward into the crevasse.

Christiaan rushed to her side and caught her just as her bad leg gave out. "You okay?"

She looked at him with those gorgeous silver eyes. "I am now."

The cold refreshing mountain air made Vicky feel alive.

But lonely. So... very... lonely.

Pushing hard, she headed back down Mt. Shasta, the cold wind chilling her lungs with every inhale. Had it only been three months since she'd rescued Christiaan not far from here? Only thirteen weeks since she'd learned her husband had never stopped loving Bri? Only ninety-two days since they'd said goodbye and returned to their respective lives?

Yes, it had been.

Crisp air stung her nostrils. She loved this mountain. She couldn't imagine being anywhere else. This is where Vicky Golden belonged.

Because Brianna was dead.

She and Christiaan had faced that reality shortly after Baz's death. A quick call to Lou had his CIA buddies on the mountain within the hour. They took charge of the situation, rounding up Duff's men here and erasing all evidence of him and his plot to wipe out this part of North America. No one would ever know how close the world came to losing half a continent because of a revenge-fueled Irishman and a resentment-filled Dutchman.

Rubbing the spot where Baz's bullet had passed through her thigh, Vicky once again gave thanks for Christiaan's quick thinking. The shot had nicked her femoral artery right above the knee. According to the CIA doctor, the belt-leather tourniquet had saved her from bleeding out. Emergency surgery had repaired the damage, and today was her first day-long hike on the mountain. Next month, she hoped to be back leading Climbing for Singles trips and the occasional rescue mission.

Vicky managed a twisted smile. *Back to life as usual.*

Christiaan, too, was back to life as usual. After her surgery, he'd returned home to bury Baz, unravel the mess his friend had created, and sort out exactly where life was headed.

Overhead, the now-familiar squawk of the red hawk made Vicky smile. The bird now seemed to follow her every time and everywhere she was on or near Mt. Shasta. Seeing the creature always brought Christiaan to mind. Vicky sighed, watching the beautiful creature ride the wind then disappear over the ridge.

Although she and Christiaan had learned a lot about each other and themselves over that fateful week, they soon realized the renewed connection they'd forged wouldn't fix everything. Too much time and even more pain couldn't change the fact that he'd failed her as a husband or that she'd betrayed him and their love. The wounds were too deep to heal.

Eventually, they decided to remain friends and see what happens. But daily phone calls had turned into weekly emails then monthly ones. Thinking back now, she hadn't heard from him in over a month.

It's okay. Really. She swallowed hard.

They also agreed with the CIA's opinion that revealing the truth regarding her death and Baz's role in it would do more damage than good for everyone involved. The agency was working quietly to infiltrate Duff's network worldwide. Neither the van Laere family or VL Holdings could withstand any more public scandal. And Mt. Shasta didn't need tabloid reporters covering it like flies on honey to find out where Brianna had been for the last eight years.

Absolutely no one would benefit from the revelation that she was alive.

So, Vicky had her life and her mountain. Christiaan had his life and his company.

Back to life as usual. Too bad her heart wasn't buying it.

"Hey, Vicky!" then static crackled over the radio clipped to her shoulder.

"What, Dean?"

"There's been a report of something downed approximately one mile north of Helen Lake. Are you still up there? Can you see anything where you're at?"

"Yep, still on the mountain. Give me a minute." Quickly, she did a three-sixty of the landscape with her binoculars. "Sorry, not a thing. No smoke. Nothing."

"Okay," he answered. "Can you head that direction and report back what, if anything, you find?"

"Sure. Vicky out."

Her breath steamed in the cold air as she picked up the pace across the lower snowfield. What were the odds that someone would crash in the same vicinity as Christiaan had months ago?

Within a mile, she crested the ridge and surveyed the landscape. Ninety yards to the east, a small helicopter sat idle. No damage. No passengers.

She radioed the location to Dean then headed down the slope. Hopefully, footprints in the snow would tell her where everyone had disappeared to.

They did. Three sets of tracks headed up to Serenity Rock. Her pulse pounded in a combination of exertion and apprehension as she turned the corner and spied the tallest man in the trio.

Piercing blue eyes. Long, straight nose. High cheekbones. Stubborn jaw. All revealed a European aristocratic lineage.

Christiaan.

Rushing to him, she jumped into his arms and buried her face in his neck. *My God!* It felt good to be in her husband's arms. "I was so afraid I'd never see you again."

He laughed. "I thought that once about you, too." Pulling her face to his, he claimed her lips and kissed her hard. Raw, possessive passion flowed between them like electricity.

As his tongue drove into her mouth, desire stronger than when they'd met fifteen years ago nearly buckled her knees. She quickly unzipped his jacket and shoved her hands under his shirt. *Damn, I want to do him right here... right now.*

Laughter in the background brought them up for air. Vicky pulled her arms down and adjusted his shirt before turning toward the other couple.

"Get a room, will ya?" Dean barked.

Rainbow laughed. "Gee, sweetie, could you at least wait until the honeymoon?"

Vicky looked back at Christiaan. "Honeymoon? What honeymoon?"

He took her face into his hands and held it gently. "*Mijn minnares*, the last several weeks without you reminded me how much I need you… want you… love you. I don't care what we decided. We *will* make this work. Somehow, we will." Dropping to one knee, he took her hand and peered up into her eyes. "My life would be so much better if you were in it. Will you remarry me?"

Vicky's gaze clouded with tears, and a gasp broke from her lips. "Yes, Christiaan Gerhard Cornelus Jan Stokman, Baron van Laere, I will remarry you."

Rainbow stepped forward with a bouquet of daisies and a book of Zen poems. "Yeah! I finally get to use my Universal Church of Life ordination." Handing the flowers to Vicky, her friend motioned for Christiaan to join them. Placing their left hands on the book, she started. "Friends, we are gather—"

"Wait!" Vicky jerked her hand back. "Before we go any further, I need to know something."

All color drained from Christiaan's face, and the vein in his neck began to throb.

"Don't worry. I'm no longer going to build a geothermal industrial park at Mineral Springs. Instead, I want to turn the property into a couples retreat. A place where husbands and wives can come together to focus on communication, rekindle their passion, and maybe learn a thing or two about conservation and Shasta folklore. Sound good?"

"Sounds great, but that's not what I want to know." She took a deep breath. "Who are you marrying? Brianna or Vicky?"

Looking deep into her eyes, he cupped her chin in his hands. "Both."

Suddenly, the last fifteen years slipped away like snow on a sunny day. All the pain and suffering, struggles and misunderstandings disappeared. Today, at this very moment, it felt like a new beginning for them, their love, and their future. The sooner they got started, the better.

"Let's do this." Placing her right hand back on the book of poems, she used her other hand to put Christiaan's on top.

"Friends, we are gathered here today with this incredible couple for a very important moment in their lives." Rainbow smiled, then turned to Christiaan. "You have something you'd like to say to your beautiful bride?"

"Yes, I do. *Mijn minnares*, once I promised to love, honor, and cherish you 'til death us do part. Then I let business, people, and others' expectations take over and didn't realize I'd lost you until you were gone." He paused to wipe a tear from his cheek.

"Eight years ago, I learned not even death could extinguish my passion for you. Three months ago, God handed me a second chance to love you like you deserved to be loved. For the rest of our years together, whether that's five, fifteen, or fifty, I promise to never let you go. *Ik hou van jou.*"

Vicky giggled. "I love you, too."

"Do you have anything you'd like to say to your groom?" Rainbow urged.

"Yes, I do." Vicky paused to settle the butterflies in her stomach. "*Mijn minnares*, fifteen years ago, I, too, promised to love, honor, and cherish 'til death us do part. Eight years ago, I let my insecurities, my jealousy, and others' lies take over and walked away from the best thing that ever happened to me. Three months ago, God handed me a second chance to love you like you deserve to be loved. I promise, for the rest of our lives, I'll never fail our love. *Ik hou van jou.*"

"That was sappy," Dean said. "Real sappy."

"Idiot." Rainbow punched his arm. "You guys, that was so beautiful." She sniffled. "So beautiful. You're beautiful. Okay, let's make this official. Got the rings?"

Christiaan slipped the chain hanging from Vicky's neck

over her head, then unclasped it to remove the slender band. Taking her hand, he slipped the ring onto her finger. "With this ring, I thee wed... again."

Wrapped in a cocoon of euphoria, Vicky pulled Christiaan's ring off his finger, kissed it, and then slid it back on. "With this ring, I thee wed..." She laughed. "Again."

"By the power vested in me by the Universal Church of Life, I now pronounce you husband and wife. Christiaan, you may now kiss your bride."

The squawk of a red hawk pierced the moment. Overhead, two birds lazily soared back and forth together. "Ah... look," Vicky purred. "She found her mate."

"And so did I." Christiaan gathered her into his arms. "Now, what about that kiss?"

He pulled her hard against him and captured her lips. Although they'd kissed a thousand times before, this one was far better than any previous. Emotions whirled, mixed, and washed over them like morning clouds at the top of Mother Shasta. Their love had endured and would until the end of time. It wouldn't be sunsets and roses all the time, but they'd learned the most valuable lesson of love.

Believe in it. Trust in it. And, with it, you can climb mountains.

What God hath joined, let no man put asunder.

About The Author

When she's not in her writing chair, ANNIE OORTMAN is usually found on her bicycle seat or in her hiking boots, gallivanting around the breathtaking Utah countryside creating more and more story ideas to bring to life for her readers.

You can find her online at www.annieoortman.com.